THE WALKING BREAD

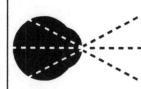

This Large Print Book carries the
Seal of Approval of N.A.V.H.

A BREAD SHOP MYSTERY

THE WALKING BREAD

WINNIE ARCHER

WHEELER PUBLISHING
A part of Gale, a Cengage Company

Farmington Hills, Mich • San Francisco • New York • Waterville, Maine
Meriden, Conn • Mason, Ohio • Chicago

GALE
A Cengage Company

**LIBRARY OF CONGRESS CIP DATA ON FILE.
CATALOGUING IN PUBLICATION FOR THIS BOOK
IS AVAILABLE FROM THE LIBRARY OF CONGRESS**

ISBN-13: 978-1-4328-5676-2 (softcover)

Published in 2018 by arrangement with Kensington Books, an imprint of Kensington Publishing Corp.

Printed in Mexico
1 2 3 4 5 6 7 22 21 20 19 18

*In memory of my great aunt Sarah Sears,
matriarch of the SOSS*

Our sunshine, now and forever

CHAPTER 1

When the town of Santa Sofia committed to something, they went at it whole hog. Whether it was the Winter Wonderland Festival, Dia de los Muertos, the Holiday Tree Lighting, or the spring extravaganza — the Art Car Show and Ball — no stone was left unturned. No expense was spared. And no other town or city would outdo our little beach haven.

The Art Car Planning Committee had hung vertical flags on every stoplight promoting the event; they strung banners across major intersections, they updated the Upcoming Events page of the town's website, and the event had its own dedicated website sponsored by local businesses. To Santa Sofia residents, the Art Car Show was akin to Mardi Gras in New Orleans — minus the beads, bar crawls, and raunchy Bourbon Street shops and paraphernalia.

It had always been one of my favorite

events when I was a teenager. Of course I felt that way about each town celebration when we were in the midst of it. But the Art Car Show was truly one of a kind. Other cities had similar events, of course, so ours wasn't *literally* one of a kind, but it was unique in that we had the ball on the last day of the event, our car parade ran on a street parallel to the Pacific Coast Highway, the backdrop of the cars being the Pacific Ocean, and, well, it was just *ours.* Santa Sofia has just a few celebrations like this, but the few we have are spectacular.

On top of all that, my brother, Billy, had been entering cars in the competition since he was seventeen years old. He worked on them all year long, breathing life into them with a passion unrivaled by anything else — except, perhaps, the love of his life, Emmaline Davis. The efforts of his first few years were rough. He hadn't come into his own yet in terms of understanding design and having a big-picture vision, but by the third year, his former art teacher at the high school had offered to help him. The two of them worked nonstop for months, and the end result had been incredible. The junker he'd bought at auction had been transformed into an under water kaleidoscope of color and design. The entire car had become a three-dimensional representation of coral reefs, seaweed, saltwater fish, and octopi. The hood had become an expanse of white-caps, and from the "water," an open-mouthed shark emerged in all its glory. Steven Spielberg would have been proud. Billy had paid attention to every detail, from the rows of teeth to the nuanced menace in the shark's eyes; it was lifelike and magnificent.

He'd come in second place.

The winner, Maxwell Litman, had also used an ocean theme, but his had been a single mandarin fish. Just like Billy, he'd paid attention to every detail. From the color patterning to the bulging red eyes, black pupils, and the odd dorsal-like fin, it looked like something an imperial empress from an ancient Chinese dynasty might have worn. Max Litman's mandarin fish was vivid and bright. Orange swirls overlaid the brilliant blue background. The sides of the car sported pelvic fins, which were what the actual fish used to walk along the ocean floor. The roof of the car was the top of the fish, its striped dorsal fin moving in the breeze as it would gracefully sway in the water. It was a sight to behold, and even Billy admitted that Max's car had deserved first place.

But the next several years sparked a troubling suspicion. Whatever theme Billy chose for his car was the exact theme on which Max Litman also based his design. If Billy created a landscape from *Star Wars,* Max transformed his car into Yoda. When Billy had created a giant Easter bunny carrying a basket of colorfully dyed Easter eggs, Max had used the same idea, but had taken it in a different direction. He'd crafted an enormous bluebird flying above the car, a giant twig in its mouth. The car itself was a nest, and spilling from it was an array of speckled eggs in muted hues. It was Easter representing rebirth rather than the whimsical child-centered direction Billy had gone.

"He's stealing my ideas," Billy told me after he lost to Max yet again. This time, Billy had turned his car into Medusa's head, the snakes writhing realistically. And Max Litman had created the god's majestic castle atop Mount Olympus, Zeus himself standing in front, arms raised, a crackling lightning bolt in hand.

"There's a spy," I said. It seemed ridiculous that Max would go to such lengths to undermine Billy's chance of winning, but like I said, the people in Santa Sofia took their events very seriously.

Billy had nodded gravely. "I think so, too.

There's only one possibility," he said.

I knew exactly where he was going with his theory. The art teacher who'd been helping Billy for years. "Mr. Zavila," I said.

Billy's shoulders sagged. He was my brother and I knew him better than anyone. He felt betrayed by a teacher he'd trusted. "It has to be."

So we'd set up a sting. Four months later, which was eight months before the Art Car Show — because it took that long to design and bring that vision to life — Billy had invited Mr. Zavila over to help him brainstorm. While they'd met in the garage, I'd waited down the street in my car. Now that I thought back about it, I realized that *that* had actually been my first stakeout, not the one I'd done with Penelope Branford not so long ago. I guess I'd been harboring investigative tendencies for longer than I'd thought.

When Mr. Zavila had left our house that day, I let him get to the stop sign at the end of the street before I pulled out and followed him. Billy and I hadn't been sure Mr. Zavila would go straight to Max Litman, but since Billy's ideas and his plan for his next art car were fresh in the art teacher's mind, it made sense that he would.

He drove through Santa Sofia, traveling

inland, skirting around the downtown area and heading for one of the more upscale neighborhoods, Malibu Hills Estates. It was, I remembered, an area that Max Litman's company had developed. He built high-end houses in and around Santa Sofia, and this had been the first gated community in town. People had been up in arms about the name. If towns could have rivalries, ours was with Malibu. We were a cross between Santa Barbara and San Luis Obispo. We were hipster and low-key, whereas Malibu was pretentious and elite. Apparently Max Litman felt Santa Sofia needed to get a little ritzy, but people did not want to have anything remotely related to Malibu in their town. There had been quite a few proposals: Emerald Acres; Sea Blue Manor; The Woods of Santa Sofia. But in the end, Max Litman had won the battle of the names.

I stopped half a block down, watching as Mr. Zavila turned into Malibu Hills Estates Surely he didn't live here. On a teacher's salary? No, I reasoned. This had to be where Max Litman lived. But Mr. Zavila's arm emerged from the driver's window and he entered a code on the keypad outside the gate. Either he actually *did* live here, or he and whomever he was here to see — presumably Max Litman, but I couldn't make any assumptions yet — were such good friends that he had the entrance code.

Then again, if Mr. Zavila *was* a spy for the developer, then it stood to reason that he would be privy to such information.

As the gate slowly swung open, I pulled up right behind him. He drove through before the gate had fully opened, leaving me plenty of time to drive right on through as if I belonged there.

I kept a safe distance from Mr. Zavila, wending my way around the curves and trying not to appear as if I was following him. Which wasn't particularly easy given I was in a car, in plain sight, in a neighborhood where nobody else was out and about.

I slowed a bit more, putting even more distance between Mr. Zavila and me, and looked at the houses. They were sprawling Mediterranean estates with velvety green lawns, elaborate fountains, pillars, and cascading trees. So this was how the other half lived. I could see the appeal, but me? I preferred the Tudor I'd recently bought in the historic part of Santa Sofia. It had character and charm, both of which came with age. All the houses on Maple Street told the tales of all who'd lived there, who'd experienced joy and pain, success and loss, love and heartache. My street told the stories of the past, and I was a part of that.

I peered into the darkness, realizing I'd lost sight of Mr. Zavila. Refocusing on the road — and cursing under my breath — I drove another half mile, heaving a sigh of relief when I spotted his car. It was parked in front of a house that looked like it belonged in Bel Air or, well, Malibu Hills. Even though I preferred a different kind of neighborhood, the place had a certain appeal. Like so many of the others homes, a huge fountain adorned the front entrance. This one had an enormous stone base and a three-tiered centerpiece, each piece resembling a nineteenth-century washbasin, the largest bowl at the bottom and the smallest at the top. Water cascaded gracefully over each stone vessel, the effect of which was both calming and majestic. An abundance of colorful impatiens circled the base, completing the grand front-yard centerpiece. The house was the biggest on the street. Its façade was a rich terra-cotta-colored stucco, intentionally distressed to make it look classically old. Wrought-iron half-circle faux balconies framed each of the upper windows. They looked as if they had come straight out of the French Quarter in New Orleans. I marveled at how willingly people paid good money to make something new look old.

I drove past the mansion, because that's what it was, slowly making a U-turn at the end of the block and coming back down the street. To anyone watching, it would look like I was searching, but not finding, a particular residence. Once again, I rolled past Mr. Zavila's car, catching my breath when I caught sight of two men. They hadn't been there when I'd driven by the first time, but they'd materialized, walking around the fountain, heading down the cobbled driveway. The fancy streetlights illuminated the men enough for me to instantly recognize them both. Mr. Zavila, of course, and as suspected, Max Litman.

In that moment, I knew that Billy and I had been right; Mr. Zavila was a spy, and Max Litman's Art Car victories over my brother year after year were not due to his own ingenuity. No, they were the direct result of insider information.

It was Santa Sofia subterfuge at its finest.

After I'd told him, Billy had, of course, changed his entire plan for his art car that year. He'd set Max Litman up, telling Mr. Zavila that the theme for the year was the Teletubbies. And then he'd let the art teacher down gently, confessing to him that things were rough at work, and he just couldn't afford to pay for his assistance anymore. It wasn't a lie. Billy had started his own construction company and the early years had been rough going. He'd almost thrown in the towel several times, but he persevered.

The art car battle with Max Litman was proof of his tenacity. While his nemesis created life-sized Teletubbies to sit atop his car, Billy created an amazing Lego façade for his. Despite the tight business budget, he scoured Craigslist and eBay for any and everybody selling Legos. In the end, he'd barely had enough, but he'd done it. His car looked straight out of Legoland. The townspeople had been awed by it. Kids wanted to touch it, to ride in it, to add to it with their own Legos. Poor Tinky-Winky, Dipsy, Laa Laa, and Po. Nobody cared about the Teletubbies. All they wanted was to touch the Lego car.

I smiled at the memory. Billy had grinned giddily. In that moment, he didn't care whether he won or lost. He'd captured the imagination of every Santa Sofian, and that was his reward.

His giddiness, however, was short-lived because as much as his car had deserved the blue ribbon, he *hadn't* actually won. It was a travesty, but for some reason it seemed as if my brother, Billy Culpepper, would never have a fair chance. That had been five or six years ago.

He'd taken a hiatus for a few years, purely out of frustration, but after our mom's death, Billy had picked up where he'd left off. Now the event was around the corner and he was more determined than ever. Our mother had loved the Art Car Show and Ball more than any other Santa Sofia event, and no one had rooted for Billy more than she had. Now, he was determined to win first place in her honor. "This is my year," he said as I crouched in front of his creation and snapped a picture. "I can feel it."

Emmaline Davis, the love of his life — and the town's deputy sheriff — folded her arms and lowered her chin, shaking her head. "You're a glutton for punishment."

But Billy just shrugged. "Maybe, but seriously, look at it." He swept his arm wide so she would direct her attention to the car. "There is no way Max Litman's car is better than mine. No. Freaking. Way."

I had to agree. All of Billy's cars had been incredible, but this one . . . this one was far and away the most artistic creation he'd ever built. And, on top of that, it truly did honor our mother.

But Emmaline had always had both feet

firmly on the ground. Where Billy saw situations in varying shades of gray, Em tended to interpret things as black or white. "His cars have never been better than yours," she said. "That is not the issue. You know my theory. He's got a judge in his pocket."

Neither Billy nor I could disagree with her. It made sense. But it also meant there was nothing left to say. If Em was right, then for as long as Max Litman entered a car in the Santa Sofia Art Car exhibition, Billy was destined to come in second place.

I had a week to finish documenting the various elements of the Art Car Show and Ball, including several of the planning meetings with the core planning committee, which included Penelope Branford, my favorite octogenarian, my neighbor, and my surrogate grandmother; Bernice Green, a local business owner who went by the name Bennie; Crystal Bozeman, a young mother of twins; Jesse Martinez, the most sought-after mason in the construction business — and one of the most eligible bachelors — in town; and Justin Griffin, a luxury car salesman at one of the few auto dealers in Santa Sofia. They were an amiable group, so the photographs of their meetings had been easy and, if I was being honest, mundane.

But I documented them nonetheless, and the photos had gone up on the event website.

I'd taken pictures of the venue, the signs and banners posted all over town, and I had visited several of the entrants. But Billy, naturally, had a starring role in my photographic narrative. I'd taken shots of his unadorned car, an old Nova he'd gotten dirt cheap at auction, and then step by step as he painted a base coat and crafted the centerpiece, which this year was an enormous book. He'd chosen to replicate *Through the Looking-Glass,* which had been one of our mother's favorites. The hood of the car served as a platform. He created a ramp, which allowed the book to lay at an angle, open to the page where Alice is asking Humpty Dumpty about the bit of the nonsensical poem "Jabberwocky." I knew that Billy had specially crafted wooden frames for the open book cover, papier-mâché for the pages, vast amounts of modeling clay to create depth in the edges of the pages, and paint.

One of my favorite resulting pictures was of him crouched over the giant book, a high-quality, thin-bristled paintbrush in his hand. It took him too many hours to count, all of which were after work and into the wee hours of the morning, or on weekends, foregoing other activities in favor of the task at hand. He had penciled the words first; then letter by letter he copied the entire excerpt from chapter 6 in *Through the Looking-Glass* onto the two open pages. He started at the beginning of the scene with Alice asking Humpty Dumpty to explain the meaning behind the poem "Jabber wocky." Letter by painstaking letter, Billy painted the entire scene, from "Twas brillig, and the slithy toves/did gyre and gimble in the wabe;/all mimsy were the borogoves;/ and the mome raths outgrave" to Humpty Dumpty's explanation of the various port- manteaus and Alice's declaration that she'd read the poem in a book.

I slipped into the memory of my mother reading those pages to Billy and me, her voice falling into a steady rhythm of those nonsensical words. They came alive for us, though. We didn't need to know what they meant to understand the feeling behind them.

Now, looking down at the art-car version of those *Through the Looking-Glass* pages, and knowing that the portmanteaus had been one of my mother's favorite things to teach, my eyes pooled. She'd been gone more than a year now, but she was never far from my thoughts. Or from Billy's. Despite the passage of time, he still couldn't express his emotions over losing our mom, but the concept behind and the execution of his art car showed just how deeply he felt the loss. He'd poured his feelings right into the words on the pages.

Billy had gone inside for a few minutes, so I pushed my own emotions aside, snapping pictures of the paint cans stacked precariously in one corner of the garage, the piles of newspaper scattered around, and the copy of *Through the Looking-Glass* that Billy had referred to. I flipped through the pages of the book, finally turning to the inside front cover. There, in a slightly left-slanted writing, which was half cursive, half printing, was my mother's writing. The inscription was dated and written to Billy:

My darling boy, may your days be filled with whimsy, and may you always slay the Jabberwocky. Like Alice, I'm always just beyond the looking glass.

Happy Birthday.
                              With love, always ~
                                            Mom

Once again, my eyes teared up. It hadn't

been prophetic, although in retrospect it certainly seemed to be so. I wanted to snatch up the book and hold it close, as if that would somehow make the inscription for me, as well as Billy. I racked my brain, trying to remember. She had given us both books over the years; it had been her thing. She wanted to share her love of reading with us, and she also wanted to let us experience her favorite books so that we could talk about them with her. Now, thinking back, I suddenly understood. The books she'd given us helped us to know her better, even now. If we pulled them all out, it would be like getting a glimpse into her soul. They would, I realized, help us rediscover parts of her long forgotten from our childhoods. And they would let us learn new things that she'd never revealed to us. We'd see her through the lens of the books that inspired her, that spoke to her, that moved her.

As I ran my fingers over her handwriting, committing the words to memory, I heard a movement behind me, followed by my name. "Ivy —"

I whirled around in surprise, my camera-carrying hand raising instinctively, my finger depressing the shutter button. My dad smiled and turned to Billy's art car.

At the same moment, Billy emerged from

the house, saw our dad, and rushed forward. My heart lurched upward, catching in my throat. Our father wasn't prepared for the scene Billy had created. I moved toward him. "Dad —"

But Billy and I were both too late. He was already in front of the car, his smile turning to pride as he took it in. He moved closer, looking at the enormous book Billy had created, squinting slightly as he started to read. And then suddenly his face collapsed.

"The 'Jabberwocky,' " he said, his voice low. He didn't move. Didn't turn away from the car. Instead he took a step closer and laid one hand on the painted lines. "Your favorite."

"Dad," Billy said, coming to stand beside him, but whatever he was going to say faded into nothing. Our father, we both realized, wasn't talking to us. He was talking to his wife . . . to our mother.

"I'm sorry —" Billy started, but our dad shook his head slightly and put his arm around Billy, gently squeezing his shoulder.

"For what? You love her. She would have been so prou—" He stopped as his voice started to break. He gathered up his emotions and continued. "I can just imagine her seeing this and —"

"She'd recite the entire poem." I closed

my eyes, seeing her standing here with us, speaking the senseless words Lewis Carroll had written. I could recite most of it, too, because my mother had loved it so much, but the second verse had always stuck with me. I spoke it aloud, feeling the rhyme, and the strength of the description, and the portmanteaus.

Beware the Jabberwock, my son!
The jaws that bite, the claws that catch!
Beware the Jubjub bird, and shun
The frumious Bandersnatch!

It had been years and years since I'd thought of the poem, but hearing it spill from my lips brought it back, word for word. It was an indelible memory and I couldn't help but smile.

"I never understood it," Billy said. " 'The vorpal blade went snicker-snack.' The 'Tumtum tree'? 'Galumphing?' " He shook his head, looking utterly bewildered. "Those aren't words."

My dad's voice suddenly rang through the garage, louder and clearer than it had been a moment ago. He recited the two verses Billy had been referring to:

He took his vorpal sword in hand:

Long time the manxome foe he sought
So rested he by the Tumtum tree,
And stood a while in thought.

One two! One two! And through and
    through
The vorpal blade went snicker-snack!
He left it dead, and with its
head He went galumphing back.

"Words or not, your mom thought they
were magical," he said when he finished.
"Can't say that I understand it either, Billy,
but for the first time, I think I get it."

He gave Billy's shoulder another squeeze
and walked around the car, taking in the
other details. I met Billy's eyes. It had taken
a long time, but we could finally talk about
our mother — and our dad could talk about
his wife — without breaking down or being
overwhelmed by grief. It felt like a pivotal
moment.

Billy attended to a detail on the front
bumper of the car as I walked next to my
dad. The entire thing was filled with whimsical features from *Alice's Adventures in Wonderland:* spotted mushrooms, teacups and a
teapot, a stopwatch, a crooked top hat laying on a grassy expanse, a small bottle with
a label that read: DRINK ME. I took pictures

of each element.

Our father was a man of few words. Billy and I waited for him to finish his slow perusal of the car. Finally, he rejoined us at the front end. "Nice job, son," he said, then patted Billy on the shoulder. "You'll take it this time."

I agreed 100%. Billy's Jabberwocky car was already impressive. By the time he finished, it would be spectacular. This was going to be his year.

CHAPTER 2

If Penelope Branford was my surrogate grandmother, then Olaya Solis, proprietor of Yeast of Eden, Santa Sofia's premier bread shop, was my honorary aunt. She'd been one of the first people I'd connected with when I moved back home. She'd shared her love of baking bread with me, and I'd run with it. Some people saw a therapist. Some did retail therapy. But for me, being in Olaya's classes and then helping out at the bread shop had helped me heal. I'd done baking therapy, and it had worked like a charm.

Olaya had a love of caftans and she kept her softly curled silver hair short. On so many women, the color would add ten years, but on Olaya it worked. "Who has time to do the hair color?" she'd once asked her sisters. "I am too busy baking the bread. You, you can keep your hair pretty brown, *pero* I am not going to fight against the

27

Mother Nature. She will do what she will do, and I will, how do you say? Embrace it."

Her philosophy on age was just one more thing on a long list of what I liked about Olaya Solis. I was thirty-six, so she had close to thirty years on me, but I planned to adopt her attitude about getting older. You can't change it, so why fight it? Mrs. Branford had a similar outlook. "You're only as old as you let yourself feel," she'd told me. I was almost fifty years her junior, and she seemed to have as much energy as I did. Whatever water she was drinking, it was her Fountain of Youth. If I could, I'd bottle it up and store it for my future self.

Exactly one week before the Art Show festivities would begin, I began my documentation of the art cars themselves. I started my day at Yeast of Eden, arriving at five o'clock in the morning. Olaya was tireless when it came to baking. She lived and breathed flour and yeast and long rises. She gave 100% to every single thing she did. Sometimes I looked at her clear skin and her bright eyes and wondered if she even slept.

Normally I'd have stayed at the bread shop until noon, but today I was photographing the first of the art cars. Many of the local entries were already complete, registered, and were being housed in an airplane hangar on the outskirts of town. In one week's time, they'd be driven through town in a parade, the townspeople cheering from the sidewalks on either side of the road. I was itching to get an early look, and by nine-thirty, Olaya's calvary had arrived in the form of her two sisters, Martina and Consuelo. They took over the baking and I raced home, switched out my pink Yeast of Eden T-shirt for a white blouse and a long soft gray cardigan, and changed into jeans. Standing at my closet, I considered my shoe options. I knew I'd be running around here and there, taking a million more shots than were necessary, and I anticipated needing to crouch down to get the best angles as I chronicled the features of each car. If my feet weren't happy, I'd pay the price. I settled on my favorite pair of Taos sneakers and was good to go.

I harnessed Agatha, my little fawn pug. The bread shop was one of the few places she couldn't tag along. Pets in a bakery? Not such a good thing. But there was no reason she couldn't come with me now. I couldn't actually keep her by my side while I worked, but my dad had agreed to be the solution. We would meet up at the hangar, where he would supervise Agatha. He'd get to have a sneak preview of some of Billy's competition, Agatha got to go on an outing, which she loved, and I had both of their company. It was a win-win-win.

I had never been inside an airplane hangar. I knew it would be huge, but that was an understatement. It was gigantic. Enormous. Massive. Walking through the door made me feel like Alice falling down the rabbit hole, shrinking until she was a miniature version of herself. On one side of the building were window-lined offices. The rest of the space was open with exposed steel rafters framing the arched ceiling. Ten cars were lined up in two rows along one side of the hangar. A Cessna Skyhawk sat on the other side. Its wingspan had to be close to forty feet, the length closer to thirty. It didn't have the height of a commercial aircraft, but the hangar looked as if it could house a fleet of Cessnas, with an intercontinental jet thrown in for good measure. Relative to the vast space, the art cars looked like Matchbox vehicles.

My dad arrived, looking better than he had in months. He'd undergone a transformation since my mother's death. His dark hair had turned to salt and pepper, his skin had taken on a sallow pallor, dark circles rimming his eyes, and his cheeks had become starkly chiseled versions of their former selves. But looking at him now, I could almost see the healing happening almost before my eyes. There was still a feeling of melancholy hanging over him like a dark cloud, but his face had started to fill out again, the color had returned to it, and his eyes had lost the vacant look they'd taken on. He no longer resembled a zombie cast member from *The Walking Dead.*

"Do you know who owns the hangar?" I asked him.

He stopped to think. "It's privately owned, I think. The space is rented out pretty regularly. It's been used for all kinds of things. From vintage markets your mom used to love to come to, to police auctions — Billy got a beat-up old car or two through those," he said with a laugh — "to the Education Foundation Las Vegas Night."

It was an amazingly interesting setting for any of these events, and so much more. An art gallery, for example, with local artists displaying their work. I'd sign up in a minute. They walked by my side as I started each vehicle's documentation with the registration tag taped to the inside of the driver's side windows. Each tag had the Santa Sofia Art Car Show logo, the car's "name," and the registration number. Once more cars were registered, the tags would help me keep them straight. It provided me with an extra level of organization.

The first car in the row looked as if a bunch of people took a few cans of earth and military-toned paint colors and did a Jackson Pollock number on it. It was dubbed the "Camo-Car." My dad nodded at it, chuckling. "It's okay, but your brother's *blows* it away," he said, emphasizing the pun.

I rolled my eyes. "Funny."

He bent down to scratch Agatha's head. "It was, wasn't it, Ag?"

The pug just looked up at him with her bulbous eyes.

"Ag?" I asked. I was pretty sure my dog's namesake, Agatha Christie, never went by Ag.

My dad stood and walked up to the next car. "It's a private nickname. Don't you worry about it."

I considered arguing the point, but my dad seemed almost happy. He angled his head down to talk to the dog as they walked, and he was smiling. If he wanted to call my dog Ag instead of Agatha, who was I to argue. The pug didn't seem to mind. Her tail was a curlicue — a sign she was safe —

and she trotted happily alongside my dad.

The next car in line was called "The Mosaic." Every square inch of it, including the tire rims, was covered with either a piece of broken mirror or a jagged bit of colored glass. Each of the fragments fit together like a puzzle, nary a gap between any of the shards. It had to have been painstaking and exacting work to get each piece to fit so perfectly. In the end, the car looked like an exquisite work of stained glass.

One by one, I went down the line. An old VW Beetle painted in red and white, with a nearly identical car somehow attached to the hood, upside down, creating a mirror image of the original; a replica of a supermarket shopping cart built on a pickup truck's chassis; a tiny smart car, the roof piled precariously with vintage suitcases. Each art car was unique and detailed, each, I imagined, expressing some element of the owner's personality.

My dad and I approached the next car registered for the parade. Agatha, who had been trotting along happily, suddenly stopped dead in her tracks. "Come on, girl," my dad said, tugging the taut leash.

She didn't budge.

"Agatha! What are you doing?" I patted my open hand against my thigh. "Let's go."

But instead of launching herself forward, as she normally would have, the little pug sat down.

I stared at her. Agatha was a high-spirited pug, but she was also well trained and obedient. This was not normal behavior for her. I slung my strap over my head, securing my camera across my body to protect it as I crouched down in front of my dog. "What's going on, girl?" I asked her. She didn't understand my words, but by the way she tilted her head and looked at me, I knew that she was responding to the soft and questioning tone of my voice. She blinked, yelped, and directed her globular gaze toward the next car in the parade line. In true attack dog form, she bared her tiny teeth, but any menace was diffused by the one-sided Elvis-style curl of her lip.

She was telling me something and I couldn't ignore her. I stood, looking for the registration and car number, but as far as I could see, it wasn't attached. The car was a giant face — or what was left of it. I registered the strips of skin torn away from the skeletal structure, the bone structure revealed beneath the rot, and its wide, dead-looking bloodshot eyes facing the sky. Two bottom teeth were missing, what should have been a fleshy pink tongue was a mottled gray, and half of one nostril was cleaved, fake skin flapping as if would rip free any second. Not even the curling hair was normal. It was crafted of what looked like modeling clay — a lot of it — and while the original color was black, the majority of it was tinged a dull and muddy-looking gray. I moved closer, walking around it. The ears were carved with exacting detail, but they, too, were mangled, part of one lobe shredded, the other missing a chunk. The strands of hair poking out from the inside were visible and distinct.

It was a zombie, and a disconcertingly grotesque one at that. No wonder Agatha was spooked.

From the grass, Agatha stood next to my dad, her tail no longer curled, but hanging straight down behind her, the sneer still on her smashed face. Even from where I stood, I could see her tiny teeth. Most of the art cars entered in the contest had a light and whimsical sensibility, and many had a meaningful message, like Billy's did. But this one was dark and menacing, and even Agatha got that from where she stood.

As I walked around to the other side, I caught a glimpse of the rotted black teeth. The gums were stippled with that same muddy gray color. I felt my nose twitch and my own lips lift in disgust. Zombies were more popular than ever, but even so, this one was hard to look at. From inside the cavernous mouth, I caught a glimpse of a pair of sneaker-clad shoes, as if the human-turned-monster was eating or swallowing a body.

I gave an involuntary shiver, but steadied myself. Despite the alarming nature of this particular art car, I readied my camera. I definitely wouldn't feature it on the event website, but I had to document it just like the others. Backtracking slightly, I took pictures of the ear and the hair, then made my way around it to capture the back of the head.

Next I headed to the front of the art car. Turning to face it head-on, I shook away the unease sliding through me and took a few shots. Agatha growled a warning as I moved closer. My dad was crouched down next to her, his hand on her back, but she would not be calmed. She lurched forward, tugging hard on her leash and knocking my dad right off of his feet. She was only nineteen pounds, so he managed to keep his grip on the lead, but my little dog was determined. She backed up and then charged forward again, barking, her chin raised aggressively.

I shushed her, but her reaction sent another shiver down my spine. Something about this particular art car had raised her hackles and since she didn't know a zombie from a bone, it was something else that had her spooked.

I stayed on alert as I approached the mouth of the zombie again, zeroing in on the makeshift body presumably being eaten alive. The tableau reminded me of the scene from *The Wizard of Oz* after Dorothy's house fell on the Wicked Witch of the West. All that remained were two legs and feet, the toes pointing up toward the roof of the mouth.

Agatha continued to growl. I nodded at her, patting the air to calm her down. "It's okay, girl," I said, but something deeper than the disturbing image was bothering me, too. I moved closer to the open zombie mouth and peered in. The feet were attached to a pair of pants. I'd expected them to be flat against the pink tongue, but they were stuffed and disconcertingly lifelike.

Who was behind this monstrosity of an art car? I had just depressed the button to snap another picture when something from underneath one of the legs caught my eye. I moved closer. Adhered to the gray and mottled tongue, and only partly visible under the khaki pant leg, was the corner of a registration tag.

Agatha was barking, alternately trying to spin around in circles and break free of her lead, but my dad held tight. I ignored her, instead directing my camera, zooming in, and depressing the button to take a picture of the inside of the zombie's mouth. After I'd captured several images, I brought up the digital images. I'd expected the faux body being swallowed to flatten into nothing, but it didn't. I hadn't noticed it with my naked eyes, but enlarging the image on my camera screen revealed much more. The figure in the art car display had a torso. Shoulders. A head. I zoomed in and drew in a sharp breath when I realized what Agatha had already sensed. The figure wasn't a fabricated body at all. It was flesh and blood.

I acted quickly, digging my cell phone from my back pocket and dialing 911 as I simultaneously hiked my leg up to one of the gaps in the zombie's mouth. I pushed myself to a crawling position and got my bearings, putting my camera near one of the rotten zombie teeth, pressing SPEAKER on the phone, then tossing the cell down as I navigated the pliable foamy flesh of the giant tongue.

"Ivy!"

I turned my head to see my dad standing in front of the open mouth and calling to me, but before I could tell him anything, a woman with a calm voice answered my call. "911. What's your emergency?"

I drew in a mouthful of air, breathing out to steady my voice. The words poured out of my mouth, telling her where I was and what I was doing. "He's not moving."

The operator didn't miss a beat. "Can you see if he's breathing?" she asked, her voice unruffled.

"Hang on." My knees sunk into the soft substance of the tongue, slowing my forward movement. I clawed my way forward, finally able to reach out my hand to place on his chest. No movement.

"We have your location, ma'am," the operator said after I told her. "We have a team en route." As I exhaled, she continued. "Is he breathing?" she asked again. "Can you check his pulse?"

I was way ahead of her, but before I could check for a beating heart, I had to be able to reach a wrist or his neck. His head wasn't visible, but I had already backed up, grabbed his legs, and tried to pull him, feet first, toward the opening of the zombie's mouth. Because of the squishy tongue, I wasn't making much progress.

Somewhere in the back of my mind, I heard the operator's composed voice still talking, as well as the faint sound of sirens. I couldn't focus on either. I grunted, exerting as much effort as I could, but the limp body only moved an inch or so. After another try, I sat back on my haunches, but then, from out of nowhere, two male hands reached past me and grabbed hold of one of the man's legs. I jerked in surprise, but didn't bother to look around to see who it was. Instead, I grabbed hold of the man's other leg. As if we'd counted down in a quick one-two-three, we pulled together and suddenly, with our combined effort, the man's body sprung free of its trapping. I lurched back, but quickly recovered, able to see his neck. I reached out to put two fingers to the carotid artery. I waited, holding my breath, hoping for some sign of life, but there was nothing. "No pulse," I finally told the operator. In the next moment, three things happened: The sirens that had been distant a few seconds ago now blared from the street outside, my brother's voice came at me saying, "What the hell . . . ?" and I finally registered the face of what I now knew was a dead man.

It was Max Litman.

CHAPTER 3

The next fifteen minutes were a blur. The EMTs were suddenly there, elbowing me out of the way. I looked around for Emmaline Davis, Deputy Sheriff of Santa Sofia, my best friend since forever, and after years of unrequited love, my brother's girlfriend. After a few minutes, I spotted her walking toward the zombie car, grim determination in her stride and her expression. Clearly she wasn't pleased with another murder happening in her town any more than I was.

She was in civilian clothes — jeans, a fitted T-shirt, and sneakers — and her black hair hung in tight spirals, framing her mocha-colored skin and her heart-shaped face. She was clearly off-duty, and second in command, but when something happened in Santa Sofia, Em was the go-to person.

She raised her arm when she saw me, turning her open palm to me so I'd stay put.

She needn't have worried; I'd found the body so I wasn't going anywhere. As if out of nowhere, a crowd of people formed. I peered outside the huge opening to the hangar and saw a line of art cars waiting as if they were stopped at a red light. I flipped my wrist to check the time on my watch. 10:30 — the prearranged time the hangar would be open to allow more finished art cars into the protected space. Or maybe it was just that people sniffed out murder like mosquitos smelled blood.

"Ivy."

Someone called my name as the EMTs started their emergency process on Max Litman, taking his vitals and trying to resuscitate him. One of them, a middle-aged woman, shook her head, but the other, a young man, wasn't willing to give up. He proceeded with chest compressions, the woman squeezing the rubber sphere on a resuscitator, forcing air into Max's lungs.

Again, the sound of someone calling my name echoed in my mind, but I was mesmerized, hoping Max wasn't actually dead. I hadn't liked him much, and he'd been a thorn in Billy's side forever, but none of us wished him ill, and certainly not dead.

"Ivy!" Billy's voice in my ear yanked me out of my thoughts, and his hands on my shoulders practically wrenched me off my feet. I grabbed the strap of my camera as Billy hauled me off the zombie's tongue and back onto solid ground, catching me before I could fall.

I didn't know why Billy was here, but it didn't matter. I nearly fell into his arms in relief. "It's Max Litman," I said. Since I'd entered the mouth of the zombie, I had ceased to hear Agatha's barking, but now that I was safely away from Max's body, I registered her frantic yelping. She hadn't seen me yet, and when she did, her yowling stopped and she spun herself in circles, twisting herself up in her leash. Her tail curled and she abruptly sat and tilted her flat face up to me.

I reached down and scratched her head, all the while watching the EMTs from the corner of my eye. They had given up their resuscitation efforts. There was no question; Max Litman was dead.

From behind me I heard a man's voice. "Murder."

I spun around, hoping I'd heard wrong. The sheriff spoke to Emmaline in a low voice, but I was close enough to make out some of what they were saying. "Ligature marks on his neck . . . no more than twenty-four hours . . . keep everyone out. . . ."

Murder. I repeated the word over and over in my mind. Violent loss of life was becoming an unwelcome reoccurrence in my life, For such a lovely coastal town, lately Santa Sofia had become a hotbed for unsavory death, and somehow I seemed to be in the thick of it once again.

Time seemed to stretch as I told my father and brother what had happened. The rest of the police had arrived, hot on the tail of Emmaline, red and blue lights circling from atop their cars, the quick burst of a siren cutting through the air. A moment later, two officers were cordoning off the area. I'd watched enough crime television to know that they wanted to prevent any contamination of the scene.

Once again I heard my name. This time I didn't recognize the voice. While Em made her way to the zombie car and Max Litman's dead body, I searched the throng of people, looking for familiar faces. The crowd had swelled to more than thirty or forty folks, but no one seemed to be focused on me.

Still, I heard it again. "Ivy Culpepper? Is that you, darlin'? My God, but you are a sight for sore eyes!"

I zeroed in on the direction of the voice, and it suddenly dawned on me who it belonged to. Dixie Mayfield. I'd photographed a lot of people over the last fifteen years, trying to capture some truth about them, something underneath the persona they put on for the world. The pictures I'd taken of Dixie were among my favorites. When I'd first met her, she'd been medicated, lost inside herself. She'd exuded sexuality, but she was melancholy at the same time. Despite the juxtaposition, there was nothing hidden — no masked version of herself that she showed to other people. She was authentic. Unique. An old soul. She could have been the reincarnation of Rita Hayworth with her contoured jawline and sultry eyes.

"Dixie!" I sounded more enthusiastic than I was, not because I wasn't glad to see her and to know she was okay, but because I was focused on the police milling about and Em crossing the parking lot and heading our way.

Dixie wove through the group of people between us until she stood in front of me. I'd photographed her wearing a full slip, listening to Billie Holiday, looking like a pin-up girl from the 1930s.

The dress she wore now reinforced that image. It boasted cap sleeves, a sailor collar and necktie, a beautifully placed drop waist with a wide black band, and an array of romantic ivory flowers gracefully cascading over the black fabric. It was either a meticulous remake of a dress from the 40s, or it really was vintage. Either way, it suited her. Her T-strap, round-toe black shoes and the gentle finger curls in her tawny hair completed the outfit.

She wrapped me up in a big hug as if we were long-lost friends, and I realized that a physical connection with someone else could feel like a jolt of energy and a reaffirmation of life. I also realized that that reminder was exactly what I needed after seeing Max Litman's lifeless body. I released her after a moment, her warmth sticking with me as if I were wrapped up in a flannel blanket. "What are you doing here?"

I looked over her shoulder at the growing crowd. It had been just a spattering of people a short time ago, but had somehow multiplied. Morbid curiosity, I thought, shaking my head.

"I had to come, darlin'. Word is all over town."

"How?" I gawked, although I knew the probable answer. Nearly everyone had a cell phone, which meant that word of Max Litman's death had been nearly instantaneous.

She flashed a coy grin. "Cell phones," she

said, confirming what I already suspected. "And truck drivers, of course. Those *Smokey and the Bandit*–era CB radios? They might as well be a phone tree."

"They're still around?" I had no specific knowledge, but I'd have thought they'd gone the way of the dinosaurs.

"They are alive and well in the trucking world."

I didn't know how she was privy to such information, but I also didn't need to know. The people were here and they weren't going anywhere. Dixie was talking again, filling me in on her life since I'd seen her last. The medications she'd been on at the boardinghouse where we'd first met had aged her face and her mind. Now that she was on new medication, the cobwebs in her head were gone, her skin glowed radiantly, and her eyes shone clear and bright.

"I'm in my own place now. And I have a job! I'm a receptionist. Small local business, but I am gainfully employed, which is something I couldn't say a few months ago." She flipped her hair and gave a suggestive smile. "It has its perks, too. I'm going to buy a house, Ivy. My own place. It should have happened a long time ago, but I've been at the mercy of others for far too long. I'm taking my life and my destiny into my own hands."

Dixie was a success story. Sometimes things didn't go as planned, and sometimes murder got in the way, but as long as the innocent bystanders didn't turn into collateral damage, I'd count that as a win. "You're resilient and pretty amazing, Dixie," I said, meaning every word of it.

"Why, thank you, darlin'," she said, preening; then she added a healthy dollop of sultry attitude into her voice. "As I always say, 'You only live once, but if you do it right, once is enough.' "

Where had I heard that before? I searched my memories and then snapped my fingers. "Mae West!"

She put a dramatic hand on her hip. "She may have said it first, but I'm living proof."

The commotion from all around us had faded as we'd talked, but now it came back into sharp focus. A car door slammed. An engine revved. "Quite the *calamity*," Dixie said, drawing out the last word. She threw a look over her shoulder toward the crowd behind her, turning back to me with a hurried whisper. "I heard that you discovered the body? Is it Max Litman? That's what people are saying."

Traveling with the lightning speed of a small-town rumor, the story would be in the newspaper by the end of the day. I had no reason not to fill her in, so I did.

"He had it coming, I guess," she said after I confirmed it, more to herself than to me.

I looked at her, startled. "Why do you say that?"

"He was a liar and a scoundrel," she said. "I don't imagine too many people will be sad that he's dead."

I had limited knowledge about the man's interaction with others, but her words struck me. Billy wasn't the only one with a grudge against Max Litman. "Did you know him personally?" I asked.

"I knew him once upon a time," she said. "We dated, if you could call it that."

"Really?" I asked. My curiosity piqued. Dixie was so sophisticated and belonged to another era. Max Litman, on the other hand, had been rough around the edges. They seemed a very unlikely pair.

From the wry curve of her lips, I knew she'd heard the disbelief in my voice. "He used to be more Johnny Cash than Willie Nelson, you know. Back in his younger days. Fancied himself a ladies' man, you know — at least when it suited him. Wined and dined and generally did his best to sweep a woman off her feet. I fell for it, hook, line, and sinker. Shame on me. I didn't know the depth of his inability to care for other people or what was truly inside of him."

I pulled up a mental image of Max Litman, not as the dead man I'd found in the zombie mobile, but as the man who'd been the thorn in Billy's side for so long. He was unnaturally tan, had shoulder-length gray hair that he kept in a ponytail, matchstick legs stuck out from the wide legs of the khaki shorts he always wore, and his portly stomach made him seem a bit off balance. As if it had a mind of its own, my hand cupped the side of my face. I shuddered at the memory of him leaning in to give each cheek a slobbery kiss with his gray peppered scruff. Who could ever see him as a Casanova? It just didn't quite compute. And Max Litman as Dixie's first love was an idea I *really* couldn't get my head around.

Dixie seemed to read my mind. "He was a good-looking man in his younger years. His appearance changed quite a lot. But one thing I've learned over the years, my dear, is that one rarely changes who they are inside, and even if they try to hide it, they end up revealing themselves one way or another. Max didn't much care about other people. If it didn't benefit him, he simply did not — *does not* — invest."

"Narcissistic?"

She nodded slowly. "I would say so, yes. Everything was always about him. His self-worth always seemed to come from the outside. How much money he accrued. How much property he held. How many women. Typical scenario of an insecure man."

"But he wasn't . . . he didn't look —"

Her expression changed, as if she'd just realized something. "The way he looked, with his shorts and his hair and all that, I think it was like a test. If he could make all these high-profile business deals and get all these women, no matter what he looked like, then it boosted his ego even more."

I considered Dixie's point. "So he thought that if he could still get beautiful women to be with him, then it would tamp down his insecurities. Prove he was worthy somehow."

"Yes, exactly. His life, you know, has always been about show. Do you want to know what *I* think?" she asked, her hand pressed dramatically across her chest.

"Absolutely," I said, glad to be getting such insight into who Max Litman was instead of focusing on the picture of his dead body I had in my mind.

"He never cared if women were with him because of his money. In fact, I think he preferred that. Real emotions were never his strong suit. I saw that early on. I was his eye candy, even back then. He thrived on people admiring him, whatever the reason. His money made him feel powerful. From my recollection, he felt his bank account let him control the women he was with," she said, then gave a matter-of-fact shrug. "Which I guess he did. He could dangle the purse strings and they'd jump, or he could yank them closed to punish them."

Dixie's gaze drifted back to the zombie car. The paramedics had Max Litman's body on a stretcher. As they lifted it slightly, sliding it into the back of the ambulance, it hit me again how final death is. Max had been here, alive, smarmy with his kisses, devoting all his energy to best my brother and win the Art Car competition — and now he was gone. It was cliché, but I couldn't help internalizing how fragile life is.

"Did *you* know him?" Dixie asked, but before I could answer, Emmaline walked toward us, her face grim. The sheriff was by her side. From what Em always said, Sheriff Lane had hung up his proverbial handcuffs when he'd inherited a tidy sum from his grandparents. He no longer felt the need to work terribly hard and preferred to do his job from behind his desk. But for better or worse, Max Litman was a Santa Sofia icon. His death brought out the big guns. Em and Lane came right up to me and the sheriff cut to the chase. "What happened here?"

He'd already decided it was murder, but I was glad that he wanted more information before making a proclamation like that public. I felt like a broken record, telling the same story over and over, but this time it really mattered. I recounted the details for them, beginning with my photographing the art cars, Agatha's reaction as we approached the zombie rendition, the feet sticking out from the back of the throat, and my realization that those feet were actually attached to a real body.

"You didn't see anyone around?" Em asked when I was finished.

I thought back, mentally scanning the road I'd taken to the hangar. Other than my dad, no one else had been around. I didn't know why, but the one detail I omitted was that Billy had appeared suddenly, helping me pull the body from the car. "Not a soul," I told her.

The sheriff scanned the crowd, cupping his hand over his eyes, a scowl on his face. "He could be here," he said. He wasn't out in the field much — that's why he had Emmaline — but his skin had the golden bronze of someone who spent hours in the sun. I'd made that comment to Em the first time I'd met Sheriff Lane. "Golf," she'd said. "He spends a lot of time on the links."

Despite being out of practice, he stepped right into the lead role. "Start talking to people," he said to Emmaline. "You take the left, I'll take the right."

"Yes, sir." As he headed into the gathering crowd, she took me by the arm. "This isn't good, Ivy."

Fear seemed to tint her grimace. "I know."

She pulled me aside and out of earshot. "We found something."

The thinly veiled fear in her voice sent a chill down my spine. I wasn't sure I wanted to know, but I asked anyway. "What?"

"Down in the back of the zombie's throat we found a copy of —"

She stopped suddenly, drawing in a deep breath through her nose. "Of what?" I asked, urging her to continue.

"A copy of *Through the Looking Glass,*" she finished. She shook her head as if she still couldn't believe it. "*Through the* freaking *Looking Glass,* Ivy."

Her voice trembled slightly as she spoke, but her pointed look felt like a knife through my heart because I knew what her conclusion was. "And you think it's Billy's?"

She bit her lower lip before answering. "I don't think, Ivy, I know. It has the inscription from your mom."

I felt the heat leave my face. *Oh God, oh God, oh God.* This could not be happening. I racked my brain, trying to come up with a logical explanation for why Billy's copy of *Through the Looking Glass* would be in Max Litman's art car, but I was at a loss. I knew what Em was getting at and I understood the panic I could see rising in her because it swelled in me, too.

She voiced what I already knew. "Billy's going to be the prime suspect in Max Litman's murder."

CHAPTER 4

The news of Max Litman's death had cast a pall over the very idea of the Art Car Show. The pervasive attitude was that the event should be canceled, but the planning committee disagreed. They'd acted quickly, meeting and discussing their options. The day after my discovery of the body, Penelope Branford, my sometimes partner-in-crime investigator, made the announcement at City Hall in front of a small crowd. Her basic wardrobe consisted of velour leisure sweat suits in every possible color. She was an octogenarian and adhered to her generation's rules of propriety. For the announcement about the Art Car Show and Ball, she'd chosen a subdued dark gray ensemble. It was true to her style, but showed her respect for the dead at the same time.

Mrs. Branford had long ago retired, but her years of teaching meant she was no stranger to public speaking, even if her oratory had typically been directed to teen-agers. She hadn't lost her poise or confidence. She clasped the wooden handle of her cane as she walked to the front of the crowd. Her walking stick was usually for show, but at this moment, I thought she actually needed it to help keep her steady. She spoke into the microphone, reading a prepared statement written by the committee. Despite the distress on her face, her voice rang out over the loud speakers. "The Art Car Show and Ball was Max Litman's favorite Santa Sofia event. He gave everything he had to crafting his art car, and his time, effort, and creativity paid off. He's won year after year after year. His trophies are displayed at the Litman Homes office. He took great pride in his success, and his creative entries in the event will be missed."

Whether or not they *personally* knew Max Litman, most everyone in town knew *of* him. He was a Santa Sofia fixture, a savvy businessman, and a cutthroat real-estate mini-mogul. I knew he'd screwed plenty of people over the years with his real-estate deals, so he wouldn't be missed by everyone. Still, Mrs. Branford's words were appropriate. She would honor the dead man by assigning him dignity and respect, whether it was deserved or not. She was not one to speak ill of the dead.

The official statement continued. "We, the Art Car Planning Committee, believe Max would not have wanted the event canceled. In fact, we are certain he would have insisted it go on as planned. And so it shall."

The crowd stirred, a few people clapped, and others responded with a yes or a nod of a head. Mrs. Branford continued. "We are dedicating this year's event to Maxwell Litman." She looked to the sky, palm open. "Rest in peace."

The people around me mumbled, but it was more an acknowledgment that she'd spoken than an echoing of the sentiment. My gaze met Emmaline's for a second. She broke the connection, her eyes finding her boss. He was not focusing on Mrs. Branford, but, once again, was focusing on the crowd. Emmaline backed away from me, focusing her attention in the same direction. I knew my old high school friend well. Like me, she was wondering if Max Litman's murderer was still here, blending in with the people of Santa Sofia.

My childhood home on Pacific Grove Street sat atop a small hill. Billy and I had spent our youth playing kick the can with the neighborhood kids, riding bikes in a zigzag to get up the incline of the road, and later, when we were young adults, sitting in the backyard with our parents, our dad grilling, our mom pulling weeds or planting a flower or reading a book. The memories had turned bittersweet after my mom died. My dad had struggled to move on, but now, finally, he was starting to adjust to his new normal without the woman he'd spent the better part of his life with.

I caught a glimpse of him standing at the living room window as I pulled up in front of the house. He held the door open for me as Agatha and I walked up the entry path. I gave him a peck on the cheek. "Hey, Dad."

He wrapped me in a quick hug, his arms tight for a beat before letting me go and leading me into the heart of the house. I let Agatha out of her harness before turning to Billy and Emmaline. They sat side by side on the sofa, their hands intertwined. Even in the dimly lit room, Emmaline's beautiful coffee-colored skin was in sharp contrast to the ivory slipcover. My brother's tanned face was still several shades lighter than her darker complexion, but somehow they almost blended together. Their children, if they ever tied the knot and went in that direction, would be exquisite.

They both straightened up when they saw

me. "Hey, sis," Billy said. He smiled, but it was forced, any trace of mirth nonexistent. It hadn't taken long for him to become a person of interest in Max Litman's death. The book with the inscription found at the scene, the theme of Billy's car, and the very public battle between the two men over their art cars had led the sheriff to the obvious conclusion. And now the pall of Max's death and the community's suspicion of Billy was taking its toll. Dark circles formed rings around his eyes and his cheeks seemed hollow. He was tall, handsome, and vibrant, so to see him looking so distraught made my heart sink. I knew he'd had nothing to do with Max's death, yet the people of Santa Sofia were judging him, and they were falling on the side of guilt rather than presumed innocence.

I sank down onto the couch on the other side of Billy and took his free hand in mine. I think we were afraid to look at each other for fear of the floodgates of our emotions breaking open, so we stared straight ahead. "We'll figure this out," I said.

Emmaline echoed my words, but from my peripheral vision, I saw Billy shaking his head. "People already think I'm guilty. Even if you find who did this," he said, turning his head toward Em, "my reputation is shot.

What if I lose my business? Who's going to contract with me now?" His voice turned bitter. "He's dead, but he's still screwing with me."

I squeezed his hand, trying to be reassuring. A businessperson's reputation was everything, so his worry was justified. "Anyone who knows you knows that you could not have done this."

"Maybe," he said, but he gave a half-hearted shrug. "But it'll always be in the back of their minds."

Nothing I said would make him see things differently, so I changed the subject. "Look, someone killed Max, and it wasn't you, so let's think about this. Surely he had plenty of people who didn't like him."

Emmaline turned to face him, tucking one foot under her. She was in her deputy uniform with crisply pressed navy pants and collared shirt. She was a tough woman, fighting crime on a daily basis in Santa Sofia, but at the moment she looked so vulnerable. My heart was breaking for them both. "The department is already on it. I have people making the rounds. A team is digging into Litman's business dealings. We're doing everything we possibly can."

Billy's hand tightened in mine. I glanced at him. His jaw pulsed with tension. "But nothing yet?"

She shook her head. "Ivy, listen," she said. "I need your help."

I'd known Emmaline longer than I'd known anyone in my life, with the exception of my family. She was the closest thing I had to a sister. I'd take a bullet for her. "Anything," I said.

"I need you to be my eyes and ears."

"What do you mean?"

Billy pushed himself off the couch and turned to face Emmaline and me. "She means she wants your help catching a killer."

My dad was up on his feet and charging forward before I could react. "Now wait just a second," he said. "One of my kids in trouble is enough. Ivy doesn't need to be involved."

Billy was nodding alongside my dad. "Exactly what I've been saying," he said with a pointed look at Emmaline.

"You're innocent, Billy. I know it. You know it. But I'm too close to this. Lane even said so. We need an objective view."

Billy scoffed. "And Ivy's going to be objective?"

Em threw her hands up. "She's already in the thick of it. She's documenting the cars and the event. She's —"

"I'm right here, you know," I said, cutting her off. The three of them turned to me. Billy frowned. My dad's forehead crinkled with concern. Emmaline's eyes had turned glassy. I ignored them all. "I am perfectly capable of making my own decisions, and I am also perfectly capable of being objective, even where my brother is concerned."

This time Billy grimaced. "You mean the brother people think is capable of murder?"

"One and the same." I turned to Emmaline. "I'll do everything I can."

CHAPTER 5

I dug my hands into the bread dough, kneading, kneading, kneading. With each squeeze of my hands, I exhaled. I was waiting for a stroke of brilliance. For an idea about how to prove that Billy had nothing to do with Max's death, but the aha moment didn't come. I had to go about things with as much logic as I could muster, which wasn't easy given my current desperate need to save my brother from the hell he was going through. I'd told Emmaline, my brother, and my father that I could be objective, but my emotions still flared. I muttered aloud, listing any and everything I could think of as a possible reason behind Max Litman's death. "A shady business deal?" Seemed pretty likely. "Had one of his bevy of beautiful women turned on him?" Possible. There wasn't a disgruntled ex-wife. A long-lost child come back for vengeance seemed overly melodramatic and unlikely. So what else? A mob hit? But I laughed that idea away. Organized crime in Santa Sofia was about as likely as the Loch Ness Monster emerging from the Pacific Ocean.

There was no way to know the truth, at least not at this moment. I needed to do exactly what Emmaline had asked me to do. I needed to keep my eyes and ears open to see if anyone knew anything; then I had to dig deeper into his life. "What were you hiding, Max?" I plunged my hands deeper into the soft goop of dough. I repeated his name over and over and over, as if saying it would somehow give me answers.

A hand gently touched my wrist. *"M'ija,"* Olaya Solis said, and I blinked. She stood beside me. She was a vibrant-color person, usually wearing bright pigments. Today was no exception. Her tunic was a floral pattern with a black background that she paired with dark pink leggings. The soft curls of her iron-gray hair were pulled back with a black cloth headband, and her gold-flecked green eyes were laced with compassion. "You are thinking too much."

I considered that. Over the last few months, Olaya had become my rock. Santa Sofia had always been a peaceful seaside town, but when crisis had recently overshadowed that peace, she'd been there to keep everyone even-keeled. She'd kept me grounded, even in the face of my mother's untimely death. She was right! Was I over-thinking things?

"Ivy, Max Litman was not a well-loved man in Santa Sofia. The police, they will find who did this."

"But what if they can't?" I asked. It was rhetorical. Of course Olaya couldn't answer that any more than I could. But it seemed to reason that if Billy was the prime suspect and no other motive surfaced, then he'd take the fall.

Olaya removed her hand as I grabbed the pliable mass in my bowl and plopped it onto the floured counter. I patted the dough, folded one section over another, and pressed, adeptly turning it as I kneaded the flour in. After the remaining stickiness disappeared, I put the dough back into the bowl, turned it over, seam side down, brushed it lightly with oil, and then covered it with a towel.

"M'ija," Olaya prodded. She knew me well enough to sense I wasn't telling her everything.

I leaned against the counter, wiping my hands on one of the bakery's standard Kelly-green dishtowels. "Emmaline asked me to dig around. I'm *going* to dig around,

66

but . . ."

She dipped her chin slightly, considering me. "But what?"

"But I'm not a detective and I don't work for the police department," I said. My words were a rationale for my insecurities. I'd gotten involved in local mysteries before and neither one of those things had stopped me. This time, however, the stakes were higher. I couldn't fail.

"You have done it before. You will do it again," Olaya said, echoing my thoughts. And I would. Somehow.

CHAPTER 6

The discovery of Max Litman's body the day before had prevented me from finishing photographing the early art car entries. Given that the event was to go forth as planned, I needed to get back to it — with new eyes and a new perspective.

I had no doubt that the police had scoured every bit of the hangar looking for clues. I didn't hold out much hope that I'd find something the police hadn't, but no stone unturned, and all that. My motivation, after all, was pretty strong. I called Emmaline, ready to convince her that I needed to finish taking pictures of the art cars. She wanted my help, but that didn't mean she could easily let me into a crime scene. But she surprised me. "I'll meet you there in an hour," she said in a hurried whisper.

I left Agatha at home this time, arriving at the hangar just as Emmaline pulled up. We moved in tandem, as if we were synchronized swimmers, stepping out of our cars, shutting our doors, circling to the fronts of our cars, then turning to face one another. "You look like I feel," she said, working hard to control the shaking in her voice.

Tossing and turning all night had left dark circles rimming my eyes, my loss of appetite had made my skin sallow, and I looked drawn and tired. Em's eyes were bloodshot and red-rimmed, her chocolate-colored skin, usually dewy and fresh, had lost its luster, and she looked like she hadn't slept in a week. "Ditto."

We both managed faint smiles and then gave up, falling into each other's arms and giving in to our emotions. After a minute, she extracted herself, ran her fingertips along the edge of her hairline, and blinked back any more tears. "I'm off this case," she said.

I stared at her, my blood pounding in my ears. "What do you mean?"

She threw her hands up, frustrated. "Lane says I'm too close to it, which is total bullshit. *Everyone* in town is too close to be objective. Even the city. Even our *department,* for God's sake. Max had his hand in a lot of pies, and a lot of them were rotten."

Emmaline was Sheriff Lane's right hand. His number one. The person he depended on most. For him to remove her from this murder investigation was serious, but I knew why. She was too close to it because of Billy. My voice dropped to a shattered whisper. "Lane really thinks Billy did this?"

She turned and walked, her arms so tightly crossed in front of her that her body seemed to shrink from the force. And then she stopped. Her back expanded as she breathed in and she turned to face me. She opened her mouth to speak. To answer my question. To say whatever it was she needed to. But she couldn't make the words come out. Even from where I stood, I could see her eyes fill, her lips part, her chin quaver. In the end she just nodded.

And my heart broke. My brother was the furthest thing from a murderer. Suddenly my commitment to be Emmaline's eyes and ears around the Art Car festivities hardly seemed enough. I didn't know how I was going to do it, but I wouldn't sleep until I found out the truth. We had to figure out who had killed Max in order to free Billy from the sheriff's — and the town's — condemnation.

We managed to gather up all our emotions and tuck them away to deal with later, focusing instead on our scrutiny of the hangar. I retrieved my camera from my car as Emmaline dug a set of keys out of her pocket and headed for the hangar's side office door. Something occurred to me, though, and I stopped her before she could unlock it. "Wait."

She stopped, the key in the lock. "What?"

"If you're off the case, who's in charge now?"

She grimaced. "Lane took it over."

My eyebrows shot up. From my experience and from Em's stories, Robert Lane didn't get directly involved with the goings-on in town. He was the politician, schmoozing and delegating, while Em was the brains and the muscle of Santa Sofia Sheriff's Department. "He's actually leading the investigation?"

She nodded. "Which tells you how worried he is. Bad PR for the department if we can't solve it. Bad PR for the department if the deputy sheriff's boyfriend is the main suspect. Bad publicity no matter which way you slice it."

"But I thought he didn't get his hands dirty."

"He doesn't." She swept her arms out to her sides, opening them wide as if she were gesturing to the whole property, or maybe even to the city. "He doesn't do . . . this. He doesn't investigate a missing tooth, let alone a murder. But he thinks proving Billy's guilt is the lesser of two evils."

"And you'll get in the way of that."

"I need to prove Billy's innocent. We have opposing goals. He's cut me off at the knees."

From the outside looking in, people thought Robert Lane called the shots, but from the inside looking out, I knew better. Emmaline ran the department. She did everything. Her boss was a figurehead, putting in the least amount of effort, but reaping the maximum benefit. "Does he even know what to do?" I asked, my fear for Billy at the forefront of my mind. Not that there was a playbook for solving a murder, but some general investigative skills were essential.

She shook her head as she threw up her hands. "I have no idea. He speaks at events and the Rotary Club and has long lunches and golfs." And then she grabbed my wrist. "I'm worried, Ivy."

Two questions hung between us, left unspoken. Did Lane have what it takes to solve a murder and exonerate Billy? And would he even try?

"How are you able to let me in if you're off the case?" I asked as Em turned the key. The last thing I wanted — and that she and

Billy needed — was for her to get reprimanded, or worse, fired, for breaking the rules of her job.

She smirked. "I told him the cars needed to be photographed for the committee. They already processed the hangar, so he didn't have any reason not to approve it. I have to use everything at my disposal to my advantage before he —"

"Before he what?" I asked.

"Before he realizes that I'm smarter than he is. Before he realizes that I didn't stop."

She took a breath. Closed her eyes. "Billy asked me to marry him."

My heart instantly swelled, but just as quickly, a vice gripped it, squeezing until I thought I might explode.

"We're supposed to spend our lives together. To have kids and grow old together."

And it could all be ripped away from them.

"I am not going to leave *that* in the hands of Robert Lane."

"Good," I said, and I knew she'd be like a dog with a bone, unwilling to give up until she had sucked out every last bit of marrow.

"Do you remember those old Nero Wolfe novels you turned me on to in high school?" she asked.

"Of course," I said, suddenly knowing

73

exactly where she was going with this. Nero Wolfe was a fictional detective who tended to orchids, was a gourmand, and was loathe to leave his New York City brownstone. Yet, there were always crimes to be solved. What was a brilliantly eccentric armchair detective to do? Rely on someone else to do the legwork, namely Archie Goodwin.

Em wasn't going to stop her investigation. "I'm Nero," she said.

But if she got stalled, I'd be there. "And I'm Archie."

Our gazes met, a silent affirmation of our common goal. Once she pushed the door open, I followed her into the hangar's office and through to the main area. Everything looked exactly as it had yesterday, with the glaring exception of Max's missing car. "They took it for evidence," Em said.

"To the county?" I asked, knowing that Santa Sofia was too small to have a forensics team.

She answered with a low "Mmm-hmm."

We took our time, walking around each car, taking in every detail. I took picture after picture after picture so I could finish documenting the artistic details I hadn't finished the day before. I'd hoped to make some discovery the police had missed. Em and I scoured the area around each car, but nothing was out of order. As we came to a stop in front of Billy's Jabberwocky car, the reality of the situation hit me in a new way. Someone had managed to get into the hangar, kill Max, and stage the body as if it were part of the art car. Not only had Max been murdered, Billy had also been framed. It was a layer of malice I hadn't thought of before.

I started with the most obvious question that needed answering. Was Max killed and put into the zombie mouth of his car before or after it was brought here? Unfortunately, that wasn't a question we could answer. Maybe after the county forensic team dug into things, they'd be able to make that determination, but from my novice point of view, I couldn't say.

I put my camera on top of Billy's car and walked the perimeter of the room. I studied the hangar with the hypothesis that the killer had come here either knowing Max was already in the car, with Max dead, or with Max still alive. Each of the scenarios was as likely as the next. I'd initially thought that the most likely entry possibility was that he — or she — had come in through the front entrance, which looked like a massive garage door. I hadn't noticed it from the outside, but from the inside, I could tell it was bisected horizontally. Five yellow straps, each starting at the top of the door and hanging horizontally, wound around clamping devices along the bottom. From what I could gather, the control panel next to the door controlled the door's movement. Pressing the top button would cause the two halves of the door to angle out as the pulleys forced the halves to collapse together like the folds of an accordion. Even if someone could open them from the outside, which didn't seem possible, having the hangar wide open and on display was pretty conspicuous. Unnecessarily risky, especially if Max had unwittingly come here with his killer.

Emmaline had moved to the now-empty space where Max's car had been the day before. She stood, hands on hips, turning in a slow circle, but like the rest of the hangar, there didn't seem to be anything amiss. Not a single clue about what might have happened.

"If we assume that the killer actually was here, how could he have gotten in?" I mused aloud as I came back around to Billy's car.

"Based on that scenario, he'd have to have a key to the office door we came through, would need to know how to open the hangar doors, and have the key, or" — she pointed toward the hallway connecting the office and the bathroom — "he could have come in through the window over there. Which only makes sense if Max was here and the killer needed to sneak in undetected."

I thought about that as I went to take a quick peek. A window, smack in the middle of the wall between the office and the bathroom, was taped up with a square piece of thick plastic. "Was it broken?" I asked.

She hadn't moved from the spot where Max's car had been. "Yes," she said. "But it's odd. The glass was on the outside, rather than the inside. So let's assume that the killer was already here somehow, but he couldn't get out through the hangar door or the office door. His only other option was the window?"

"That still leaves the question of how he would have gotten in here in the first place, and was Max here, or did the killer haul in the body to stage in the car?"

I peeked into the bathroom, quickly cataloging the room. A small sink was mounted to the wall. A simple mirror hung above it. A utilitarian shelf held a plastic pump bottle of soap, a roll of paper towels, and three rolls of toilet paper. Whoever had used the toilet last had left the seat up and had forgotten to flush. I shook my head. Men.

Back in the hallway, I looked more closely at the window. Spreading my arms, I gauged the size. It wasn't a huge opening, but it was plenty big. An average-sized man or woman could certainly fit through. Easy in, easy out. Emmaline's supposition about the way the window was broken stuck with me, though. Something didn't compute about it. I spun around to head back to the wide-open space of the hangar, but stopped short, nearly barreling into Emmaline.

"Whoa," she said, back-stepping to avoid a full-on collision.

She registered the expression on my face. "What?" she asked.

I gestured toward the blocked window. "Didn't an alarm go off when the window was broken?"

"Apparently it wasn't armed. We talked to the guy who manages the hangar. He said the alarm is always armed when no one's here."

"Always, but not yesterday."

"He says it *was* armed when he left. He's the one who set it."

I followed Emmaline and headed back to the hangar. We both gravitated to Billy's Jabberwocky car.

"Do you think Max was killed here?"

Em shook her head. "I don't think so, Ivy."

Emmaline had a sixth sense for things like this. Even without an explanation, I would believe her, but I asked anyway. "Why?"

"Mostly a hunch. Usually the cars are driven here by a towing company. Lane is looking into that. Max wouldn't have any reason to be here —"

"Unless he tagged along with the car transport. Which I wouldn't put past him. He was obsessed with winning, so would he leave his car in the hands of some strangers?"

She considered this. "Good point."

"Or," I said, another possibility surfacing, "he and his killer could have both come with the towing company."

"Or he could have been killed somewhere else and the killer came along with the cars, stayed behind, and put Max into position."

"Do you know the towing company that brought the cars?"

"Mike Moreno was working on that," she said as she pulled her cell phone from her pocket and pressed a speed dial number. "Moreno," she said after a few seconds. "Quick question. Did you figure out who brought the first round of cars to the hangar?"

She listened, but looked at me, the smooth skin of her forehead furrowing. "So Litman arranged it?"

"Arranged what?" I asked in a stage whisper.

She held up her finger, started to say something to Moreno, but then, like a flipped light switch, her expression changed. Fire burned underneath her coffee skin and her eyes flared. The tone of the conversation changed and it was painfully obvious that Mike Moreno was no longer on the other end of the line. I knew my friend nearly as well as I knew myself. In some ways I probably knew her better. She was livid, but she swallowed her fury, somehow managing to control her voice. "Yes, sir," she said. "I know, sir."

As she listened, she met my gaze, her jaw tensing. I jumped to the only possible conclusion. Emmaline Davis was not one to kowtow to authority, which was one of the reasons she majored in criminal justice in college and went into law enforcement. She had always wanted to be the one in charge, even when we were kids. Her career as deputy sheriff let her be the boss in her day-to-day life. The only person she had to answer to, and that she'd call "sir," was Robert Lane. I raised my eyebrows in a silent question, but her response to me was a quick shake of her head; then she was speaking again. Explaining. "The commit-tee's photographer needed to —"

She yanked the phone away from her ear as a voice boomed, sounding like it was coming from a bullhorn instead of a cellular device. "Davis, do you think I'm an idiot, or are you just trying to get yourself fired?"

Em put the phone back to her ear, a flush creeping up her neck. "Sir?"

Even then, I could hear his side of the conversation. He growled in exasperation. "I am well aware that the committee pho-tographer is the prime suspect's sister. Your *fiancé's* sister."

Emmaline cupped her hand across her forehead, pressing her fingers and thumb to her temples. "But, sir, I think Litman was ki—"

"Goddammit, Davis," he interrupted. "You are off this case."

She winced, pulling the phone clear of her ear again. "I know, but —"

He cut her off again. "If you know, then why are you there? Get back here. Now!" he bellowed. "Are we clear?"

"Yes, sir," she said through a grimace. She hung up and turned back to me. "He's a little upset."

"So I gathered," I said.

"I'm not supposed to be here."

"Right."

"We're having a banner week, aren't we?"

"We're going to figure it out," I said, squeezing her hand, hoping against hope that I was right.

CHAPTER 7

Olaya Solis was like my Yoda. She'd taught me not only about bread, but also about life. In baking, you took a starter and from that, sourdough bread was born. It was a cycle, but instead of starting with a handful of ingredients, transforming them into a loaf of bread, I was starting with a set of clues, and I'd end up identifying a killer. By the time I was done, Billy would be exonerated.

After our morning excursion to the hangar, Emmaline headed back to the sheriff's station to get chewed out by Sheriff Lane, and I drove along the PCH thinking about what I knew so far and where to go next. I let the fresh salt air waft into the car through my open window, cleansing my mind and my body. And then, out of nowhere, I had a sudden hankering to bake. To try using the sourdough starter I had fermenting in my kitchen. I craved the smell of yeast, and I craved a piece of crusty sourdough bread slathered with butter.

Making sourdough bread was a process. And it was as much an art as it was science. I couldn't wait until I could spring for a proofing box. In the meantime, I kept my starter in a large glass bowl. I'd been feeding it, letting it bubble, and rise, and foam. Because of the cool temperature in my house, the starter had taken almost two weeks to be strong enough to use. Today was the day I'd be making sourdough bread.

It didn't take very long, as it turns out. I mixed the dough, shaped it into two ten-inch oval loaves, and set them aside to rise. After an hour, it was ready to bake. Thirty minutes later, the scent of baking bread filled the kitchen. The loaves were a deep golden brown when I pulled them from the oven. As good as they smelled, I didn't actually want to eat any. I left them on a rack to cool, got back into my car, and headed to Ocean Drive. A few minutes later, I pulled into the back parking lot of Yeast of Eden. The discovery of Max's body had zapped my appetite, but suddenly I craved one of Olaya's skull cookies. She made them every other day, hiding them amidst the bread shop's daily offerings like Easter eggs tucked away for children to find. And that's exactly what happened. Little eyes would light up with excitement when they spotted one of the decorated cookies, modeled after the Day of the Dead sugar skulls, tucked behind a loaf of rye bread, or poking out from behind a mass of scones or croissants. Yeast of Eden didn't make the traditional sweets that a bakery did. "I make artisan bread," Olaya said. "I must stay true to my passion and my culture." Her sugar skull cookies were the exception to her rule.

They weren't overly sweet, but the taste of the sugar cookie was so satisfying. And right now I needed that type of satisfaction.

I walked in through the back entrance, straight into the kitchen. The bakery racks overflowed with baguettes, boules, rustic loaves, croissants, and a number of other Yeast of Eden offerings. I searched high and low, but there were no sugar skulls to be found.

Bypassing the office and the ovens, I abandoned the kitchen and went to the front of the bread shop. As always, the lobby was abuzz with bread lovers. Mandy, a young college student who'd been working at Yeast of Eden, manned the cases, along with a part-time high school student, while Olaya worked the register. Together, they were a well-oiled machine.

I took my place at the end of the line to

wait my turn, standing behind a woman holding a toddler in her arms. He looked over his mom's shoulder, his slobbery mouth chomping down on three of his chubby fingers. His deep brown eyes were red-rimmed. I scrunched my face up, blew a raspberry, and made googly eyes at him.

With one hand still in his mouth, he balled up the other and rubbed his tired eyes. His lips quavered, pulling into a frown, then a smile. "It's okay, buddy." I quickly scanned the bread case, spotting a sugar skull cookie next to the salted pretzels. I waved my hand to get Mandy's attention and pointed to the cookie. She made a face at me like, *really, you're going to take one of the kid cookies?* I notched my head toward the little boy. It looked like he'd given up the battle between laughing and crying. He was winding up, ready to drop his jaw and belt out a toddler-sized wail.

The little boy's mom bounced him up and down on her hip as Mandy handed me the cookie. I held it up for the little boy to see and, like a light switch turning off, his cheeks pulled up and his cry turned into a laugh in that way that exhausted two-year-olds can.

"Excuse me," I said as I tapped the woman on her shoulder. "Is it okay if I give —"

The words froze on my lips. The little boy's mother was Laura, Miguel's sister — who happened to hate me with a fiery passion.

The little boy reached his chubby, slobbery hand toward the skull cookie.

"Hi, um, Laura," I said, anything more intelligible failing me.

"Ivy," she said. The disdain dripping from her voice matched the expression on her face.

"Cookie." The little boy lunged toward me, his arm outstretched. "Cookie?"

I raised my eyebrows at Laura. Her answer was a grimace as she snatched the colorful skull from my hand. But then she turned to her little boy, her scowl turning into a compassionate smile, and offered it to him. At long last, he took his slobbery fingers from his mouth, giggled, and clapped his plump hands together. And then he took the cookie from his mother and started gnawing on it.

"Your bread," Olaya said from behind the cash register. She held out a brown gift-style bag, a sticker with the Yeast of Eden logo stuck on the front. Three baguettes artfully emerged from the top, looking like they came from a French sidewalk patisserie.

Laura readjusted her baby boy on her hip

and handed Olaya a twenty. Once she had her change, she threw me a pointed look, grabbed the twine handles of the brown bag, and strode straight out the bread shop door.

"Am I supposed to —" I looked at Olaya. "Does she want me to —"

The door, newly adorned with a bell, dinged and Laura stuck her head in. "Ivy."

"— follow her . . ." I finished, knowing the answer to the question was yes.

"Good luck, *m'ija,*" Olaya said with a wink.

"Mmm." I needed answers, not luck, but Laura couldn't give them to me.

The bell had barely dinged behind me when Laura whirled around, wagging her finger at me. "You . . . you —"

I held my palm up to her, resisting the urge to grab her flapping finger. "Laura, come on. High school was a long time ago. Can we just move on?"

Her little boy kicked his legs, happily gumming the skull cookie. His free arm flailed around haphazardly. Laura tried her best to contain him, but he bonked her on the back of her head. "No, Mateo," she scolded. She released her grip, letting him slip down her body. He landed on his feet, wrapping one arm around her leg to hold himself steady, still working his way through the cookie.

"I'm trying, Ivy. I really am," she said. "But I've hated you for so long."

Hate was such a strong word. "Laura, I never —"

"I know, Ivy. I know. You broke his heart —"

"No, Laura." I stopped her. "I did *not* break his heart. You actually did that all on your own." Not long ago, Miguel and I had figured out the truth about the end of our high school romance. He'd raced out of town, the dust from his truck's tires coating me in a cloud of despair. But he'd left thinking that I'd betrayed him, spending years in the military, almost as if he'd been trying to force me out of his mind once and for all.

Until we'd both come back.

Laura had done her best to scare me away from Miguel, telling me that he wanted nothing to do with me, telling him that I was sure to dredge up old wounds and break his heart again. "I get it," I said. "You were his baby sister, and I was stealing him away from you. So you lied." She'd told Miguel that she'd seen me with someone else. He'd had a teenager's broken heart based on her jealous lies, and they'd festered for years.

She dropped her head, looking tortured.

She was at battle with the emotions that had turned her against me for so long. It was as if a demon inhabited her body and was fighting to stay in. But finally, Laura won. Her eyes glassed over, her lower lip quivering. "I never meant to . . ." she started, her entire demeanor shifting before my eyes. The blame she'd been holding on to dissolved until all that was left was the ache on her face. Her voice dropped to a whisper. "I didn't mean to, you know?"

She'd been an adolescent. Of course she hadn't thought about the repercussions of her actions. Even if she'd thought about them, she wouldn't — couldn't — have foreseen all the fallout. "I know."

"He's my big brother. I just — you —" She paused, trying to gather her thoughts. "I thought I could keep him for myself. I didn't know he'd leave. I didn't know you meant — mean — that much to him."

I hadn't, either. All I'd thought as he'd driven away was how little I must have meant to him. Laura and I had both been wrong. "Have you talked to him about it?" I asked.

"No, because he's doing that *thing,*" she said.

I knew exactly what *thing* she was referring to. Miguel had a way of shutting down.

Everything seemed okay on the surface, but underneath, whatever was bothering him festered, and those buried emotions, whatever they were, seeped into his attitude like toxic water leaching through the soil. "It's like a lake that's been dredged, Laura. It all came to the surface again, but he'll get over it. Just give him time."

She nodded, her face sullen. I heard the distant caw of a seagull; the whir of cars rolling past. From the corner of my eye, I caught a blur of something blue at the curb. Recognition registered and I reacted without thinking, lunging, my arm outstretched. Laura registered what was happening at the same moment. "Mateo, stop!" she yelled, just as my fingers clamped around a fleshy little arm.

Everything came back into focus. Mateo tottered on the curb, one foot dangling, the other rooted only because of my grip on him. "Coo-coo-coo . . ." he said, reaching toward the street, his fingers opening and closing. The half-eaten sugar skull cookie lay in a mushy mess out of his reach.

Laura scooped up her son, squeezing him against her. "Don't do that, boo. You scared me."

The corners of his mouth had turned down and he looked like he was winding himself up for a wail, but Laura held him close. Little Mateo managed to rein in the cry he'd been about to unleash, gnawing on her shoulder to pacify himself. She pressed her open palm against his back, rubbing it in a slow circle. He gurgled, his gummy saliva leaving a wet spot on his mama's shirt.

I laid my hand on his back, as much to soothe him as to soothe Laura. For the last twenty years, she'd held me responsible for her brother leaving. The last fifteen minutes had been a breakthrough. I felt as if a ton of bricks had fallen from my shoulders, so I could imagine the relief she felt. "You have a little girl, too?" I asked.

Laura wiped away a tear. "Andrea," she said with a smile. "Mateo's eighteen months. Andrea is two and a half."

"You are one busy mama," I said. She was a few years younger than me, but looked worn-out. Still, it was an exhaustion that I wanted to experience. To know what it felt like to have a child growing inside of me, to give birth, to hold a precious newborn against my breast. Motherhood. My biggest regret was that I hadn't given my mother grandchildren.

I didn't know if it was in my future. Looking at Mateo, I certainly hoped that it was.

"She's with my husband," she said.

"Father-daughter date."

Those three words took me back. I'd started going to Valentine's dances with my dad when I was four years old. It was an annual event, and it went on for years. We added on ice-cream dates, roller-skating in the summer, dinner once a month, trips to the library. I looked forward to those times more than anything, until I decided that the idea of a date with my dad was for little girls. At eleven years old, I was far too grown-up.

A warm glow washed over me. Suddenly I wanted nothing more than to go on a date with him again.

As if it had been choreographed, my phone rang at the exact same moment that Laura's did. She dug hers from her giant black purse, which doubled as a diaper bag — or the diaper bag that doubled as a purse — and I pulled mine from my back pocket.

Laura cuddled Mateo against her shoulder as she took her call.

"Ivy, you there?" Miguel's voice was in my ear.

"Yes, sorry. Hey."

"Any news?" he asked, referring, I knew, to Billy and Max's murder.

I sighed. For the few minutes Laura and I had been talking, I hadn't thought about my brother and the murder rocking our small town, but now it all came back like a cannonball hurtling through the air, hitting its target head-on. "Nothing noteworthy."

"I'm on my way back from the city. Walk on the beach later?"

"Definitely," I said. He knew how the sound of waves crashing or the feel of sand between my toes could alleviate my worry.

Suddenly Laura was by my side. "Is that Miguel? Can I talk to him?"

Before I could hand over my phone to her, though, Miguel's voice snapped in my ear. "Is that Laura?"

"She wants to talk to you," I said, knowing that talking to his sister was the last thing he wanted to do. I was the reason he and Laura were at odds, but it was high time they mended fences.

He was silent for a beat. "Where are you? Why is she there?"

"At Yeast of Eden. To get bread, like everyone else. But, Miguel, we talked. It's okay. Really."

Another beat. "How —" he started, but before he could formulate his question, Laura snatched the phone right out of my hand.

"Miguel, Sergio got called to take another truckload of cars. I need to get Andrea from him, but my car's in the shop. It won't be ready for a few hours."

Miguel said something that caused Laura to bite down on her lip. Her eyes turned glassy. She pivoted until her back faced me, lowering her head. "I know. I'm sorry," she said, her voice shaky. She listened and nodded while Miguel said something else. "Me too."

And just like that, it seemed their walls had come tumbling down. She didn't need to say more than that. He was ready to forgive her. At long last, the past, it seemed, was behind us.

Laura fell silent, listening to whatever Miguel said next, and then, in the middle of her tears, she laughed. She met my gaze, nodding and smiling, the emotions I imagined she'd had bottled up for twenty years bubbling to the surface. It seemed to be the way of things with the Baptistas and the Culpeppers. We suppressed our feelings, or buried things we didn't want to face, but then, once the dam broke, it all came pouring out in one glorious mess.

Laura adjusted her hold on Mateo, repositioning him so he fit more snuggly on her hip. "I will," she said; then she handed me back my phone.

"Hey," he said. His voice seemed lighter

somehow, as if the burden that had visibly been lifted from Laura's shoulders had also floated right out of him. It was just the two of them — Laura and Miguel Baptista — against the world. I'd seen it with my own eyes back when we were kids, and here it was again. Ultimately, nothing could tear them apart — just like nothing could tear Billy and me apart.

Laura caught my eye. "I have to go," she said, but she looked around as if she were lost. "How are we going to get sissy?" she said to Mateo in a low voice.

"Hold on," I said to Miguel, refocusing on Laura. "I can take you," I told her. Another peace offering.

"Are you sure?" Laura asked. "I hate to ask —"

"Positive." It would give me something to do and a little distraction just might open up my mind to some new avenue to pursue.

"My husband, he can't get his flatbed through town here," she explained.

"It's no problem."

The relief on her face, though, told me that it was a big deal. "Thank you," she said.

I responded with a smile and a nod before my attention was drawn back to Miguel. "I can thank you personally," he said in my ear, a good dose of flirtation — and suggestion — in his voice.

"That could be arranged," I said, grinning to myself for the first time in a while. The sooner, the better.

CHAPTER 8

Sergio Morales reminded me of Pitbull, the rapper, not the dog breed. He boasted the same faint stubbly mustache and narrow soul patch shooting down from his lower lip and had the same build. He was on the short side, about five foot seven, from my estimation, but his demeanor was big and bold.

He had been leaning against a flatbed truck, arms folded over his chest, when we drove up, but pushed himself to standing as we parked. He might have looked a tiny bit menacing had it not been for the wide smile adorning his face, the little wave he offered to us, and the little girl in a yellow dress spinning in circles in front of him. She was a miniature version of her mom, from the waves of her dark hair to the amber of her eyes. Andrea, I presumed.

Laura's mini-me stopped to stare as I got out of the car, but the second Laura's feet hit the ground, she jumped up and down, clapping her hands. "Mama! Mama! Mama!" Laura scooped her up as I got Mateo out of a booster car seat we'd managed to borrow from Maggie at the bread shop. Turns out she often drove her baby brother here and there.

Just like Andrea had beelined for her mother, Mateo zeroed in on his father. "Papapapapa!" He reached for him, practically lunging out of my arms.

Sergio strode forward, taking him from me and flying him above his head like an airplane. Mateo squealed happily. "Hey, buddy," Sergio said as he lowered the boy to eye level. "Been a good boy for Mama?"

Mateo threw his head back, nearly leaping out of his dad's arms, but Sergio was an experienced dad. *"Calmate,"* he said as he put his hand on his son's back. Mateo shoved his fist in his mouth, slobbering away as he gummed it.

"Babe," Laura said, Andrea holding on to her hand. "This is Ivy Culpepper."

Sergio cocked a brow. *"The* Ivy?"

"The one and only," I confirmed at the same time Laura scolded him with an indignant, "Sergio!"

Her husband stepped back before she could take another backhanded shot at his arm. "Whoa there. Can you blame me for being surprised? You two have been mortal enemies for, what, like, twenty years? And now she's giving you a ride. *Es un milagro,*" he said. He winked at her, then held out his hand to me. "*Mucho gusto.* Sergio. Nice to meet you."

I shook his hand, instantly liking his easy laughter and the affection he clearly had for his wife. "Mortal enemies might be a little strong," I said, although it was 100% true given that, until I'd run into Laura recently, I hadn't even known there was any sort of problem between us. "But I'm glad for the miracle."

I took in the size of the truck and the trailer hooked up to the hitch. It wasn't like a flatbed semi, but it was plenty big to haul a decent-sized load in and around Santa Sofia. The spring breeze fluttered a white sheet of paper from the bed of the trailer, skittering it onto the ground nearby. There was something familiar about it. I bent to pick it up, immediately recognizing it — a registration tag for the Art Car Show, the ones that the committee required be displayed on the front right area of the car.

We were in the parking lot of Baptista's, nowhere near the hangar where the already-registered art cars were being kept, but I put two and two together. Laura had said her husband was a truck driver and that he was doing a local job, covering for a friend. "You haul cars," I said.

"Sometimes," he nodded.

My heart beat faster. Was it serendipity that Laura had brought me to her husband, who just might know something that could help me? "Do you take art cars to the hangar?" I asked, trying not to sound too anxious.

"Yep, my third trip in the last few days," he said. "Pretty tragic about that man who died."

"Yeah, definitely." I forged ahead with the question burning on my tongue. "Did you happen to bring his car — Max Litman's car — the other day?"

But instead of affirming, he shook his head. "Nah, I've been filling in for a buddy," he said, "but not since last week. Not connected to the art cars. He took the first round to the hangar. It's his business."

I was disappointed, but also not surprised. It would have been way too easy if Sergio had some of the answers I needed. "I'd love to talk to him," I said.

Mateo airplaned his arms, one of them thunking against his dad's head. Sergio grimaced, clasping his hand around his son's wrist. *"Cuidado, m'ijo,"* he said.

Mateo propelled his body away from his dad, his arms flying again. Laura lurched forward, grabbed him, and lifted him out of Sergio's arms. "You're a rascal," she said, half scolding, half laughing. "Let's look at the flowers," she said, putting him down and grabbing his hand to keep him steady on his feet.

I watched the interaction between Laura and Sergio. The lift of an eyebrow between best friends could convey an entire paragraph worth of conversation. The pursed lips between a mother and child spoke volumes. A single look between a husband and wife, like the subtle glance that passed from Sergio and Laura, expressed understanding. My former husband and I had never gotten to the point where we developed that form of communication. In a fleeting thought, I wondered if Miguel and I ever would.

Sergio winked at Laura as she held Mateo tight, ushered Andrea forward, and strolled away from us. He looked back at me. "It's eaten her up, you know, all the stuff between you and Miguel. About everything that happened back when you were all kids."

"I know. But it's all good now."

He folded his arms across his chest. "She

ended up with an ulcer. Miguel doesn't even know that." He looked across the parking lot at his wife and children, his expression soft. "All these years, it's torn her up from the inside out, her guilt over breaking you and Miguel up."

"It was a long time ago —"

"But it drove Miguel out of town. Into the military, no less. If anything had happened to him, I think it would have destroyed her."

I remembered her outright disdain when I'd seen her at the Winter Wonderland Festival not long ago. There had been no love lost. This turnabout — the burying the hatchet — had come out of nowhere.

"Self-preservation," he said, as if he could read my mind. "We've been married almost eight years, and we've known each other for a lot longer than that." He chuckled. "Sometimes I have no clue what's going on inside her head, but then there are other times when I can seriously read her like an open book. When you moved back here, it pretty much turned things to crap for a while. She lost it. She went back and forth between thinking that the past was going to bubble right back up, or that it wouldn't, but that she'd be looking over her shoulder, sure it was just a matter of time before it all went to hell. Basically, she didn't want her brother to know that she'd lied. Stupid after all these years, but baggage is baggage. It keeps the therapists in business."

I started to speak. To say that Laura had been a kid. That it didn't matter, but Sergio held up his hand, palm out. "I know, believe me. I've been telling her for years that she needed to tell him what really happened, but she wouldn't do it. She was afraid. She painted you as a villain back then. She thought that doing it again could give her a little time to figure out what to do."

Sergio wasn't judging his wife. He was just being brutally honest. "She was ready to let it go, though. We just talked. Finally."

He shrugged. "Like I said, sometimes I have no idea what goes on inside her head. Keeping you and Miguel apart didn't work, so I think she just threw in the towel. I think she finally decided to just come clean."

It had taken her a long time to get here, but at least she had.

Sergio took his cell phone from his pocket, tapping his thumb against the touch screen. A moment later, he held the phone out for me to see. "Nate Allen," he said. "Allen Trucking. Want me to share the contact?"

I answered by giving him my cell number. "Thank you, Sergio."

He gave a single nod. "Thanks for accepting her apology. I think my life just got a lot easier," he said, with a wink.

I hoped mine had, too.

CHAPTER 9

Crime drama TV shows made solving murders look so simple. A clue was discovered that led to another clue, which in turn led to yet another, and before long, a suspect was targeted, alibis were discounted, and a murder was solved. Badabing, badabam, badaboom . . . done.

It didn't happen that way in real life. At least not in *my* real life. I'd been the one to discover the body, and other than the *Through the Looking Glass* book connecting Billy to the crime, not a single other clue had been unveiled. With Emmaline's help, we had gotten back into the hangar to reexamine the crime scene, but other than the broken window, we'd come up empty-handed. Knowing who brought the cars to the hangar was the first actual connection someone had to the scene of the crime. If the police already had this information, I didn't know about it. I channeled my Archie

Goodwin, texted Emmaline my next move, and formulated a semblance of a plan. First order of business was a trip to Allen Trucking Company. Next, depending upon what information, if any, I gleaned, I planned to stop by the Litman Homes office. Between the two, surely I'd be able to learn something about Max and who — other than Billy — could be a viable suspect in his death.

I dropped Laura and her kids back at the bread shop and then made a pit stop on Maple Street to collect my partner in crime. I'd called ahead, and Mrs. Branford was waiting on the curb for me. Today her standard velour sweat suit was dark gray, a stark contrast to her snowy hair. She leaned on her cane and reached for the door handle before I'd even rolled to a complete stop.

I slammed on the brakes. The car lurched forward before it stopped altogether, but Mrs. Branford was none the worse for wear. "Did you get caught behind a train?" she asked after she strapped herself in, an unfamiliar tone in her voice.

As a lifelong Santa Sofia resident, she knew perfectly well that that the town did not have a rail system. I cocked an eyebrow at her. "There was traffic."

"Hmm."

"Seriously. An accident on PCH has things backed up."

She stared straight ahead. "So where are we going?"

I shot a puzzled glance at her. My, but she was salty today. I might have thought she didn't want to do any crime-solving today, except that, despite her bad attitude, I knew that she did. She lived for this kind of thing, sometimes dragging me into something I thought we'd be better off avoiding.

I pulled away from the curb, heading east, but avoiding PCH by going through town. "Allen Trucking Company."

She harrumphed again, but I ignored her bad mood, chalking it up to a poor night's sleep. I filled her in on the sudden turn-around with Laura and the fact that Sergio knew the guy who'd hauled Max Litman's art car to the hangar. "Maybe he noticed something, but doesn't *know* that he noticed," I finished.

"Ivy," she said with a shake of her head. "You can't barge in and ask a person if they know something they don't know they know. That is a completely muddied thought."

"Of course I'm not going to phrase it like that," I said, suddenly on the defensive and thinking that this is what it must have felt like to be one of Penelope Branford's high school English students on the receiving end of her disappointment.

"Good, because we have to think this through. Your brother needs you."

"This is the *only* thing that's been on my mind," I said. "The sheriff took Emmaline off the investigation. It's just me."

"Then we need to get serious."

The traffic light turned red and I slowed to a stop. "Mrs. Branford, what in the world is wrong?" I asked, concerned. She was as sharp as a tack, but was her shift in attitude a sign that her old mind was slipping? Or . . . Oh my God, was she sick?

I looked at her, waiting. She drew her lips in and closed her eyes for a moment. The light turned green, so I drove, still watching her from the corner of my eye. Finally, when she still hadn't spoken, I pulled over, put the car in park, and placed my hand on hers. "What is it? Are you okay?"

Finally, she let out a heavy breath. She had one hand over the other, clamping the handle of her cane. "I heard from my boys today," she said.

Her oldest son, Jeremy, lived and worked in banking in San Francisco. Peter, her youngest, was a computer programmer who lived abroad. He worked virtually and had never laid claim to one specific locale. He climbed, surfed, biked, and generally lived outdoors when he wasn't tethered to his computer.

I waited. She loved to hear from her children, so there had to be more. Something was upsetting her. "Today is the anniversary of Kat's death," she said, her emotions barely under the surface.

A vice gripped my heart. Her daughter, Katherine. She'd fallen victim to cancer long ago, but, had she lived, she would have been fifty this year. Mrs. Branford didn't talk about her daughter much; in fact, for the first few months after we'd met, I'd had no idea she'd even had a daughter.

Not long ago, Mrs. Branford had paid me the highest compliment by telling me that I reminded her of her headstrong and bold Kat. She'd described her as quick-witted, book-smart, intuitive, and wise, all things she felt I embodied, as well.

Losing Katherine had left a hole in her. It had nearly driven her husband, Jimmy, into another woman's arms. But they'd survived, the love they had for Kat like the circling light from a cliff-side lighthouse, guiding them through their daily lives until they were safe and could emerge from the fog.

"And neither the angels in heaven above, /

110

Nor the demons down under the sea, / Can ever dissever my soul from the soul / Of the beautiful Annabel Lee." She spoke softly, but I'd heard enough to recognize the line from one of Edgar Allan Poe's most famous poems. Poe had written of a romantic love, but the sentiment was universal. Not even death could break the eternal love between a mother and a daughter. I felt that with my own mother. Sometimes I thought Mrs. Branford coming into my life, and me coming into hers, was serendipitous. Neither of us could replace the people we'd lost, but we were surrogates for each other.

Still, there were no words. Nothing I could say would lesson her grief. I waited in silence, ready to take my cue from Mrs. Branford. It took her a few minutes to gather herself, but finally, she closed her eyes and exhaled again. "I'll always miss her," she said. "The day that marks her passing is the one day I allow myself to slip back in time. To grieve. Some years it hits me harder than others."

"I know," I said, squeezing her hand. The loss of my mother hit me harder on some days than others. I'd seen the same struggle in my father and my brother. Something would trigger a memory and then, bam, we were shot right to that empty hole inside, the one that would never be filled.

We sat in silence for another few minutes before I squeezed her hand in solidarity and support. I started the car and resumed our trip to Allen Trucking Company, the air between us clear, our purpose renewed.

A short time later, we pulled up to a grouping of warehouses. Allen Trucking Company was housed in the last space in a row of attached rental spaces, the modest sign the only evidence that that particular spot was occupied by a business.

"This is it?" Mrs. Branford peered out the car window, her eyes pinched to block out the bright light of the sun. "This man, this Allen. Do you really think he knows something about Max's death?"

That was the one-hundred-twenty-thousand-dollar question. "I hope so."

She threw open the car door, swung her legs sideways, leveraged herself out with her cane, and started for the nondescript door.

"Mrs. Branford, wait," I said, slamming the car door behind me and hurrying to her side.

"No time to waste, Ivy, my dear," she said, her voice and sass back to their normal tenor. "If the man from the trucking company can help, then we must talk with him, posthaste."

"Right, but Mrs. Branford, you have to be careful. You're —"

"— not in the ground yet," she finished; then she raised her cane, rapping the base of it against the door.

No answer. I tried next, pounding with my fist, but still nothing. "Let's check around back," I suggested. The words were scarcely out of my mouth before she was already walking to the end of the building, swinging her cane, and making a sharp turn at the corner. She was incredibly agile for her age. I speed-walked to keep up with her, turned the corner, and nearly ran right into her. She'd stopped short, but I caught myself before I took us both down. Looking up, I froze. Three men stared at us from in front of a low flatbed truck. We stood staring at each other until one of them finally strode toward us. "Can I help you find something, ladies?"

I circled around Mrs. Branford and met him halfway. He readjusted the ball cap on his head, lifting the brim slightly so I could see his eyes. "I'm looking for Mr. Allen? Allen Trucking Company."

"Which one?" he asked, looking over his shoulder at the other men and then back at me.

That was a good question. Given the fact

113

that I didn't know there was more than one possibility, I didn't have the answer. "The one that drove Max Litman's art car to the hangar."

"Right." He notched his thumb toward the other men. "Nate, these ladies *need* you," he hollered.

The three of them snickered.

Seriously? I crossed my arms and gave them a death stare. Juvenile. But Mrs. Branford was not in the mood for male shenanigans. I'd caught a glimpse of this side of her in the car a few minutes ago, but now she embodied it fully. She wasn't going to let them off so easily. She lifted her cane, pointing it like a sword at the men. "You need to learn respect. Has the recent downfall of prominent men taught you nothing?" she snapped. "This is about a murder. It is *not* a joke."

They reacted as I imagined her students did when she'd taken them to task. The three men stood up straighter. The one we had been talking to removed his hat, holding it by his side. The others strode over to us, their gaits purposeful.

One of them, the man with heavy stubble and dark brown hair in a buzz cut, looked a little unsavory. But he was the first to extend his hand to Mrs. Branford. "We meant no disrespect, ma'am."

Looks can be deceiving. I reminded myself never to judge a book by its cover.

"I suggest you think before you act next time. Mrs. Branford's stern voice and lips drawn into a tight line more than conveyed her dismay, but she finally nodded an acknowledgment of the man's apology and lowered her cane.

The same man turned to me. "What can I help you with?"

I looked at the three of them. "Are you Nate Allen?"

"That's me."

Finally. Maybe now we'd get somewhere. I cut to the chase. "Sergio Morales gave me your name. Mind if I ask you a few questions?"

He drew his head back slightly, narrowing his eyes. "About what?"

"Max Litman."

I took his silence as acknowledgment.

"Sergio said you took Max Litman's art car to the hangar?"

He rocked back on his heels, plunging his hands into the pockets of his jeans. "That's right."

In and of itself, that confirmation was nothing to get overly excited about. Still, I was hopeful that it would be a boon for potential progress in the investigation. "How does it work?"

"How does what work?" he asked.

"I mean, how'd you get the job? And did Max meet you when you loaded it up?" That was the big question I wanted answered. Had the man already been dead and posed as a corpse when his car was taken to the hangar? Or was Max alive and well when Nate Allen picked up the car? Was he killed in the hangar, or brought there after? Knowing the answer to that could help focus my unofficial investigation.

"Max always uses — er, used — me to take his car. Been doing it for years. I don't think he trusts — trusted," he corrected, scratching his head — "anyone else."

"So he's the one you arranged the pickup with?"

"Right. He coordinated with the others. I just load 'em up and haul 'em away."

"And that day? The day you took Max's car to the hangar?"

"It was a light load. A few other cars were already there when I delivered."

"So you just took Max's car?"

He shook his head. "Two cars. Max brought his the day before the delivery. He was supposed to meet me for the haul, but he was a no-show."

It struck me as odd that Max would trust a complete stranger with his art car. If he knew he couldn't be there, why wouldn't he have rescheduled for a later time, or even for the day before?

"What was the other car?" I asked. Who did he trust to make sure his car was safe?

Nate shrugged his burly shoulders. "Don't remember the guy's name. He just showed up with the car and I hauled it away. Something to do with a book."

I froze. Mrs. Branford put her hand on my arm. "What book?" I forced out the words in a whisper.

"Shit, I don't know. Books aren't my thing."

I wasn't sure I really wanted the answer, but I pressed anyway. "Do you remember anything about the car itself?"

He snapped his fingers as if it just came back to him. "Tim Burton."

"Tim Burton?"

"Mrs. Branford knocked her cane against the ground, her voice in rhythm with it. "Tim Burton and Johnny Depp."

Nate snapped his fingers and grinned. "That's it! *Alice in Wonderland*. Max didn't show, but the other guy did."

My pulse flared, blood pounding in my ears. I couldn't find my voice, but Mrs.

Branford knew exactly what was on my mind. She moved closer to me, clasping my hand. "What other guy?" she asked, although we both knew the answer to that question.

Nate pinched his eyes, thinking. He turned to the man with the ball cap. "What was his name?"

But it was the third man who took a step forward. "I remember him," he said. "His name, it was Billy."

CHAPTER 10

I called Billy the second Mrs. Branford and I had rounded the corner and were clear of Nate Allen and the two other men. He answered on the fourth ring, his voice low. Angry.

A knot formed in the pit of my stomach, but I forged ahead, doing my best to keep my voice calm. "When was the last time you saw Max Litman?"

He sighed, the tone of it clearly irritated. I pictured him dragging his hand through his hair in frustration. "What?"

I felt bad for him, but I needed an answer. "Just tell me. When was the last time you saw him?"

He let out a heavy sigh. "Ivy, I can't deal with this right now."

"You don't have a choice." I closed my eyes for a beat, willing my voice to remain steady. "You didn't tell me that you were the one who met Nate Allen."

"Nate *who*?"

"Allen. Nate Allen. Allen Trucking Company. The guy who hauled your art car — and Max's — to the hangar."

"O*kay,*" he said, drawing out the word. "So?"

"That's a problem, Billy."

"And why is that, Ivy? Another nail in my coffin?"

I shuddered at the reference. "As a matter of fact, yes. That truck driver puts you as the last person to see Max's car before it was taken to the hangar, and that's where his body was found. Max was a no-show meeting the truck driver. Why did he not show up? It begs the questions of whether or not Max was already dead, and if so, was his body already staged in the car and no one noticed? And, see, here's the problem, Billy. If he was still alive, why wasn't he there to see his award-winning car loaded and then unloaded at the hangar? And why were you, his nemesis, there? And if you *were* there, which we now know you were, and Max was already dead, you could have put his body there."

A heavy silence fell between us. "So that's what you think," he said, more disgusted statement than question.

I realized how what I'd said must have

sounded. "No, it's not what *I* think. It's what *other* people might think, Billy. Why were you there?"

"Max texted me. Said he had the transport arranged, but he couldn't make it. He asked if I could. He said he'd bring his car earlier, so there'd be no problem there. I figured I could drive my car the short distance to the pick up location, then let the truck load them on the flatbed and take it from there."

"I didn't know you two were text buddies." It came out more like an accusation than I'd intended, but I let the words hang there.

"Yeah, Ivy. All those years of him besting me, it was all a ruse. We were secretly great friends." His sarcasm dripped like honey from an overflowing pot.

I didn't care that it came out wrong. "Since when does he text you?"

"Never. That was the first and only time."

I wanted to bang my head against the steering wheel. "Billy, that's important information! Does Em know?"

He exhaled, heavy and downtrodden. "No."

"Oh my God, Billy. Oh. My. God." I held my cell phone away from my ear for a second, bugging my eyes at Mrs. Branford. She raised her snowy eyebrows, her forehead

121

crinkling into a roadmap. This was turning into a bad TV show.

"It was free transportation of the car, so I took it."

"So you didn't actually talk to him?"

"I did not talk to Max that day, or any other. I did not see Max that day, Ivy. *He texted me.* He said he couldn't make it. He asked me to meet the guy. *He* arranged it, I didn't. But it sounds bad, doesn't it? I know it does, so I didn't tell Em. How could I?"

Knowing that he was innocent, I really couldn't blame him. If it had been me, what would I have done?

"I've replayed every minute of that day, wondering if I saw something that just didn't register. I showed up a little early. I wanted to look at his creation to see if I was really going to lose again. I looked at it, and I realized that it *was* good. Good enough to win? Probably, but not because it was actually better than mine, but because he *always* won. I walked around and around it. The details were great, you know? I waited while they were loaded and I followed him to the hangar. The guy there let us in, then locked it up after the cars were inside and we left. That was it. I never saw Max that day, and then the next morning you found him."

"Was there a body in the zombie mouth?"

"Are you asking me if I noticed Max was already dead and sprawled in the car, and I just neglected to mention it?"

It sounded ridiculous when he put it that way, yet people sometimes didn't realize that they'd seen something until their memory was jogged. I didn't know if him being certain about the body being there — or the body not being there — would help him one way or another. Still, it felt like something we should try to be definitive about. I pressed. "Think, Billy."

"Don't you think I have been?" he snapped. "That's all I've *been* doing. Replaying it in my mind, trying to remember everything. Every drop of imitation blood. Every fake wrinkle. The red of that tongue. Did I really miss seeing a dead body right there in front of me?"

I glanced at Mrs. Branford. She had leaned her head back against the seat and closed her eyes. Her chest rose and fell in a steady rhythm. Sound asleep. Doing my best not to wake her, I slipped out of the car, gently closed the door, and leaned against it. "Billy," I said, "do you have an alibi from the time Allen Trucking took Max's car to when I discovered the body?"

Instead of an answer, I heard the reverberating sound of a boom, like he'd put his fist through a wall. "I met the truck guy, we drove to the hangar and dropped both cars off, and then I went to work."

"Work, where?" As a contractor, work could mean he went to wrap up a house remodel, headed to the city to pick up a special-order kitchen faucet, a meeting with an architect, or anything in between.

"I had a meeting with a developer. Wellborn Homes. There's a piece of land east of town. Thirty-three houses planned and they called me to bid them out."

I put a smile into my voice, happy for him that *something* was going right. A boon for my brother's business would give him something real to focus on, and that could only be a good thing. "You never mentioned that. That's great."

But my enthusiasm was short-lived. "Yeah, not so much. The second Max's body was found and I became an unofficial 'person of interest,' they ran."

"They could corroborate the timeline, though," I said, thinking aloud. "If Max was already dead and in the car when it got to the hangar, and if you have an alibi for *before* you met the truck driver and for *after* they left, then you couldn't possibly be the killer."

Why hadn't Emmaline thought of this? Or

the sheriff? It would be so easy to exonerate Billy based on his alibies.

"Right, but this is real life, Ivy. I don't have an alibi for before I met the truck driver. I was taking care of some odds and ends. Digging through my garage to find some tools I needed, stopping by a completed job site —"

"No one was there?"

"Nope. We'd wrapped up the day before, but I always take a final look around."

Disappointment flared, but I tried to stay positive. "Okay, but you met this Wellborn guy right after —"

"Yeah, except he was late."

"How late?"

I could almost see Billy shrugging. "Thirty minutes. A little more."

"Which means you have no alibi," I said.

"Which means I have no alibi," he confirmed.

I tried to bolster him up, failing miserably. I hung up, leaving him feeling worse off than he had before. A minute later, I was back in the car. Mrs. Branford was still snoozing in the passenger seat. I leaned over, pulling the seatbelt over her shoulder and snapping it into place. I had a plan, but before I executed it, I had to figure out what to do about Mrs. Branford. I weighed my choices. Did I take her home? Or did I take her with me? Either way, I'd have to wake her up. She'd stifle a yawn, spread her fingers open, and then ball them into a fist. "Working out the arthritis," she told me once. "It's like oiling a squeaky gate. I have to get the joints lubricated." And then she'd look around, shake the cobwebs from her brain, and register where we were.

Once I told her I was dropping her off at home before I went to dig around at Wellborn Homes, she'd turn right around, swinging that cane, and march back to the car. I could hear her voice. "And, what, you think I'm going to sit around at home while you have all the fun?"

So the decision was less about where to take her and more about how she'd feel if she didn't end up in the thick of things with me. Decision made.

"Okay, Mrs. Branford," I whispered. "Let's go pay a visit to Wellborn Homes."

CHAPTER 11

For the second time that day, I was waiting in line in the bread shop. I hadn't been just a customer at Yeast of Eden since I'd taken my first baking class with Olaya Solis. Before that time, I'd stood in the lobby, contemplating the myriad bread selections, struggling to choose. But after I'd learned to mix flour and yeast and water together and actually end up with edible bread — and after I'd become fast friends with Olaya — I started working in the bread shop rather than strictly being a customer.

Earlier in the day, I'd craved a skull cookie. This time I was after something different. I was a firm believer of the "you catch more flies with honey" philosophy. Bringing a box of croissants to Wellborn Homes was the honey.

With the exception of a young mother and her son, the bread shop was empty. Maggie, the dark-haired high school student Olaya employed to work part time, was crouched down in front of one of the display cases, the little boy by her side. He looked to be about four years old. He was a shy one, completely quiet, but looking intently at Maggie.

Maggie was a quiet girl, but over the time I'd known her, she had started coming out of her shell. Now her hands moved in front of her, like she was talking with them. The boy's mother stood nearby, her eyes glistening. I looked more closely at Maggie, suddenly realizing what she was doing. She was, quite literally, talking with her hands. Signing with the little boy.

The tears in the mother's eyes made sense. So did the lump in my throat. Maggie said something else with her hands, and the little boy fisted his hand and moved it, as if it were a nodding head. He and Maggie both looked up, and the mother gave the nod of approval. Maggie grinned, scooting behind the counter. Using a square of waxed paper, she reached into the display case and retrieved one of the hidden skull cookies.

The little boy's eyes popped open. His mom nodded again, both with her head and her fisted hand. And then, after Maggie handed over the cookie, the lump in my throat grew right along with the little boy's smile. Maggie got down to her knees and wrapped the little boy in a hug; the mom took his hand in hers, held the baguette she'd bought, and left the bread shop.

The second the door closed behind them, I turned to Maggie. She brushed her hair back from her face, her own eyes gleaming. "That was beautiful," I said. "Where did you learn to sign?"

She circled back behind the counter. "My brother is deaf," she said. Ah, I thought, the brother she drove around in the car seat Laura had borrowed.

Maggie looked back at the little boy and waved. It was clear her connection with him was as big a deal to her as it probably was to him.

The bell on the door dinged and a small group of people came in laughing and talking. One of them held open the door for the boy and his mother. They disappeared down the sidewalk, the little boy's happy grin lingering in my mind. I stepped aside, letting the small group of people who'd just entered go before me.

While I waited for Maggie to help them, I glanced out the bread shop's front window at my car parked along the sidewalk in front. Mrs. Branford was plenty capable of taking care of herself, but leaving her alone — and asleep — felt akin to leaving a baby unattended. From my vantage point, it didn't look as if Mrs. Branford had moved.

The bell on the door dinged again as the customers left with their brown twine-handled bags stuffed with their bread selections; then Maggie spoke. "What are you doing in front of the counter?" she asked. "You're usually back here."

I swiveled around, bringing my attention back to her. "I need a box of croissants," I said. It might have been more accurate to say I needed a box of bribery, but I was pretty sure that sweet Maggie would not appreciate the plan I was ready to put into action.

"What kind?"

I'd given this decision some thought on the drive over. Did I go with a savory mix of ham and Gruyère, spinach, mushroom, and roasted bell pepper, and Kalamata olive, thyme, and feta cheese? Or would a sweet collection with the always popular chocolate, cherry preserves with slivered almonds, Nutella, and roasted apricot be better?

"Or maybe a combination of both," I muttered.

Olaya appeared from the back. "I do not

know what these are for, *m'ija,* but I suggest you choose either savory or sweet, not both."

"Why?" I asked, at the same time Maggie asked, "Really?"

"*Porque,* the people, they will fight over them. Some will want sweet. Some will not. There will not be enough of either, and so who is made to be happy?"

She looked at us expectantly, waiting for one of us to supply the answer to her question. "No one will be happy," I said.

Maggie finished the thought. "Because there wouldn't be enough of either one."

Olaya tapped her finger against the tip of her nose. *"Exactamente."*

In a split second, I made up my mind. "In that case, I'll take a dozen sweet. Six chocolate, three apricot, and three cherry," I said, knowing that two out of four people always chose chocolate.

Maggie got to work filling a white bakery box. I handed over the money, she handed over the pastries, and with a wave, I headed off to grease a few stomachs in my pursuit of information.

Mrs. Branford still hadn't budged since she'd fallen asleep. Not when I'd stopped at the bread shop; not when my hand slipped and the car door slammed; not when I absently turned on the radio before remembering that she was there, completely zonked. I hadn't realized she was such a deep sleeper. But when the car was off and we were in the parking lot of our destination, she stirred. She sat up and immediately patted her loosened silvery curls. She looked around, her gaze stopping on the Max Litman Homes sign. "Aha. I'm ready." She turned to me, her already wrinkle-ridden brow furrowing even more. "What am I ready for?"

I pointed to the two businesses. "I came to talk to someone at Wellborn Homes. They're Billy's alibi — sort of." I spun my head to look at the Litman Homes building. "I didn't know they were side by side."

"Which is very convenient." She threw open her door, used her cane to leverage her way up and out, and was halfway across the parking lot before I'd grabbed the box of croissants and caught up with her.

I expected her to slow down at the curb, but she swung her cane at an angle, dropped it down, and once again moved up and forward in one fell swoop. Spry. There was no other way to describe the woman, and — not for the first time — I hoped I'd have half as much energy as she did when I was in my ninth decade.

Once I'd seen both builders in one location, I had debated which to go to first. Mrs. Branford made the decision for me. She went straight for Wellborn Homes, yanked open the door, and then stood back. "After you, my dear."

I looked at her with what I was sure was an expression of awe, and skirted past her. The lobby was devoid of people. So much for winning people over with baked goods. There was, however, plenty to look at. The builder had pulled out all the stops, show-casing every one of their high-end finishings for prospective clients — hardwood floors, heavy wrought-iron light fixtures, thick carpet with a heavy carpet pad beneath it. Every bit of the place screamed expensive.

We heard the click of shoes and then a woman's voice. "Can I help you, ladies?"

That voice. I stood up straighter, as if a string attached to my head had yanked me upright. I turned around slowly. "Dixie?"

Her eye twitched with . . . surprise? Or was it dismay? But then she was rushing forward with open arms and the only emotion I got from her was happiness. "Ivy!"

I gestured wide with my free arm. "This is where you're working?"

"For a few months now," she said; then she lifted her eyebrows and her mouth curved flirtatiously. "Between you and me, darling, it's paid off already."

So many things were rushing through my mind. First was what a crazy coincidence it was that Dixie worked for Max Litman's business neighbor and, presumably, rival. Second was why she had failed to mention it when I'd seen her at the scene of the crime.

"I don't believe I've had the pleasure," Mrs. Branford said.

"Dixie lived at the Thompson boarding-house," I said, jogging her memory.

The skin around Mrs. Branford's eyes was creased, but it smoothed out as her eyes opened wide. *"But soft, what light through yonder window breaks?"* she said, her voice quiet. Reflective. And then it hit me. Dastardly Mrs. Branford. Allusion and the English teacher. I'd told her about seeing Dixie, backlit through a second-story window, and so she pulls out her Shakespeare references. "Of course I have *heard* about you," she said to Dixie, "but our paths have never crossed."

Was that true? Our last adventure had taken both Mrs. Branford and me to the boardinghouse where Dixie had lived. I thought back, though, realizing that Mrs. Branford hadn't actually been with me when I'd met Dixie.

"They've crossed now."

Mrs. Branford switched her cane to her opposite hand and shook Dixie's proffered hand. "They certainly have."

If we weren't talking about an elderly old woman and a middle-aged throwback to the golden era of Hollywood, I'd have thought the two of them were sizing each other up, complete with puffing chests and peacock feathers splayed, jockeying for position. I intervened with a formal introduction. "Penelope Branford, this is Dixie Mayfield. Dixie, Penelope."

Dixie sashayed to the granite bar that was set up as her reception area. "Are you in the market for a new house?" she asked.

"No, no," Mrs. Branford tsked. "We're in the market for information."

I swung my head, bugging my eyes at her in silent communication. Being so forthcoming hadn't been my plan, especially once I'd laid eyes on Dixie. It wasn't that I *didn't* trust her, but, well, I didn't know her well enough to say that I absolutely *did.*

Although I knew Mrs. Branford understood me, I hadn't actually expected her to respond in the way I wanted her to. She was emboldened and had taken on my determination to absolve Billy of any wrongdoing. Which meant she would completely ignore me if she had a different idea than I did.

Dixie perched on the leather-seated stool at the counter, glancing at the other stools, then back at us. We took her cue, sitting down. I slid the box of croissants to her. "We got these for . . . well, actually, I thought more people worked here. You now have a lot of croissants," I said, smiling.

She lifted the lid to take a peak, licking her plump red lips. She pulled a tuft of the flaky bread from one of them, her eyes rolling up as she let it melt in her mouth. "The boss will *definitely* appreciate them," she said with a wink.

The room was open, but the air felt heavy. "Dixie, why didn't you tell me you worked for Wellborn Homes?"

She arched one brow, looking from me to Mrs. Branford, then back to me. "Is it important?"

"Maybe," I said, but Mrs. Branford cut me off with a curt, "Of course it's important."

I'd been wrong earlier. She wasn't back to her old self; she had morphed into a bulldog with a bone.

"My brother actually met with Mr. Wellborn about a job," I said.

Dixie's smile didn't betray any concern over our question about her not mentioning where she worked. "Recently?"

"Last week, in fact," Mrs. Branford said.

I leaned forward on my elbows. "And then Max Litman died and the job went away. I'm just wondering why he'd take the job away after Max died, given that they were competitors."

"Darling, you know I can't speak for Mr. Wellborn," she said, as she jiggled her computer mouse. The screen came to life, she logged in, and a moment later she looked up at me, and for the briefest moment, her gaze was more intense. "Is your brother Billy Culpepper?"

I nodded.

"I remember the day he came in." She gave another flirtatious wink. "He's a good-looking man."

I forced a smile. "I'll tell him you said so."

Mrs. Branford leaned toward me. "She's a little old for Billy," she whispered.

Dixie cleared her throat. "Beauty and age are not mutually exclusive."

Mrs. Branford conceded the point. "True enough."

"Beauty knows no age, now does it?"

Mrs. Branford and I startled at the unexpected baritone of a man's voice, but Dixie just looked up, batting her eyes and giving a throaty laugh. "Why, Mr. Wellborn. I didn't expect you back so soon."

He let the door slam behind him and waved her away. "It's hard to stay away — from work." He added that last part, but I didn't think it was work he couldn't stay away from. Dixie might be older than Mr. Wellborn, as Mrs. Branford so indelicately pointed out, but she truly was a beauty. "Don't mind me, ladies." He strode across the room and disappeared briefly into another room, reappearing with a folder tucked under his arm.

"Do you need anything else, sir?" Dixie said, sounding as if she were propositioning him rather than being a good secretary.

Mr. Wellborn was attractive — dark hair, straight nose, not quite six feet. He looked to be somewhere in his late forties, but from the curve of his smile, he appreciated her pinup girl style. "Nope, I'm all good, Dixie. But thanks."

He headed toward the door. "I'll be back in a few hours."

"Wait, Mr. Wellborn?" I jumped up. "I'm Ivy Cul—"

He'd been reaching for the door handle, but suddenly stopped, his hand midair. The rest of my name froze on my lips. He turned around, his eyes narrowed. "I'm sorry, Ivy

— ?" His voice had become oddly disquieting.

From Mr. Wellborn's reaction to just hearing my last name, I realized that I had to change my tactic. Yes, I had to help Billy, but I couldn't go about my investigation with that angle. People didn't want to help a guy some thought could be a potential murderer. "Ivy, Cullison," I said, blending the tail end of my mother's maiden name, Madison, with mine.

He visibly relaxed. "Pleasure to meet you, Ms. Cullison. Did you have a question Dixie couldn't help you with?"

Dixie started. "They're not he —"

"No, not at all," Mrs. Branford said, cutting her off. She stood and faced him. "She's been very helpful. It's just, we're —"

Mr. Wellborn looked at her. A moment later his jaw dropped. "Mrs. Branford? Is that you?"

She stared; then, leaving her cane behind, she crossed the room to peer up at his face. She snapped her fingers. "Twelfth-grade English," she said. "About thirty years ago, I'd wager."

"That sounds about right. I can't believe it's you." He laughed, looking a little sheepish. "No offense, I liked you, but I hated your class."

139

"None taken. Not everyone likes Joseph Conrad, Thoreau, and Márquez," she said.

"All I can say is thank God for Cliffs-Notes."

Mrs. Branford stepped back, trying not to look offended. She didn't quite pull it off. "I accepted that kids relied on those long ago. You certainly weren't the first, nor the last," she said. When she'd said that not everyone enjoyed classic literature, she wasn't being facetious, just matter-of-fact. "But you can make up for it now."

He grew wary, the lightness he'd had in his step when he'd first entered all but gone. "Oh yeah? How's that?"

I took my cue. My story wasn't really a lie, but more of a stretching of the truth. "I'm documenting the Art Car Show and I'm trying to get a little more information about Max Litman."

Mrs. Branford shot me a quizzical look, but from her nod, I knew she finally understood the direction I was going and that she'd play along. "Such a tragedy," she said, shaking her head sadly. We hung our heads. After a moment of silence, I cleared my throat.

Mr. Wellborn let out a heavy sigh. "Huge loss for the community. I can't quite wrap my head around the idea that he's gone."

He looked appropriately somber. His voice held a degree of sadness. But something about the way he spoke belied a different sentiment.

"Were you good friends?" I asked, watching him closely.

And there it was. It was brief — maybe no more than a split second — but he hesitated before he answered. "Sure, of course we were friends."

So far he hadn't asked why we'd make that assumption or why we were so interested, so I forged ahead while I could. "He didn't have many, from what I've heard."

Mrs. Branford snorted. "And by that she means that he preferred the female persuasion."

Mr. Wellborn dipped his head in agreement. "That's true enough."

"I didn't realize his business was right next door. I would have thought you'd be rivals rather than friends."

Mr. Wellborn shifted his weight from one foot to the other. "Friends might not be the right word, exactly," he admitted after a moment.

"Truth be told," Mrs. Branford said, "I didn't like the man."

Dixie tossed her hair back. "I did not care for him, either." She glanced my way, meet-

141

ing my eyes in a way that made me think she was trying to help me get information, even if she didn't quite know what I was after.

I held up my hand. "Me, three."

Mr. Wellborn grimaced. "Then I guess it's unanimous."

"I thought you said you were sort of friends, Johnny," Mrs. Branford said, pulling his first name out of thin air.

"Never reveal all your cards," he said cryptically.

I understood that philosophy completely. Mine were held close to the vest, too. The box of croissants still sat on the granite countertop. I picked it up, offering one to Mr. Wellborn.

His eyes opened wide. "Are these from —" He picked one and took a healthy bite. "They are," he said, his words muffled. "Mmm. Yeast of Eden."

"You're a fan?"

"That place has the best bread I've ever had. Ever." He reached for another before he'd finished the first.

I hoped he'd reveal at least one of his cards after being buttered up with the croissant. "I've heard Max was a wheeler and dealer," I said.

Mr. Wellborn grunted, flicking a croissant

flake from his lip. "He was a crook, plain and simple."

That was more direct than I'd anticipated. "I knew him as a liar, but a crook?"

Mrs. Branford jumped in again. "What did he do?"

That was all the prompting he needed. "What didn't he do?" was his cryptic answer.

"Come now, Johnny, you can't tease us and then not deliver," Mrs. Branford scolded playfully.

Mr. Wellborn smirked. "The guy swindled me out of one hundred twenty thousand dollars."

All of our jaws dropped, but Mrs. Branford took her next cue and launched into a scolding. "Johnny, Johnny, Johnny, one hundred twenty thousand dollars? How?"

"It was supposed to be an investment. A condo development along Oceanside Drive. There were four of us."

"You pooled your money?" she asked.

He took another bite of croissant, grimacing before continuing with his mouth full.

"That would have been better. We each contributed one hundred twenty thousand. Max was supposed to invest it with a developer."

We were all on the edge of our seats. Max

Litman, the swindler. That had the makings of a motive. "But he didn't?"

He swallowed, shaking his head. "Who knows."

Dixie had disappeared into a back room, returning a minute later with four bottles of water. She passed them around, one for each of us, laid out a stack of napkins, and then reached for her own croissant. She pulled off a piece with her fingers, placing it neatly in her mouth. No flakes on her lips. "There was no investor?" she asked once she'd washed her bite of croissant down with a dainty sip of water.

"I never met him," he said. "It was some Japanese investor. At least that's the story Max spewed."

"You didn't believe it?" Mrs. Branford asked.

He polished off the last of his second croissant. "What I believe — no, what I know — is that the money's gone."

"Wait." Dixie flipped her hair back as she worked through whatever she was thinking. "If there was no investor, and ten of you invested one hundred twenty thousand each, then you're saying that Max stole more than a million dollars?"

"We had the law on our side, but we could never prove it," Mr. Wellborn said. "Max said he was taken to the cleaners, too, but —"

"But you don't believe it," Mrs. Branford finished.

"I have an easier time believing that he figured out how to steal our money than that he was duped in an investment scheme by someone else. If there was a scheme, and I think there was, he was behind it."

"Who were the other investors?" I asked. More potential suspects.

"Unfortunately, I have no idea. We were all silent investors. To *protect* us, he said."

"And there's no way to get it back?" Mrs. Branford asked.

"If there was, it's dead and buried with him." He clutched the folder he'd come for. "At least someone else can win that damn car contest," he said as he headed for the door.

"You're not a fan?" I said, leaping through the opening he'd just presented.

"Everyone should have a passion," he said. He glanced at Mrs. Branford. "Even if it's British literature and poetry."

We all smiled at that. That he felt comfortable ribbing his former English teacher endeared him to me just a little bit. I sensed there was a "but" coming, though.

"But Max was obsessed with that stupid

contest. Art car this and art car that. It'll sound coldhearted, I'm sure, but I am not going to miss that. He wouldn't have won this year anyway."

"Why wouldn't he have won?" I asked. Billy's car was amazing, but there was no reason to think anything would be different this year. Plus I was fairly certain he hadn't seen Billy's car to be able to make such a pronouncement.

"There's been a change in the voting committee membership this past year," he said. "I've been on it for years. No plans to leave. But a few others were ready to retire, so to speak."

And suddenly my head was spinning. "Wait. I thought the planning committee voted on the winner."

Mrs. Branford looked at me as if I were daft. "That would be a very overt conflict of interest, Ivy. There is a completely separate voting committee. We have a selection process and we've done our best to make it fair."

Mr. Wellborn scoffed. "It hasn't been fair in years."

It wasn't hard to believe what he was alluding to, especially since I'd hypothesized this scenario for years. "So what you are saying," I said, "is that Max Litman bribed the voting committee every single year?"

"I haven't seen it firsthand, if that's what you mean," Mr. Wellborn said, "but that's what I've heard."

"From . . . ?"

It was a fill-in-the-blank moment, but Mr. Wellborn didn't bite, and his forthrightness came to an abrupt halt. "Ladies, what exactly are you looking for?" He looked at me. "How is this helping you to document the show?"

"I'm just trying to get a clearer picture of him," I said. "I want to get to the core of who he was, not just who he was on the surface."

He looked skeptical. "For the Art Car Show?"

"He won every single year," I said, ignoring the fact that those wins had not been honest. "And he even *died* in his car."

"He was ruthless, and he would do anything to win. It finally came back to bite him in the ass. Now, if you'll excuse me, ladies —"

I held my palm out to him. "Mr. Wellborn, wait, please."

"I'm done, Ms. Cullison. I appreciate what you're doing, I guess, although I don't quite understand it, but I'm not going to waste any more time on Max Litman."

I didn't want to, either, but I didn't have the luxury of going to a meeting and putting the murder out of my mind. My head hurt from trying to make sense what any of this meant. I'd known Max Litman was not an honest man, but the depth of his dishonesty was a bit mind-boggling.

Suddenly my thoughts went in an entirely different direction. I looked at the man heading for the door, a chill running over my skin. He clearly had no love lost for Max, ratting him out about the failed condo investment and the art car voting scandal. I drew in a stabilizing breath. The man had thrown out enough bait about potential other suspects with motives, but what about himself? Could *Wellborn* be the murderer?

I circled back around to the reason I'd come here in the first place. Billy. Wellborn had left Billy in the dust after the murder. Initially, I'd thought that was out of some inexplicable loyalty to Max, but now I knew there was no allegiance to the dead man. There was only justified betrayal. It seemed most likely that he's nixed any agreement with Billy so his company wouldn't be associated with someone he thought might be capable of murder. Self-preservation.

Dixie had been silent during our exchange, but now she stood, walking with her boss to the door. She shook her head, looking forlorn. "What in the world has happened to our quiet little town?"

He scoffed. "Don't be delusional, Dixie. Every city . . . every town . . . hell, every *place* has an underbelly. You're experiencing ours for the first time, but it's been here all along."

"Oh Lord," she said. I could imagine her fanning herself and placing the back of her hand to her forehead à la Scarlett O'Hara. "I don't know about you all, but I'll feel a whole lot better when they figure out who killed Mr. Litman. When they have a suspect."

Mr. Wellborn was halfway out the door, but he stopped and turned to face her. "They do, Dixie," he said.

The hair on the back of my neck stood on end and I closed my eyes to ward off what I knew was coming. And then he spoke the name I had prayed he wouldn't.

"Billy Culpepper."

Chapter 12

I left Wellborn Homes feeling dumb-founded. My brother was innocent, so how could everyone think he was capable of murder? Especially when there were potentially four other suspects?

Mrs. Branford and I walked the short distance to the Litman Homes office. Stucco walls, red tile roof, manicured landscape. The entire place looked more like a home development than a business complex. A few cars dotted the parking lot. Given the absence of its owner, I thought the place might be locked, but we were in luck. The handle turned and we walked right in.

And abruptly stopped short.

The lobby of Max Litman's business was the polar opposite of the office we'd just come from. Conversation with Dixie, and the brief encounter with Mr. Wellborn, was the extent of the activity in the latter. But from the looks of it, I'd have said that nearly every law enforcement officer in Santa Sofia was in the Litman Homes office, and they appeared to be scouring every square inch of the place. There hadn't been a single police cruiser in the front parking lot. There had to be a back lot, I realized, just as there was at Yeast of Eden.

I didn't know many of Santa Sofia's finest, but I recognized a few of the people Emmaline worked with. I'd run into them here and there, both in the bread shop and in connection with some of the crime solving I'd gotten wrapped up in. There was no sign of Emmaline, which came as no surprise, but I spotted Sheriff Lane right off the bat. He fit in at the crime scene about as much as a banana fit in with a head of cauliflower, a bundle of broccoli, and a bushel of Brussels sprouts. He covered his balding head with a Santa Sofia Sheriff's Department ball cap, and his uniform was ill-fitting. I'd guesstimate that he'd put on about ten pounds since he'd first gotten it and hadn't replaced it with one in his actual size.

Someone from the depths of the office gave a low whistle. Everybody stopped for a choreographed beat, looked at Mrs. Branford and me in the doorway, and then promptly went back to what they'd been doing. All except the sheriff himself. He sauntered over, his belly taking the lead. "Ladies, this is a crime scene. I need to ask you to leave."

You'd think that leaning on a cane would make a person shorter, but not so for Mrs. Branford. She clutched the handle, her knuckles turning white from the force of her grip, pushed up, and held her head higher. "You can ask," she said, "but that does not mean your wish is our command."

I allowed myself a quick second to gawk at her. My sidekick's feisty mood was still front and center, and she was taking no prisoners. For his part, the sheriff looked like he was winding up, ready to lambast her for her cheek. I cleared the tickle from my throat to distract him. With any luck, he'd excuse her sassy remark and not kick us out on our behinds.

"I found the . . . er, Max's body," I said, in case he'd forgotten. Which, of course, he hadn't. Santa Sofia was touristy during certain parts of the year, adding significantly to the day-to-day population, but it was also a small town where everyone (or close to it) knew your name.

"I know you did, Ms. Culpepper. And while I appreciate your interest, your help is not required. We need to do our job now."

"I know, it's just —"

"There is no 'just,' Ms. Culpepper," he said slowly. "You are not involved in this case."

Technically, he was right. But emotionally, he was as far off the mark as a person could be. "But I *am* involved. My brother —"

"That's the problem right there. Your brother is currently our prime suspect, as I'm sure Deputy Sheriff Davis has informed you, therefore you cannot be here." He looked over his shoulder, notching two fingers. A uniformed officer, one I didn't recognize, appeared by Sheriff Lane's side. He held his arms wide, ushering us backward and right out the door. It closed with a quiet whoosh, but it might as well have slammed with a resounding bang. Mrs. Branford and I were left standing on the sidewalk staring at each other.

Chapter 13

I felt as if I were climbing a never-ending mountain. No matter what I did, or which way I turned, I wasn't able to grab ahold of anything that could propel me to the summit. I wasn't done trying, though, so I made a split second decision on what Nero Wolfe might have Archie Goodwin do. I dragged Mrs. Branford on another adventure. I drove the same route I'd traveled years ago, when I'd followed the high school art teacher, Mr. Zavila, to his duplicitous meeting with Max Litman to give him the goods on Billy's car. I took us inland, to Malibu Hills Estates.

Just like I'd done years ago, I waited nearby until an unsuspecting resident pulled up to the gate and inputted their passcode. Once the gate swung open and the car passed, I kicked my car into drive and slipped unnoticed into the upscale neighborhood.

"Very industrious," Mrs. Branford said.

It was meant as a compliment, but all I could muster was a nod and a grimace.

She patted my leg. "Don't lose hope, Ivy. You'll figure this out. *We'll* figure it out."

I liked her spirit, and her faith. Giving up wasn't an option; therefore, I *would* succeed. There really was no other choice. "I think I've been going about this wrong," I said as I drove. In the years since I'd been here, the trees and the landscaping had matured. The properties maintained their high-end luster, but at the same time, they looked lived-in and loved. I didn't spend time goggling them, however. I didn't remember exactly how to get to the Litman house, so my energy was spent trying to recollect which way to turn and when. I'd find it eventually.

Mrs. Branford, though, was taking it all in for the first time, oohing and aahing from the passenger side at every massive Mediterranean estate, every pillar and fountain dotting the properties we passed, every expanse of flawless emerald lawn and picture-perfect flower beds blooming with explosions of color. "Lovely," she said, more to herself than to me.

I hadn't expected her to like the neighborhood, with its new construction and story-less homes. I replied anyway. "They are beautiful."

And then she shrugged and gave a half frown. "Pft. If you like this sort of place."

Her abrupt shift gave me whiplash. "You don't?"

"Pft." This time the sound was twice as loud. "If I did, I would be living in a place like this. Jimmy and I made our choice years and years ago. We wanted to raise our kids in a house that had history. On a street with character. We made our choice. And I don't regret a single minute of a single day we've spent on Maple Street."

After circling around and around, driving down streets I'd already been on, I was ready to pull over to look up Max's address. Once I had it, I'd be able to queue up Google Maps. Before I stopped, though, I finally spotted it. I came to a stop in front of the massive house Max Litman had built for himself. I'd forgotten just how pretentious the terra-cotta-colored house was, what with its stucco walls, massive fountain, and pillars. The tiered centerpiece of the fountain still cascaded water over the sides of each of the washbasin vessels. It must be on a timer, I realized, but with Max gone, shouldn't they be turned off?

Just like I had when I'd first laid eyes on

this house, I drove past it, made a U-turn at the end of the street, and parked just opposite the house. "It fits him," Mrs. Branford said, and for the third time that day she swung herself out of the car and was halfway across the street before I managed to get myself out of the driver's side and catch up to her.

I touched her lightly on the shoulder once I reached her. "You have to stop doing that," I scolded.

She turned, still walking, but directed her innocent gaze up at me. "Stop doing what?"

"Leading the charge. Beating me to our destination. Risking an injury."

She waved away my concerns, never stopping the swing of her cane or the lightness of her step. "Finally, things are getting interesting. Maybe Max has a mail-order bride tucked away. Or maybe he's been laundering money and has a whole counterfeit money machine, or whatever those counterfeiters use. Diversification, you know."

"Seems a little unlikely on both counts," I said.

"I concede the point, but my excitement remains. There could very well be something of interest in Max's house. Something that might take the focus off of Billy. Or something that could point us in the direction of Max's murderer."

Which is exactly why I'd driven us here. "There's only one problem," I said. "We can't actually go into the house."

That brought her up short. She turned around to face me. "That *is* a problem, isn't it?" But then she swung her cane again, directed herself toward the house, and was off again.

"You are not breaking and entering," I said, wagging my finger at her back as if she were a child.

She threw up her hand and waved nonchalantly — an acknowledgment of sorts — but didn't turn around to quell my concern. We walked up the driveway, circled around the fountain, and stopped on the far side. I hadn't gotten this close to the house the first time. Now I tilted my head back and stared up at it. The home's features, from the off-white stucco, the red tile roof, and the wood-framed windows to the rose bushes, the lushly planted pots, and the neatly trimmed boxwood shrubs, were elaborate. It wasn't over-the-top gaudy with everything gold and ornate, but it still screamed money. Apparently, Max didn't believe in subtlety.

"I'll stick to my Maple Street house with

the slanted porch and ancient wood," Mrs. Branford said.

"Me too," I said. I would never trade my Tudor for a McMansion. Or for any mansion. "Still, it is pretty in a Richie Rich kind of way."

"I will concede to that," she said.

"Wait here," I said. I left her on the solid ground of the driveway and tiptoed onto the grass. It was broad daylight, but I crept along the perimeter of the house like a cat burglar. Sheriff Lane had sent us packing from Litman Homes, so to speak, but he hadn't said a word about staying away from Max's house. I might be splitting hairs, but I was going with the philosophy of asking for forgiveness rather than permission. I might not be able to get *inside* the house, but if I could sneak a peek, who knows? Maybe I'd learn something.

I went from window to window, cupping one hand over my eyes to block the sun, but the glare made it impossible to see inside. The windows were completely blocked. If Max had taken the time decorating the interior of the house as he had with the details outside, it was probably gorgeous, and well worth protecting with some high-end window coverings. I might not want to live in such a place, but I was never opposed to educating my taste.

It didn't look like that would be happening today. I walked back across the grass, sidling up next to Mrs. Branford. "Nothing?" she asked.

"Nothing."

"And I don't imagine you want to scale the fence into the backyard."

I couldn't help but laugh. "Uh, that would be a hard no, Mrs. Branford."

"Penelope."

She had been trying to get me to call her by her first name, but I couldn't do it. I'd met her as Mrs. Branford, and Mrs. Branford she would stay. I was the ghost to her Mrs. Muir. "Mrs. Branford," I repeated.

I started back to the street, guiding her by the elbow, but she pulled free. "We can't leave yet," she said.

"But there's nothing left to do here."

Mrs. Branford, however, seemed to have her own agenda. She swung her cane, turned on her heel, and walked straight to the front door, pausing only slightly to get up the two curved steps. "Of course there is," she called over her shoulder; then she knocked on the door with the handle of her cane.

"Are you hoping Max's ghost will answer the door?" I asked, coming up beside her, my hands on my hips.

"Of course not, Ivy. I haven't gone senile, for heaven's sake."

"Then what?" I asked, but my question was answered half a second later when the front door jerked open.

Mrs. Branford teetered, her orthotic shoes no match for the surprise of seeing a frazzled-looking blonde, her arms full of clothes, suddenly staring at us. I had no time to formulate a thought about who she was or why she was at a deceased man's house because Mrs. Branford was going down. "Oh oh!" Her body moved from its center of gravity, angling left . . . left . . . left.

I lunged, crouching and positioning one of my legs under her to block her fall, grabbing her arm at the same time. It slowed her, but I felt myself going down, too. And then suddenly, I wasn't. The woman standing in the threshold of Max Litman's house had dropped the load she'd been carrying and had Mrs. Branford by her other arm. The woman was thin, but she was stronger than she looked. She hauled Mrs. Branford upright; then Mrs. Branford stretched her arm out to me, dragging me up right beside her.

"I do not know who you are, my dear,"

Mrs. Branford said to the mysterious woman, "and while my orthopedic surgeon may not be happy, *I* thank you for saving my left hip."

"Is it the doctor who won't be happy, or the insurance company?" the woman muttered in a tone that suggested she had some less-than-positive personal experiences with both.

Mrs. Branford responded without missing a beat. "The doctor for the blow to his Porsche payment, and the insurance company for just . . . losing."

And then the woman arched her eyebrows and dipped her head as if she were saying *touché*. "I don't know who you are, old woman, but I like you."

Mrs. Branford threw her shoulders back, lifting her chin indignantly. "Old woman?"

The woman had bent to retrieve some of the clothes she'd dropped when she'd saved us both from meeting the stone porch, but Mrs. Branford's words had wiped the brief moment of levity off her face. She blinked rapidly and her lips quivered. "I-I-I'm sorry," she said, stumbling over her words. "I don't know what came over me."

She was younger than I'd initially thought. Maybe early thirties. From my viewpoint, there were only two logical possibilities for

162

who she was and why she was here. Either she was one of Max's girlfriends, or she was his daughter. Since he didn't have children, at least as far as I knew, I went with the former as my prediction.

But I let the interaction between Mrs. Branford and the woman play out before I tried to confirm. Mrs. Branford did not disappoint. She waited just long enough for the poor woman to sweat; then, diabolical creature that she was, she threw her snowy head back and guffawed. "Young lady — and I call you that honestly, because you *are* a young lady compared to me — I *am* an old woman. I can't hide it, so I choose to embrace it. Now, what do you have there?" she said, pointing her cane at the clothing scattered around.

I watched the woman carefully, noting two things. Number one, she had definitely been crying. Her eyes were red-rimmed and her tears had left tracks on her cheeks. And number two, she was up to something.

She looked around, guilt painted on her face. "Um, clothes?"

A few things had been flung my way. I bent, picking up a brown and rust-colored scarf, as well as a cami, and a creamy white pair of gauze palazzo pants. From the looks of her wardrobe, I was leaning toward a live-in girlfriend. Another of Max's secrets, it seemed.

"Are you going somewhere?" I asked, handing over the garments.

Once again, she was flustered. "Oh, well, yes, I'm just getting some of my things. I don't, you know, live here."

I'd learned that staying silent was an excellent tactic for getting information. People didn't like silence, and they'd eventually fill it. I caught Mrs. Branford's eyes, communicating that idea with my eyes; then I nodded — and waited.

The woman didn't say anything for what felt like a long minute. It felt like a game of chicken and I was just about to blink, but she finally spoke. "I'm an . . . advisor," she offered, but instead of being an answer to something, the statement left me with questions. She was an advisor for Max? In what capacity? And did she dispense that advice while lounging by the pool? Did she do more than advise?

Mrs. Branford placed her open palm against her chest. "I'm Penelope, and this is Ivy."

"Vanessa," she said, nervously running her tongue over her lips.

"What kind of advisor?" I asked, hoping she'd just answer my questions and not ask any of her own — like who we were and why we were there.

She hesitated long enough that I feared she might not answer, but then she did. "I'm a . . . spiritual advisor."

Somehow, I managed to keep my jaw from dropping. My mind had hypothesized long-lost daughter to Vegas bride. After she'd uttered the word *advisor,* I'd even entertained the idea of attaching the word *financial* to it. *Spiritual* advisor, however, had never entered my mind. It had never even come close.

Max Litman had been a lot of things, but spiritual was not one of the words I'd ever heard him described as. "Does Max need spiritual counseling?" Mrs. Branford asked.

The woman threw her shoulders back. "Doesn't everyone?"

Mrs. Branford and I looked at each other. I suppose it was a valid question, what with the state of the world. Spirituality might not make anything better, but it could help a person cope.

The woman took our silence as us conceding the point. If she wondered who we were and why we were here, she didn't let on.

"So, where *are* you going?" I asked, nodding to the clothes now scattered about.

She darted her gaze this way and that.

"Did you not hear?" She slapped her open hand over her mouth. "Oh my God, do you not know?"

Of course, I knew exactly what she was going to say, but instead of playing my hand, I feigned ignorance and gave her my best blank stare. "Know what?"

She pressed her lips together, lifting her chin and giving a slow blink. "Max." Her voice cracked with emotion. "He's dead."

An odd sound, like a mewling cat, came from Mrs. Branford.

"Max is dead?" she croaked, her hand losing its grip on her cane. I stopped and stared at her, shaking my head. Maybe in astonishment. Maybe in pure admiration. This was not the first time I'd seen Mrs. Branford use her age or supposed frailty to her advantage. And just like before, it was perfectly staged.

She teetered, but I was by her side in an instant, falling into my role. "Are you okay? Do you need to sit down?" I ushered her toward the door, looking at the spiritual advisor.

Vanessa seemed frozen in place, but her eyes had grown wide. "Is she okay?"

"She will be. If she could sit down for a few minutes . . . ?"

Still, Vanessa stood stock-still. Right on

cue, Mrs. Branford moaned again. I stepped across the threshold, not giving Vanessa the opportunity to say no. "Do you mind?" I asked.

She had no choice but to move. "Right, right. Of course. I mean, no. Come in." She kicked the clothes just inside the door out of the way, standing back so I could help Mrs. Branford all the way into Max Litman's house. Just as I knew it would be, the inside was beautifully decorated. Dark hardwood trims and moldings, travertine tile, plush pile carpets. The entire space was meticulously detailed. I couldn't imagine living in such a place. There was no warmth here. No personality. No sense of welcoming, with a hearty, "Come in! We're glad you stopped by." No, Max's house presented like a picture-perfect design abode meant to sell the space and the furniture, but not really meant for living.

Vanessa led the way, taking us through the open foyer and into the adjacent living area. Pillars and archways denoted the separation of one space from another. She pointed to the massive off-white sectional sofa. "Sit. I'll get her some water."

I helped Mrs. Branford onto a firm-looking chair instead of the sofa. The open floor plan made it easy to watch Vanessa from the corner of my eye. She knew her way around the kitchen, opening a cupboard to retrieve a glass, tugging open the paneled door of a built-in freezer to get ice, pulling a dish towel from a drawer to mop up the water she accidentally sprayed onto the counter from the sink faucet.

As Vanessa came back, I refocused on Mrs. Branford. She slumped in the chair, her back curved, her head lolling. I had a moment of panic. Even when she was channeling Meryl Streep, seeing her so indisposed made my heart skitter out of control and sent cold beads of sweat down my back. I wanted her alive and well, and her current posture did not portray either of those things.

I crouched down next to her, offering her the water Vanessa had handed me. She slowly pried open her eyes, having somehow managed to make them look glassy and dazed. She laid her hands on mine, guiding the glass of water to her lips. She drank as if she were completely parched, her performance utterly perfect. Which, once again, made me wonder just how much was an act versus a reality I didn't want to see or face.

I kept my voice low as I asked, "Are you okay?" I needed reassurance.

She pushed the glass away and focused on

me. "Right as rain," she whispered; then she winked. It was too quick for Vanessa to see, but it convinced me that all was fine and we could carry on with our investigation.

I sat on the couch, staying as close to Mrs. Branford as I could. It was clear we weren't going anywhere, so Vanessa had no choice but to sit. Which she did. Before she could formulate any of her own questions to ask — namely, *Who are you?* and *What do you want?* — I forged ahead, leaning forward and painting a disbelieving expression on my face. "Max is dead." I ended on a slight lilt, framing it ambiguously. It could have been a statement or question. For some reason putting it that way made me feel a little bit better, as if I wasn't quite lying. Or not lying quite so much, anyway.

Vanessa's doe eyes grew even bigger, bright with emotion. "It's been all over the news." She leaned forward, her voice dropping to a loud conspiratorial whisper. "He was murdered."

Mrs. Branford and I both reacted, showing shock, followed by a hint of fear. "Murdered?" Mrs. Branford asked.

Vanessa nodded gravely. "And his murderer is still out there." For some reason, she had decided that she trusted us. She looked around, as I'd noticed almost all people did when they were about to reveal a secret or disclose some important bit of information. She was apparently satisfied that we were still alone and that no one had managed to break into the house unawares and sneak up behind us. "The police were here. They said it was routine and that they have to look at all sides of things, but that they have a" — she made air quotes — "person of interest."

I lowered my head, not trusting my response. I didn't want her to see my nostrils flare or my eyes flash. My skin went cold, spots dancing behind my eyes, and once again, my heart plunged to the bottom of my stomach. And then Vanessa, like everyone else, named my brother as the main suspect in Max Litman's murder.

CHAPTER 14

I took Mrs. Branford home before sitting down in my backyard. With Agatha running around in her usual circles, I called Emmaline. I filled her in on the big reveal of the investors from Johnny Wellborn, as well as meeting Vanessa, the spiritual advisor. "I never would have pegged Max as the spiritual type," I said.

"She's definitely someone we need to look into. But the other, the real-estate investment gone bad? Those people, whoever they are, have solid motives," Em said, a trace of hope in her voice.

"Exactly what I thought," I said. "So what now?" I certainly didn't know how to pursue a financially motivated crime with four silent investors involved. All I knew how to do was root around, uncovering the secrets people tried so hard to keep buried.

"I'll turn over the information to Lane and the team. If it's Wellborn — or one of the other nine — they'll be able to figure —"

She stopped, catching her words before she released them and had to try to pull them back. Because we both knew that we couldn't count on Sheriff Lane to figure things out. Nero Wolfe and Archie Goodwin. It was up to us.

"There's something bugging me," I said to her. I didn't know if it was worth mentioning, but I didn't want to keep anything back — just in case. "You remember Dixie?"

"The Marilyn Monroe look-alike? Of course. I don't think I could forget her if I tried. She's a one of a kind."

"That she is."

"What about her?" she asked, but I could tell she was still circling around the potential suspects who invested with Max Litman.

"She used to date Max back when they were both younger. And when I ran into her, she told me she got a job as a receptionist. What she *didn't* say was that the job was with Max's business rival."

Emmaline didn't react. I knew her well; she was thinking about what I'd said, pulling in her background knowledge, and formulating her ideas on the subject. "Ivy," she finally said, "how did she happen to be at the hangar that morning? The morning you found Max?"

I wondered the same thing at the time, and now I relayed the conversation I'd had with her. "Half the town showed up. Cell phones."

"Dead body found in a car in a hangar on the outskirts of town, she hears about it from someone — but who knows who? — and she hightails it out there. Why?"

That was a very good question. Although she knew Max when she was younger, she made it clear that there had been nothing between them for decades. That very well could be true, however one thing I'd learned during my own three-plus decades was that people told you what they wanted you to know, and they omitted what they didn't. Why *had* she come to the hangar? "She knew it was Max in there," I said, putting a different spin on something she'd said. "She didn't ask me who was dead, she asked me for confirmation. She told me that people were saying it was Max. What people? How would anyone have known that?"

I also remembered how Sheriff Lane had gazed out into the growing crowd of looky-loos. He'd thought the killer might still be there. What if she'd been standing right beside me the whole time?

A shudder tickled my skin. I'd just spent

the better part of an hour with her today and certainly hadn't gotten any sense of her as a murderer. Still, I knew better than to discount her; *anybody* was capable of doing *anything.*

"Looking at it objectively — and excluding Billy," Emmaline said, "we now have eleven potential suspects: the ten investors and Dixie."

"Twelve if we count Vanessa." Which we definitely should. "That's a whole lot more than we had a few hours ago."

Emmaline had been carrying a heavy load, beginning with the circumstantial evidence potentially connecting Billy to Max's murder and then the blow of not only being taken off the investigation, but the lack of control that came along with that removal. Still, having twelve people to focus on, other than Billy, had to give her a modicum of hope, didn't it? It even felt overwhelming. How were we supposed to get to one killer from twelve suspects?

Emmaline echoed my feelings with the audibly shaky breath she blew out. We didn't know the identity of nine of the investors, and motives for Dixie or Vanessa were both giant unknowns. And if I was being honest with myself, none of them took Billy off the hot seat.

CHAPTER 15

After my conversation with Emmaline, I needed a change.

I needed a distraction.

I needed ice cream.

Since the moment I'd seen Laura's husband on a daddy date with their daughter, I'd wanted to call my father. I hadn't seen him since Em had asked me to be her eyes and ears within the Art Car Show and Ball. The event itself was still days away. In the meantime I was thinking about what to do next with the information in my head. I didn't know how to figure out who the investors in Max's condo scheme were, so I couldn't do anything there. I didn't like that Dixie had not told me where she'd worked, but that didn't mean the omission was deliberate or calculated. She may not have seen a connection between Max and her employer. I had to remind myself that not

175

everything had a sinister intention behind it.

But pursuing information about Vanessa was a different story. What, exactly, was a spiritual advisor, and in what capacity had she advised Max? Learning more about her was doable. Of the three possible doors I could walk through, digging into Vanessa's background was the logical choice.

But first, ice cream.

A surprise visit to the city planner's office and a midday sit-down with my dad was exactly what I needed. It was also what he needed, although hell would freeze over before he admitted it. Owen Culpepper always gave 100% to his job; since my mother had died, however, he'd thrown himself into his work even deeper than before. He woke up early, often heading to the office before it was light outside. He'd come home late, well after the dinner hour, well after the time when he might run into neighbors out watering their lawns or walking their dogs. He avoided people these days, and since I'd bought my own house and moved out, he came home to no one. There was nothing I could do about those things, but I could drag him out in the middle of the day.

The Santa Sofia city offices were in a nondescript flat-roofed building on the west side of town. There were no tourists here; no souvenir shops where you could buy trinkets printed with SANTA SOFIA, CALIFORNIA or LIVE, LAUGH, LOVE IN SANTA SOFIA; no crab shacks on the beach. This was where the cogs of our town turned. My dad was one of those cogs.

There were a few annexes, but the city manager's office was in the main building. So many in similar jobs had short tenures, but my dad had been moved up through the ranks over the years, landing the top job ten years ago. He was half politician and have administrator, balancing the needs and fickleness of an ever-changing city council. He'd managed to have longevity in his job, something that was almost unheard of. He was smart and politically savvy, and knew how to function within the system, something that had served him well.

Because my dad had worked for the city for his entire career in one capacity or another, I'd been around this place hundreds of times. Even after my time in college and years spent in Austin, the clerks and assistants still knew me. The office manager, Sally O'Brien, had worked with my father for as long as I could remember. She had a good ten years on him and had always looked it, but after losing my mom, he'd caught up with her. His hair had turned to salt and pepper right before our eyes. He had melted away from his loss of appetite. Eventually he started to bounce back. We owed part of his recovery to Sally. She'd anticipated his needs, stayed by his side, and helped to ease him through the worst of it by providing normalcy to his days. She kept my dad's office running, even when he had been unable to. There was a lot to be said for loyalty.

She had her head down as she shuffled through a stack of papers, but glanced up as I approached. I lifted my hand in a quick wave and smiled. It took her a beat before recognition set in, but when it did, she was out of her seat in a split second, her papers forgotten. She rushed around her desk, sweeping me into a hearty embrace. "Ivy, aren't you a sight for sore eyes! I've been wondering when we'd see you around here again."

She was a robust woman, several inches shorter than me — and strong as a horse. She'd had enough strength to carry my dad through his grief, and she'd done her share of helping Billy and me, too. From organizing meals to be delivered to checking in on each of us on a daily basis, she had been a rock for us all. I'd always be grateful to her for that.

I filled her in on my photography and the bread shop, and she gave me an update on her husband, children, and grandchildren, and I promised I wouldn't be such a stranger. After another hug, I headed down the corridor to the city manager's office, stopping at the threshold. My dad sat in his black ergonomic chair. It was a luxury he'd refused to indulge in, but finally, after years of an aching back, we indulged in it for him. It was the best Father's Day we'd given him since Billy and I were knee-high to a grass-hopper. As little kids, every Father's Day was a treasure, but as adults, finding something that made a person's daily life better was immensely gratifying. And that chair had done the trick.

He had his back turned to me as he riffled through the contents in a filing cabinet drawer. I watched as he walked his fingers over the tabs until he settled on two folders. He reached his hand down, but muttered under his breath as it came up empty a second later. Whatever folder was supposed to be there was not. My dad was a stickler for organization. In that one way, he and my mother were polar opposites. She was the creative type, always leaving a trail of whatever she was working on in her wake. He, on the other hand, had a different philosophy. There is a place for everything and everything had a place. Billy and I had both ended up somewhere in the middle. Neither of us obsessed how orderly — or not — our space was, but neither did we feel comfortable in a house full of scattered *stuff*. A missing folder would annoy me, but I wouldn't lose sleep over it. That same missing folder would drive my father crazy.

He flicked his fingers over the files again, finally landing on the one he wanted. "How'd you get there?" he muttered to it, as if it had up and moved itself to a different spot in the drawer. As he turned to place it on his desk, I cleared my throat to announce my presence and stepped into the room. "Hey, Dad."

"Ivy! This is a surprise," he said. He got up, rounded his desk, and wrapped me up in a hug that lasted a beat longer than normal. Sometimes it felt as if I was his lifeline. My mom's absence hit us all in different ways and at different times. The truth was that we were all each other's lifeline.

"I'm here to steal you away for ice cream," I said.

He ran his hand through his hair. Billy had gotten dark brown waves, while I'd inherited my mother's spiraled ginger curls. But my dad's hair had turned to gray, all color wiped clean away, never to return. I'd gotten used to the change in hair color, but I hadn't adjusted to the changes in his face — from the gauntness of his cheeks to the downturn of his mouth, always a little melancholy now, to the new set of lines between his eyes from so many hours sitting, pondering, asking why. Why was it Anna who had died? Why had she been taken from him?

He shook his head. "I don't know, Ivy. I'm backed up."

I'd known he wouldn't just drop everything to take a midday excursion at my first request, but I'd come prepared for a fight and I would not take no for an answer. "The work will be here when you get back."

"It never goes away," he agreed.

"You deserve a break now and then."

"I had a long break," he said. "Months, in fact."

He was talking about the time after my mom died. "That doesn't count, Dad. You don't have to make up every hour you were gone. Your job isn't like that."

"I'm not trying to make up the time, but I have things that have to get done. I have a budget report that is due in a few days and a meeting with one of the council members later today," he said.

I knew his schedule was busy, and I'd been lucky to find him in his office rather than running around here and there, politicking, but even the head honcho was entitled to an afternoon break. "Dad, it's just ice cream. I'll have you back in less than an hour." And then I took him by the hand, dragged him out the door of his office, down the hall, and out of the building.

He'd continued to resist at first, but soon we were back in town and sitting at a cute little bistro table at our favorite old-fashioned ice-cream parlor. I had a hearty scoop of strawberry in a cup and my dad had a double-scoop hot fudge sundae. Eating the ice cream was easy. Making small talk, not so much. It didn't take long before we came around face-to-face with the elephant in the room. "So those are some possible leads," I said after filling him in, making my voice as hopeful as possible.

We were silent for a minute; then he looked into my eyes. "You being careful, Ivy?"

I met his gaze and saw his fear blazing from behind them. It wasn't just fear for my personal safety. It was fear that I wouldn't succeed. Wouldn't manage to find the truth and free Billy from the accusations and the outcome of being charged with Max Litman's murder. "Always, Dad. Nothing's going to happen to me. Nothing's going to happen to Billy." I took his hand. "We'll be okay."

He squeezed my fingers. "I hope so, Ivy. God, how I hope so."

It hadn't been the uplifting trip to the ice-cream parlor I'd hoped for, but we were together and that was what we both needed. We just hadn't known it.

An hour after I'd picked him up, I dropped him back at the city building; then I went home. Home to my old historic house on Maple Street. Home to Agatha. Home to think.

CHAPTER 16

Back at home, I set Agatha free from her crate and opened the French doors that led from the parlor to the backyard. With a cup of rose-and-lavender-infused hot tea, a hunk of the sourdough bread I'd made, a floral-covered notebook, and my laptop, I settled in at the patio table. Agatha ran around in circles, foraged in the flower beds, and eventually wore herself out, stretching out in a sliver of sunlight on the grass. While she basked in the sun, I opened my notebook and recorded everything I knew about Max Litman, so far. Done with that, I opened my laptop, opened my browser, and began my search for spiritual leadership in Santa Sofia.

I hadn't been sure how difficult it would be to find information on Vanessa, but it turns out it wasn't hard at all. Googling "spiritual advisors" led me to a series of psychics and mediums, several professional counselors, and a life coach. A life coach who was named Vanessa Rose. Clicking over to her website and seeing her photograph confirmed that it was, indeed, the same woman. When Mrs. Branford and I had met her at Max Litman's house, she hadn't struck me as overtly metaphysical — or, truth be told, spiritual, at all. But the picture painted a different story. It had been taken with an exposure that created the effect of light streaming from behind her like an aura.

Turns out Vanessa was a Certified Life Coach and Spiritual Advisor with services that ran the gamut. She could help a person build loving relationships that work; cope with "hot buttons" like managing anger, frustration, and stress; deal with grief; develop self-awareness, self-worth, and self-esteem; and more. And she could also tap into a person's psyche with her "third eye."

Vanessa Rose was a one-stop therapist without the advanced degree to support her expertise. And with the added perk of angel readings. Knowing all of this made me want to go see her again so I could dig deeper into her relationship with Max. Without the benefit of a uniform and badge, however, I couldn't compel her to talk to me. A cold call might scare her off, and then where would I be? Keeping this in mind, it didn't take long to formulate the easiest and most logical plan: I was going to contact her about her services. After all, who couldn't use a life coach?

I made the call, half expecting to get a recording, but she answered on the third ring. I introduced myself using my middle name, Anna, which was my mother's name, and Cullison, the made-up surname I'd given to Johnny Wellborn. "I've never done this before," I said tentatively. True statement.

"I hear that all the time. We'll do a complimentary meet and greet first. I'll come over, we'll talk, and determine what your needs and goals are."

Life coach/spiritual advisor/angel readers must not be in high demand in Santa Sofia, because she had availability the following morning. We made the appointment, but as I hung up, a case of nerves struck me. How far would I have to go with my ruse to get information from her about her relationship with Max?

The doorbell rang, making the opportunity to dwell on what I'd say to Vanessa short-lived. Agatha had been asleep, but the moment I stood, she popped up, following me inside. I pressed the pads of my fingers to the door, stood on my toes, and peaked through the peephole to see Miguel's distorted face. I opened the door to him, a surprised smile on my face, grabbed hold of his shirt, and pulled him in. He laughed, but only until my lips landed on his with a *God, it's good to see you* kiss.

Had it not been for Agatha, the kiss would have gone on and on, but the second she'd laid eyes on Miguel, she tilted her head back, looking for all the world like she was going to howl, but instead she sucked in a wheezy breath and let forth a lusty barrage of barks. It was hard to sustain a kiss with the cacophony of her yelps and the *clickety-click* of her nails against the hardwood floor. She raced down the hall before doubling back to repeat her greeting. She sniffed his shoes, circled around him, and lightly nipped the hem of his pants, then started the barking frenzy again. Finally, she stopped when he bent to scratch her head. "One of these days you'll love me, Agatha." He glanced up at me with a charmingly crooked grin. "So will you."

I think I already did, but I wasn't ready to confess that. That would mean truly putting my heart on the line with him, and I wasn't ready to take that leap quite yet. Instead I smiled coyly. "You think so?"

He stood, then gave me that smoldering

look he was so good at. "I *know* so."

I folded my arms and did my best to look stern, but my flirty voice gave me away. "You're a confident one, aren't you, Mr. Baptista?"

He kicked the door closed behind him and wrapped his arms around me. "Confident and patient," he said. And then he pulled me close and kissed me again.

I melted in his arms. This was the feeling I'd missed since we'd parted ways so long ago. This was the feeling I'd missed even after marrying Luke. This was the feeling I hoped I'd have with Miguel for the rest of my life. But it wasn't going to last any longer at the moment because, dammit, Agatha was at it again, sounding for all the world as if she might hack up a lung. I pulled away from him, throwing a disappointed look at my pug. "Agatha, stop!"

She let go one more, followed by a half-hearted growl. She backed up a few steps, but never took her bulging eyes off Miguel. "You're a rascal," he said to her, "but you'll come around."

We took her back outside. Miguel sat opposite me at the patio table, and once again, I told my tale about Vanessa, the spiritual advisor, Dixie and her omission, and the ten investors in Max Litman's condo development deal.

He leaned forward as I relayed the details Johnny Wellborn had told Mrs. Branford and me.

"I have something to add to that," he said.

Now I leaned forward. "About the condos?"

"I didn't know about the condo, but I might know something about the investors."

I opened my notebook, fine-tipped pen in hand, and waited. If there was something noteworthy, I was ready to jot it down.

"Running a restaurant has some perks," he said.

"Right. Like unlimited brisket queso, white queso, and Diablo shrimp tacos," I said, and right on cue, my stomach growled.

"Besides the food," Miguel said, but he laughed. "Hungry?"

Now that he mentioned it, I couldn't actually remember when I'd eaten something besides a bite of bread. My stomach rumbled again. "I guess I am."

"Let's go get some dinner, then," he said, starting to stand.

I reached over to grab his wrist. "No, no, no. Tell me first. What did you learn?"

He lowered himself back down. "I've been training this new server. He's pretty good, so today was his first solo. My mother was on the floor, too, so I stayed in my office to catch up on the billing and ordering."

"Your mom?" Her English language ability was fairly limited and I'd never known her to wait tables.

"Sitting at the hosting station and just keeping her eye on the new kid," he amended.

"Okay." I waited, pen still at the ready, while he went on with his story.

"There was some problem with the food at one of the tables. The new kid —"

"Does he have a name?" I interrupted.

"Oh yeah. Jesse. So, Jesse was dealing with that. Apparently it wasn't going well, so my mom went to see what was happening. To see if she could help.

"Jesse ended up dealing with it fine, though. My mom was heading back to the hostess station when she overheard some people talking at a table. It was pretty heated."

"They were fighting?"

He shrugged. "Fighting. Arguing. They were having a disagreement."

I rolled my hand in the air so he'd keep going. "About . . ."

"She didn't hear everything, but she did hear Max's name. They were talking about money they'd lost thanks to him and what they were going to do about it."

"The investors!"

"Possibly," he said.

He was right not to jump to conclusions, but the coincidence was too big to ignore. "But they have to be." I wrote the word *investors* at the top of the blank page in front of me, circling it three times. "What else did your mom hear? Did she see who they were? Did she recognize them?"

He shook his head. "She didn't have her glasses, so she couldn't see them well. Blurry faces. One man spoke Spanish. She heard him take a phone call. The woman had dark hair. Light eyes. One man had a hat on. Nothing else stood out."

"How many were there?" I asked.

"Three men, one woman."

I wrote that down. So half the investors got together, which meant Wellborn had either lied or he was out of the loop, because these five investors did know each other.

"Did she hear anything else?"

"Just one thing," he said.

I waited expectantly. Maybe it was the break we needed to be able to move forward and help Billy.

"She said one of them kind of laughed and said the world was better off. Then one of them reminded the guy that they still didn't have their money, and then they all got quiet again."

"Are you sure she didn't recognize any of them?"

He shook his head. "Sorry."

It was interesting information, but disappointing that we couldn't ID at least one of the people at the table. But then it dawned on me. Johnny Wellborn was one of the investors. He had said they were silent investors. He had said he didn't know who the others were. But if these people *were* the investors, had Johnny Wellborn been among them?

It stood to reason that if five of the investors knew each other, the remaining five did, too. Whether or not Johnny Wellborn was at that lunch didn't matter. The fact was, Johnny Wellborn had lied.

And then another thought occurred to me. Someone had had to pay for their meal. Or maybe they all paid separately. "Did they pay with credit cards?"

"Cash," he said, but then he smiled, a satisfied expression on his face. "Except for one."

This was good. Wellborn hadn't ponied up, but maybe this person would. I thought about all the times I'd paid with my credit card. It showed the last four numbers, but no name. Unless the waiter had a really excellent memory, the odds were slim that he'd even looked at the name on the card. "Is the signature legible?" I asked, trying to stay hopeful. Unless there was something helpful in this story, Miguel wouldn't have brought it up. I tapped my fingers on the table, waiting.

"The credit card number itself doesn't help us, and no, the signature isn't legible. It's more of a scribble. But listen, I'm not done. The new server ran into a problem running the credit card so he asked my mother to do it. She had to run the card. She's the one who took it back to the table. We have always made a point of trying to make our customers feel welcome. Like they have had a personal experience eating at Baptista's."

I'd been on the receiving end of that. Every time I ate there, they greeted me by — "Right. You thank people by their names," I said, suddenly knowing where he was going with this.

"Bingo." He pulled out a pale yellow sticky note and handed it to me, a single name scrawled across the middle of it. "My mom did what she always does. What we all do. She looked at the name on the card before giving it back with the slip to sign.

Vicente Villanueva."

My excitement felt like a million needles pricking my skin from the inside out.

The name did not ring a bell, but we had a name nonetheless. "Do you know him?"

"No, but I looked him up."

"Miguel, you're a man after my own heart."

"I already have your heart," he said with a slight grin and a quick upward flick of his eyebrows.

He did, indeed. "So who is he?"

"Turns out he's a VP for a hotel chain."

"So how does he know Max?" I asked, thinking aloud.

"How did anyone know Max?" Miguel said. "Real estate. Construction. Art cars. That was his trifecta, right?"

"Plus he needed spiritual advice," I said, telling him about my appointment with Vanessa the next morning.

He arched a brow. "So you're going to see a fortune-teller."

"She's a life coach," I said, making air quotes as I said it.

"And an angel reader. 1096," he said.

"1096?"

He circled his index finger near his temple. "Crazy."

"Ah, police code. Got it." I thought back

to my first encounter with Vanessa. She hadn't struck me as someone full of great wisdom, an angel reader who could summon the spirits of the netherworld, or a 1096. She seemed pretty normal, in fact. "I guess I'll find out."

"I'm assuming Vicente Villanueva and this life coach don't run in the same circles."

That seemed like a pretty safe assumption to me. "I guess we need to pay Mr. Villanueva a visit, don't we?"

"First we need to get you some real food," Miguel said. He stood, picked up my empty mug and the forgotten piece of sourdough bread, and headed inside. I followed with my laptop, Agatha trotting along beside me. I'd expected Miguel to put the dirty dishes on the counter to be dealt with later, but instead, he gave them a quick wash and set them to dry on the absorbent mat next to the sink.

I stood on my toes to brush my lips against his cheek. Instead of going back to the dishes, he spun, taking me into his arms. His hand splayed across my lower back, a little light pressure pressing me closer until not a bit of air could pass between us. "I like coming home to you." The tenor of his voice dropped just enough to hear suggestion laced in it; then he left me with no doubt, pulling me into a kiss.

Before I could succumb and forgo the idea of food in favor of dessert, my cell phone bleated out the ringtone I had programmed for Emmaline. Any call she made to me while Billy was a suspect was going to be about the case. I pulled away from Miguel to answer, grabbed the phone from the table, and put her on speaker.

"I gave the information to Lane," she said.

"And?"

"And he is more interested in making the clues fit his suspect rather than the other way around. We can't count on him, Ivy," she said, her voice void of emotion.

"What about the investors? Those are real people with real motives." I couldn't fathom why the sheriff wouldn't pursue that lead.

"This is high profile," she said. "He has to solve it quickly, and Billy is right there for him on a silver platter. He doesn't think he needs to look any further."

Which meant he'd feel the same way about looking into Dixie and Vanessa. He had set his jaw, dug in his heels, and had all but named Billy as the guilty party. At this point, I knew Em could talk until she was literally blue in the face and still not get Lane to budge in his stance.

Miguel spoke up. "We have a potential lead."

"Hey, sorry. I didn't know you were there, Miguel."

"No problem. Been talking to Ivy about some customers at the restaurant." He went on to tell an abbreviated version of his story. "The name's Villanueva. Vicente."

"Vicente Villanueva," she repeated. "I'll see what I can find."

We hung up, took care of Agatha, and headed out. "I need to stop by the bread shop first," Miguel said as he drove us out of the historic neighborhood.

I looked at him, surprised. Normally I was the one needing to stop here, or run in there, with Yeast of Eden always being high on my list. "I need to adjust the restaurant's bread order," he explained.

Miguel ran Baptista's Cantina and Grill like a well-oiled machine. He was part of every decision and had his hand in every part of the restaurant his parents had created. He'd recently made some adjustments to his twice-a-week order with Olaya. "The tortas are our number-one seller now," he continued. "I'm running out every single day."

"We can call it in," I said, knowing that Olaya could easily adjust the number of rectangular rolls she made for him.

"We could, but I want to talk to her about a few other things. I still want you to take photos of the restaurant, by the way. New menu. New tourist brochure for the hotels and chamber."

We'd talked about that a while back, but life in Santa Sofia had gotten in the way. I was glad he hadn't forgotten. Building my photography business would be slow going, and every job would help.

"You're adding new breads to the menu?" I asked, getting back to the reason for his visit to Yeast of Eden.

"Mexican cornbread," he said. "I'm putting a new chocolate chile soup on the menu. The cornbread would be the side."

"Chocolate and chile?" I wasn't sure what I thought of that.

"Similar to chicken mole. Blackened ancho chilis, onions, tomatoes. Just a hint of chocolate."

"Well, when you put it that way. . . ." I trailed off, my stomach growling again.

He leveled a serious gaze at me as we rolled up to a stop sign. "You have to eat, Ivy."

"I know," I said. "I will."

A few minutes later we were there. There was no parking in front, so Miguel pulled into the small lot behind Yeast of Eden. My mind flashed back to the first time I'd seen him again after returning to Santa Sofia, right here in this parking lot. At that moment, I never would have predicted that we'd end up together, yet here we were.

The bread shop was closed for the day, but I knew Olaya would still be here. Miguel and I entered through the back door straight into the kitchen. She had it set up with various baking stations, stainless-steel countertops, multiple bakery racks ready to receive trays filled with whatever came out of the oven, the professional ovens themselves, and an enormous movable mirror stationed directly above the primary baking workstation. She used this to demonstrate process and technique during the monthly classes she held.

We found her in the little office off to the side of the kitchen. The space was small. Aside from the desk chair Olaya sat in, there was only one other. I sat there while Miguel leaned against the doorframe. They spent a few minutes discussing Baptista's bread order, making adjustments to both quantity and variety. Fifty additional telera rolls were added to cover the demand for tortas. The *pan dulce* order stayed the same. They moved on to the Mexican cornbread. "I can make it in several ways," she said after he'd described the ancho chili soup. "I can layer the bread. Pour half the batter into the pan, lay down the green chilis and cheese. Pepper jack, I think. And last, I pour in the rest of the batter. That is the simple way. To be fancy, I can add jalapeños and corn, creamed and niblets. Mmm. *Que bueno.*"

"That sounds great," Miguel said. "How many —"

Olaya waved one hand in the air. "That was option one. There are others."

I drew my lips in, stifling a laugh. Olaya took her baking very seriously. If she had multiple options, she was going to share them all.

Miguel nodded. "Right. Of course. What's option two?"

"Option two is to make them as muffins with the mix-ins worked into the batter. This would be easier to handle, *pero* maybe not as pretty on the plate. This would not be my choice."

This time I did laugh. "Olaya, you are too funny. Why mention it if it's not the best way to go?"

She responded without looking up from her paperwork. "Ivy, the decision is not mine to make. I must give all the choices so Miguel can make the best decision."

"Is there a third choice?" Miguel asked.

"*Por supuesta,*" she said. "The last is a stuffed cornbread. It is layered. No, no, not layered. This one is, how do you say . . . ?" The word came to her. "Ah, it is stuffed. It has chorizo, onion, cheese, chipotle chilis in adobo, and black beans. *Pero ay mas.*" She tapped her finger against her cheek, thinking. "Ah, *sí.* Tomatoes, of course, and cilantro."

At this point my stomach had a mind of its own, rumbling steadily. "That sounds like a meal by itself."

Her eyes pinched. "Ivy, you are neglecting yourself."

"I'm going to feed her. The restaurant is the next stop."

"*Bueno. Entonces* which bread do you prefer?"

"I think you're right about the muffins. Too casual," Miguel said.

Olaya ticked off the two remaining choices on her fingers. "Simple layered or deluxe stuffed."

"I need to try them," Miguel said.

Olaya nodded with approval. It had all been a test, I realized. She already liked and respected Miguel, but I knew that his response had elevated him in her estimation. "That is the right decision," she said.

"I will make them for you."

"Perfect." He seemed to know he had passed her test, too, and smiled. After they worked out a few more details about his standing order, I stood up to leave.

She walked with us back through the kitchen. We stopped at the back door. "Do you have news?"

Miguel answered. "The name of a man we think might have invested in a deal with Max."

"A deal that went south," I added. "We are on the hunt for a man named Vicente Villanueva?"

In my experience, there wasn't much that rattled Olaya. She was calm and collected. But hearing the name cracked her veneer. *"¿Que dice?"*

We both stared at her. "Vicente Villanueva," I said. "He invested a lot of money with Max Litman."

"He lost a lot of money with Max Litman," Miguel said.

"Do you know him?" I asked, but from her reaction the answer was evident.

"Vicente Villanueva *es el novio de* Martina," she said. I didn't know much Spanish, but I understood that. Vicente was her sister Martina's boyfriend.

CHAPTER 17

Olaya had called Martina the moment we'd put together the connection between her and Vicente Villanueva, but she hadn't answered the phone calls, and she didn't text. There was nothing to do but wait.

"Food," Miguel had said once we were back in his truck. "You need to eat."

I had started to argue. How could I eat when there was a potentially viable clue that could lead us somewhere concrete? "We could —"

He held his hand up, palm out. "No, we couldn't."

I planted my hands on my hips. "You don't even know what I was going to say."

"Oh, but that's where you're wrong." He tapped his index finger to his temple. "I can see the wheels turning."

"We can find Martina, which will help us find this Vicente Villanueva guy. Which could lead us to the other investors. All of which could end up helping Billy."

"Come on, Ivy. You want to drive all over Santa Sofia looking for Martina?" He held up his hands, palms to the ceiling. "Needle," he said, raising one hand. He lowered that one and raised the other. "Haystack."

Even though searching high and low for Martina is exactly what I wanted to do, I took his point. It wasn't practical, or realistic. I had no choice but to give up the fight. "Okay. Food first, but we're talking a quick meal, not a drawn-out sit-down."

"Agreed."

Now, twenty minutes later, we were in Baptista's Cantina and Grill's kitchen. Miguel had pulled a stool off to one side. I perched on it, watching the carefully choreographed dance of the cooks and the waitstaff. They juggled steaming pots on the professional-grade stoves; a woman manned the salad and soup station; someone else handled sauces; yet another prepared desserts. Together they were a well-oiled machine.

The entire process was dramatically different from the inner workings of the bread shop. The kitchen at Yeast of Eden was calm. The long rise of yeast bread took time. The shaping of rolls and scones and baguettes was methodical and repetitive. I found the process therapeutic.

Here, on the other hand, there was a buzz in the air; the space was alight with energy. Different personalities responded to different environments and different stimuli. While I preferred the relative calm of Olaya's kitchen, Miguel clearly thrived here amid the activity of his restaurant kitchen. No matter the environment, there was something about being in a restaurant kitchen that was exhilarating. It was as if the place was filled with possibility.

Miguel knew his way around a kitchen, but I had never seen him in action. I watched him now with fascination. He checked on his staff, dipping a spoon into a saucepan to taste, nodding with satisfaction after sinking his teeth into a cherry tomato, pulling a homemade corn tortilla off the griddle. He was clearly in charge, and he was in his element. Food was in his blood. He'd grown up right here in this very kitchen. Now he'd taken it over, slowly but surely, putting his own stamp on it.

Once he was satisfied with the current kitchen operations, he set to work in a tucked-away corner of the stainless-steel counter. He started by splitting open two telera rolls from the bread shop. The knife sliced through the crispy crust of the outside, revealing the soft texture of the bread inside.

He'd pulled a few things from the walk-in refrigerator, setting them at his makeshift workstation. And then he began to assemble. First, he slathered on a spread of black beans. Next, he added a layer of perfectly fanned slices of avocado followed by finely chopped lettuce, tomatoes, and onions. My stomach growled relentlessly now, my hunger coming at me with full force.

With the tortas laid out on two plates, he took a pair of tongs and a small bowl from the stack of dishes on the open shelves above the counters and disappeared into the heart of the kitchen. He reappeared a moment later, the bowl steaming, the aroma seeping through me.

"*Carne asada,*" he said, taking a thin piece of freshly grilled beef and laying it on his cutting board. With a knife that looked sharper than any I'd ever laid eyes on, he sliced the beef, using the tongs to arrange it onto the prepared telera rolls. Finally, he wrapped each one in parchment paper, sliced it in half, and placed the two pieces on a plate.

After wiping his hands on a clean dish towel, he pulled up another stool and set the plate between us. Before he sat, he took two Topo Chicos from the beverage cooler under the counter where he'd been working, using a knife to pop off the bottle caps.

I picked up one of the two sandwich sections, tearing part of the parchment back. And then, unable to wait a second longer, I took a bite. "Oh my God," I said, savoring the first bite. "So good." My stomach thanked me; so did my taste buds.

I took another bite before I washed it down with a sip of the mineral water. "Did your dad teach you to cook?" I asked.

He sat on the second stool, picking up a jalapeño slice with one hand, holding his sandwich in the other. "Dad. Mom. *Abuela.* Pretty much my entire family."

"They taught you well," I said before taking another bite.

After we'd satiated ourselves, we launched back into the investigation. "We know Wellborn was one of the investors, and Vicente Villanueva is another. That still leaves seven more." I had racked my brain but had no clue who they might be."

"Is there a Mrs. Wellborn?" Miguel asked.

I opened my mouth, ready to say no, but I realized that I didn't actually know. I'd assumed there wasn't. He hadn't worn a wedding ring, and while he hadn't actually done anything overt, there had most definitely been some flirtation between he and Dixie. "Good question. I have no idea."

"Because if there is, we could —"

"— see if she knows anything," I finished.

There were probably several ways I could find out if Wellborn was married, but I went with the simplest. I picked up my cell phone, searched my contacts, and dialed Dixie.

A minute later, I had the answer to my question. Johnny Wellborn was, indeed, married. "I don't know," Dixie said hesitantly when I asked her for Wellborn's home address. "Isn't that private?"

"It's not top-secret information. I can find it through public records," I said, hoping that was actually true. Still, it would be so much easier if she'd just give it to me.

Turns out I didn't need to press her. "They live on a property on the other side of the interstate," she said, rattling off the address. "But you did not hear it from me."

"Got it. Thanks, Dixie."

"Wait just a minute, darlin'," she said before I could hang up. "What are you going to do?"

"The same thing I've been trying to do all along. Find a murderer."

The drive east took us to farmland and prime properties with the most expensive addresses in Santa Sofia. "Pays to be a contractor," Miguel said as we passed massive house after massive house after massive house.

That wasn't always true. Billy was a contractor, but he lived in a modest home about five miles from our childhood home, not a 4,000 square foot house on five acres in the country. "It does for Johnny Wellborn, anyway."

We found the address and turned down the paved road. Miguel gave a low whistle. "Their own moat," he said as we drove over a small bridge arched over a trickling creek.

A majestic weeping willow grew just over the bridge. It was planted far enough away so as not encroach on the irrigation, and from this vantage point, it brought a fairytale-like element to the property.

"Impressive," he said, scanning the scenery.

If you liked that sort of thing. Did he like that sort of thing? If so, that was an incompatibility. Nice as it was, I could never live out here, just as I could never live in Max

Litman's neighborhood.

We kept driving, finally catching sight of the house around a bend in the asphalt road. It was a sprawling single story with a stone and brick façade. Dark wood accents accentuated the stone. "And I thought Max's house was something else," I said.

"Big and expensive doesn't necessarily mean better. Your house, now that's a keeper."

A relieved sigh escaped me. He preferred character to expansive living. A man after my own heart. A thought suddenly hit me. I only ever saw Miguel at Baptista's, at some other location where we happened to run into each other, some prescribed place where we'd agreed to meet, or at my house. I knew he lived somewhere near the restaurant, but I had no idea where. "You've never taken me to your house," I said.

"Haven't I?"

"Um, no, you haven't." I suddenly wanted to go. To see how he lived. Did he wash his dishes after he ate, or leave them in the sink? Did he make his bed in the morning, or leave it rumpled from the night's sleep? Did he have real furniture, or was he still living like he was in college? These were things a woman needed to know about her man.

"It's kind of near the restaurant," he said.

I stole a glance at him. He had a smoldering look and there was a glimmer in his eyes that gave him the Cheshire cat mischievousness. Still, he managed to look sheepish somehow.

"Yeah, you've told me that, but where?" Baptista's was on the pier. The closest neighborhood was inland, on the other side of PCH. I wouldn't have described that as near the restaurant, but before I could inquire any more, he pulled his truck into a space on the driveway that seemed designated for visitor cars.

Even the refurbished dark wood barn-style garage doors, arched and sporting a row of windows across the top of each, were spectacular. They elevated the look of the house — as if it needed that. The sprawling single-story home was surprisingly welcoming for such an enormous place. Colorful flowers, wispy fronds from a cluster of ferns under the shaded porch, and a stone walkway leading up to the front door welcomed visitors. The landscaping on the side of the house where we were was just as gorgeous. The Wellborns had taken the time and invested the money to make the entire place a showcase.

Miguel got out of the truck, circling around to the passenger side. He put his hand on the doorframe as I pushed it open and stepped down. As we turned to face the house, a woman materialized in front of the garage. The knees of her jeans were browned from kneeling, and her dark green Hunter garden clogs were caked with a layer of dirt. She brushed her gloved hands together, a mist of dirt falling to the ground, before peeling them off. "Can I help you?"

I walked toward her, casually placing my palm against my chest. "I'm Ivy. This is Miguel."

Her eyes narrowed warily. "Are you selling something?"

"Oh no, no, ma'am —"

"Then am I supposed to know your names? Or you?"

It was a long shot that she'd be inherently trusting and accept two strangers at face value, but I'd expected her to be pleasant. My hope was dashed on both counts. "No, not at all. We were just —"

Miguel jumped in. "We know your husband, and since we were in the neighborhood, we —"

"— decided to stop by," I finished. I stretched my arm out in a friendly gesture.

She looked at it, then to my face, hesitating. Finally she stripped off her garden gloves and stepped forward to shake my hand first, then Miguel's. "Johnny's not here."

I imagined she and her husband didn't get many random visitors out here in the country, but if she thought it was odd we were *in the neighborhood,* she didn't let on. I'd been smiling amiably, but let my face fall. "That's too bad. We're sorry to miss him."

She'd folded her arms over her chest, still guarded. "What was your name?" she asked me.

Too late I realized that it would have been smart to give my Anna Cullison alias. Then again, if Mrs. Wellborn described me to her husband, my curly red hair would give me away. "Ivy," I said. "And this is Miguel. You're Mrs. Wellborn?" I asked, wanting to confirm the fact before continuing.

Her lips were drawn into a thin line. She wasn't unattractive, but the harsh manner in which she held her expression, coupled with the sharp point of her nose and her small dark eyes, didn't give her a warm and fuzzy look. She gave a curt nod to answer my question.

I had to try the softest approach I could. Bees and honey again, only this time I didn't have a box of Olaya's croissants. "We're sorry to bother you. We had a quick question for your husband."

She let out a derisive laugh. "You drove all the way out here to ask Johnny a quick question? Come now . . . Ivy, was it? What is it you want?"

"Mrs. Wellborn," Miguel said, "let me be straight with you —"

"I wish you would," she snapped.

"The investment deal with Max Litman —"

The moment Max's name crossed Miguel's lips, Mrs. Wellborn grew stiff as a board. I thought she'd been uptight before, what with her rigid spine and taut neck, but in comparison to now, she'd been positively slouching. Her jaw pulsed, her lips drawing together in a thin line. "You know about that?"

We both nodded, afraid to say too little or too much.

"Did he tell you how that man swindled us? If I could, I'd spit on his grave."

While I was taken aback by Mrs. Wellborn's anger, I understood it. Losing a hundred and twenty thousand dollars was more than a big deal. It could be life altering.

"We're well aware, Mrs. Wellborn."

"Did he also mention how *Mr.* Litman walked away from the so-called deal with a

214

cool million in his pocket? Or in some Cayman Island numbered account, anyway." Her eyes opened wide, clarity striking like a hot iron. She pointed at us, a floppy garden glove in her hand. "You're part of it, aren't you?"

Miguel and I had talked about how to answer that question. Now I forged ahead with the tactic we'd decided on. "We have a stake in that, too." It wasn't a lie; our stake just wasn't financial.

Her seething fury was palpable, but it was directed toward Max and the situation, not us. "Of course you do. Why else would you be here?"

"So I guess you haven't been able to recoup any of your money," I said, fishing.

She scoffed. "Have you?"

"Um —" I faltered, but she picked up where she'd left off.

"We tried every possible avenue, but Max was pretty damn smart. Smarter than us. Wherever that money is, we'll never get our hands on it again." She leveled her gaze at us.

"What's the quick question you want to ask Johnny?"

Miguel jumped in. "We wanted to run something by him."

"And the other investors," I added.

She wasn't moved. We clearly weren't going to be able to soften her up, so I hardened my own expression to mimic hers and nodded. Solidarity. "He screwed a lot of people. We want justice." Again, not a lie, just not the entire truth.

She grimaced. "You're preaching to the choir."

"We haven't seen any of the others," Miguel said, playing into the ruse that we were part of the elite group that had been swindled by Max. "Keeping a low profile after the loss, I guess."

Mrs. Wellborn slapped her garden gloves against her thigh. "That I wouldn't know."

"You haven't seen them either?" I asked.

"Seen them? How could I? My husband refuses to tell me who the other victims are. And yes, I do consider us all victims."

"You haven't seen Vicente around?" She gave me a blank stare. "Vicente Villanueva?" I clarified.

Mrs. Wellborn pulled on her gloves again. "Another of Max's casualties, I presume. I don't know him." She walked to the end of the garage, but stopped at the corner to look back at us. "I'll tell Johnny you stopped by," she said; then she rounded the corner and disappeared from our sight.

By the time we'd made it halfway back to

Santa Sofia, we'd almost convinced each other that Mrs. Wellborn was a pretty good suspect. She certainly had a strong motive, but we ended up dismissing her from our minds. "She's too obvious," I said. "If she'd killed him, she wouldn't be so . . . so . . . so . . ."

I was at a loss, but Miguel finished my thought. "So brutally honest about her hatred for the man?"

"Exactly."

After another few minutes, my cell phone rang. Olaya. "You should come here to the bread shop," she said when I answered. "Martina is here."

"We'll be back in twenty minutes," I said. "Don't let her leave!"

"To Yeast of Eden?" Miguel asked, confirming what he'd gathered from my half of the conversation.

I pointed forward. "To Yeast of Eden."

He nodded, flicked the turn signal down, and made the left turn to take us back into town.

CHAPTER 18

Olaya Solis had two sisters. Olaya was in her mid-sixties, Consuelo was a few years younger, and then there was Martina. The youngest Solis sister was in her late fifties. The three women were tighter than a knot, but vastly different. Olaya was bohemian, green-eyed, and statuesque; Consuelo, also green-eyed but with a fairer skin, was a casual jeans and T-shirt kind of woman; and Martina, who had a darker complexion, amber eyes, and auburn hair, was the most stylish of the three. Every time I'd seen her, she'd been put together. Refined. At the moment, however, before us in the bread shop, she was wide-eyed and nervous.

Olaya, Martina, Miguel, and I sat at one of the bistro tables. Martina leaned forward, one hand resting on top of the other. "Vicente lost one hundred twenty thousand dollars?"

"We think so," I said, "although we haven't

been able to confirm it."

She stood abruptly, her chair teetering behind her. Miguel reached over, grabbing the back and pulling it out of the way. And then Martina paced, back and forth, back and forth, back and forth. She whirled around to face us again. "All that money? For nothing?"

I nodded, wishing I could tell her something different. "He wasn't the only one."

"Who else?" she said, sitting down again.

Miguel answered. "Johnny Wellborn."

Martina and Olaya looked at one another, both shaking their heads. "I do not know him," Martina said.

"And there are more," Olaya said. "Each one put in the same amount of money?"

"One hundred and twenty thousand dollars each," Miguel said.

Martina stood again, backing away from the table. "It is all gone?"

"That's why we want to talk to Vicente," I said. "The investors gave their money to Max Litman. We don't know what happened to it after that. What we heard is that the deal went south in a bad deal. Max said he took a loss, too."

"One hundred and twenty thousand dollars, that is not a loss. That is to be destroyed." Martina's face waffled between

219

anger, frustration, and compassion. Finally she landed on the latter. "*Pobrecito*. How could Vicente keep this from me?" She spoke aloud, but she didn't expect an answer that none of us could give.

"Can we see him?" I asked.

The truth seemed to suddenly dawn on Martina. "Oh no." She backed away, her hands shaking, palms out. "No, no. You cannot think Vicente could have done this thing to Max? That Vicente could have killed him?"

I stood now, taking her hands in mine. They were cold. Trembling. "What I know is that Billy did not kill Max. I know Johnny Wellborn lied about not knowing who the other investors were. I know that there are plenty of other people who didn't like the man for one reason or another." I turned away from Martina, talking to Olaya, too. Talking to the universe, maybe. "Someone killed Max. I need to figure out who. If Vicente knows something, it could help us prove Billy's innocence."

She faced the display cases, pressing her hands to the top and stretching her arms out, hanging her head. "*Pero* it was not Vicente. I promise you that."

Olaya spoke to her sister in Spanish. Consuelo joined in, and before long the three sisters were wrapped up in a conversation I couldn't follow.

Miguel leaned toward me. "They're trying to convince her to call Vicente," he translated. "She's afraid."

I didn't blame her, but I had to believe that Martina wouldn't fall for a killer. She was a better judge of character than that. Martina had sunk down at the table again, her head in her hands. Olaya came to stand beside her. She put her hand on her sister's back, lightly rubbing it. "*Hermana,* he is a good man. Not capable of murder. If he can help find who is, then . . ."

She let the words hover in the air, let them sink into her sister. "*Claro.* He *is* a good man," Martina said. "He did not do this thing."

"Call him," Olaya urged. "Help Ivy."

Martina pushed herself upright and moved back to the table, digging her phone from her purse. After a few taps on the screen with the pad of her index finger, she held the phone to her ear.

I held my breath, hopeful that our luck was finally going to change. Vicente could fill in the blanks and tell us whatever Mr. Wellborn had left out of the story.

But Martina pulled the phone away from her ear. Her shoulders drooped, and she hung her head. *"Nada."*

No answer.

I tried to keep my expression even, to not betray my frustration. The walls of the bread shop seemed to close in around me. I felt like Alice in Wonderland as she shrinks, growing smaller and smaller, the room growing bigger and bigger, the walls distorting. I couldn't breathe. My lungs seized.

Olaya left Martina's side and came to stand beside me. *"Está bien?"* she asked. I nodded, but Olaya didn't believe it. She disappeared behind the counter, bent to pull something from one of the display cases, slipped it into a bag, and handed it to me. "For later," she said. "Trust and believe, yes? Ivy, trust and believe."

CHAPTER 19

Vanessa arrived at my house the next morning at nine o'clock on the dot. I opened the door to her, greeting her with a friendly smile, but the moment she laid eyes on me, her jaw dropped. "You?"

I smiled sheepishly. "After meeting you, I found myself wondering if I needed a spiritual advisor, and since you're the only one I know of . . ."

She looked more like I imagined a spiritual advisor might look this time around. Standing in the threshold of my doorway, she looked positively New Age. Her blond hair was pulled back into a loose bun, wavy strands haphazardly framing her face. Her long skirt dusted the ground, and her dangling bracelets and beaded necklace gave her the look of a fortune-teller.

"You're not really a friend of Max's, are you?" she asked.

"Not exactly, no," I said.

She started to back away, but I stretched my arm out, taking her hand in mine. "Vanessa, wait. Please."

She turned. "You don't really need a spiritual advisor — or a life coach. So what *do* you want? Why did you call me here?"

I could lie to her again, but I found that I didn't want to. "I need to find out what happened to Max," I said.

"But you just said you weren't friends."

"He had a big impact on my life," I said. It was cryptic, but I couldn't give her more than that. As much as I wanted it to be true, I didn't peg her as a killer. Worst case, I was wrong and had put myself in danger by having her come to my home. Best case, she had some information that would help me.

"He had that effect on a lot of people," she said, her voice almost reverent.

"I didn't think you'd come if you knew I was the same person who'd shown up at Max's door —"

"You'd have been right," she said, but her voice wasn't cutting like Mrs. Wellborn's had been. "I'll ask you again, why did you call me here?"

"The idea of a life coach *is* kind of intriguing. Everyone could use one, right?"

She finally managed a little smile. "In my opinion? Yes."

Agatha had been behind me, but scooted into view as I held the door open. I was hoping Vanessa would come in instead of going back to her car. She hesitated, but then she saw Agatha, gave a smile that reached her eyes, and stepped inside. I ushered her out to the back patio, Agatha in tow, brought out a pitcher of iced tea, and we settled in on the Adirondack chairs.

We sat in silence for a few minutes, sipping our tea and breathing in the spring air. I waited, sure she'd break the silence before long. After another long minute, she put her glass down. "Tell me about your relationship with Max," she said.

I managed a light laugh. "Where to start? He's a Santa Sofia icon. I can't really think of a time when I wasn't at least *aware* of him."

She interlaced her fingers, holding her clasped hands under her chin. "And did you like him?"

"I can't say that I knew him well enough to say whether I liked him or not as a person."

"Fair enough," she said. "Let me put it a different way. What was your general impression of him?"

I hesitated, not wanting to speak ill of the dead, and not wanting to reveal the depth of my animosity toward Max. He'd worked so hard to thwart Billy's success and had cheated people out of their hard-earned money. Finding anything positive to say was a huge stretch.

She gave her head a slight shake and waved one hand to stop me. "Clearly your impression wasn't good. I get it, but I want you to know, he *was* trying to change. He wanted to make amends to the people he'd hurt. It was an active pursuit, actually."

"What, like a twelve-step program?"

"Exactly like that. Max's life was hollow. A vacuous existence, if you will. He wanted more."

I'd often thought about how sad his life seemed. No partner. No children. No one to come home to at the end of the day. But what facilitated his desire to change? I thought about the old dog, new tricks maxim. It was true. While he hadn't spied on Billy's art car this year, the condo scam had been a relatively recent act. I had to wonder if his so-called desire to change his ways was more about having Vanessa Rose in his life than actually recalibrating the way he lived his own.

"If you weren't friends, why are you so interested in Max?" she asked, reaching down beside her to scratch Agatha's head.

After a minute, Agatha laid down beside Vanessa's chair. A few seconds later, her steady snore filtered up to us.

I saw no reason to keep the truth from her. "You know the art car competition?"

"Who doesn't?"

"My brother and Max have been what you might call art car rivals pretty much forever."

She started. "Your brother? You mean Billy *Culpepper*?"

Now I sat up. "Did Max mention him?"

"A better question would be when did he *not* mention him? Your brother was like Max's lifeline in a lot of ways. He never told me his last name, so I didn't put you together with him."

I glossed over the revelation that Max had Billy at the forefront of his mind, instead zeroing in on the other part of what she'd said. "What does that mean, that Billy was his lifeline?"

"Everyone has a lifeline. A person who pushes them, who creates a situation or situations that allow one to become a better — or sometimes worse — version of him or herself. It's a yin-yang. Balance, although often the balance is uneven. Conflict is everywhere, but the challenges we face are the things that define us. It's not really

227

about the conflicts themselves, it about how we respond to them."

"There was definitely conflict between them, but how was that a lifeline?"

"Max hit a breaking point recently. A defining moment, if you will. He had gotten to the point where he couldn't look himself in the mirror. Couldn't stand some of the things he'd done, and was continuing to do, to the people around him. Your brother epitomized that breaking point, but it was also his lifeline. If he could make amends with Billy, he could forgive himself."

The shock must have shown on my face. "Are you being serious right now?" I asked. I was having a hard time wrapping my head around the fact that maybe Max Litman wasn't as bad as I'd made him out to be in my head. Or at least that he had been trying not to be.

"Completely. He was battling demons. He wanted to reach out, but making peace with Billy was his most difficult obstacle. He apologized to others, but it didn't always go well. You are not the only skeptical one in Santa Sofia," she said, acknowledging my feelings. She was good. "He felt that what he'd done to your brother was somehow worse than the injury to those he'd taken money from. If those people rebuked him, he was afraid Billy would, too."

I had no idea how Billy would have responded had Max offered him an olive branch. I liked to think that our parents raised us with the capacity to forgive, but Max had done a good number on Billy. That chasm ran pretty deep. I also wasn't sure I completely bought the story Vanessa was weaving.

The ocean breeze picked up, bringing a chill to the air. Vanessa crossed one side of the lightweight sweater she wore over the other. "I know what you're thinking," she said.

"Do you?" I asked.

"You're wondering if Max turning over a new leaf was just pretense. A means to some other end."

God, she wasn't good, she was great. "Did you know that he spied on my brother every single year just so he could win the Art Car Show?"

She blinked slowly as she nodded. "That was one of his first confessions to me."

"It's not life and death. Billy and I, we get that. But Max was underhanded and dishonest, and he cheated every single year. He didn't care how he won, only that he did."

We fell silent for a moment. I stared at the

sky while Vanessa closed her eyes, her hands intertwined, and her index fingers steepled and pressed to her lips. "He was on a spiritual walk, Ms. Culpepper," she said.

My skepticism flared. "What does that mean? He found God? He was born again?"

"That is what it means for some," she said. "For Max it mostly meant he realized that he was walking a path that teetered between right and wrong —"

"He was walking a path that was firmly wrong," I corrected.

She dipped her chin, which I interpreted as a concession. "I was helping him build his spiritual foundation." Tears pooled in her eyes. Real emotion. "I got to know the *real* Max Litman."

After seeing her at Max's house, I'd entertained the idea that she'd been after his money — more gold digger than advisor — but maybe I'd pegged her all wrong. She dragged her fingers under her eyes, whisking away her tears. "He was a good man. He really was. He just didn't let people see it. I helped him appreciate that there is a power that's greater than man's. Greater than his could ever be. That money and winning, in whatever way he sought those things, could never give him power that would be peaceful — power with no strings attached."

Vanessa's manner was calm. Accessible. I waited, letting her gather her thoughts and continue.

"He had to understand that his way of life was poisonous, not just to others, but to himself. He had to dig deep. To take stock and find his moral and ethical deficits. Part of that process is confessing these failings to someone else. He did that with me. I saw him when he was most vulnerable. When he thought there was no chance of redemption. And then I held his hand and we prayed together."

"He told you he swindled people out of their life savings?" Ten that I knew of with the condo deal, but I had no doubt that there were others.

"He was trying to make that right," she said. "He had every intention of paying that money back to each one of those people. He was walking a spiritual path."

Again, doubt crept in. Did he really want to make it right, or was that just something he'd said to win her trust? What if Vanessa Rose was just a conquest for Max? "Do you know who they are? The people he swindled?"

Her response was a slow shake of her head. "I don't ask specific details like that."

"But he told you Billy's name."

"As I said, Billy was the lifeline."

I leaned my head back against the hard back of the chair, cursing under my breath.

She angled her body toward me. "You came to Max's house. You brought me here. What are you hoping to gain or understand?"

"He's dead, and the sheriff has Billy pegged as the murderer. I'm trying to find out what really happened. You were trying to free Max. Well, I'm trying to free Billy."

She gave me that slow blink again. "I wish I could help you, Ivy," she said. "I really do. Please believe me when I tell you that Max really was regretful."

I wanted to believe her, but I wasn't sure if I did.

Chapter 20

The lemon-thyme bread Olaya had given me the day before melted in my mouth, but it didn't instantly fill me with renewed hope. I did, however, have the strong impulse to act. Maybe her intention had not been for me to simply maintain my belief that Billy would be okay, but believe it enough to get out there and fight.

So fight I would.

Miguel was at the restaurant. It could run without him, but only for so long. Olaya couldn't leave the bread shop. What I had in mind might require some stealthy sneaking around, so I opted not to risk Mrs. Branford's hips. I even considered summoning my dad as my sidekick, but in the end, it came down to either Billy or Emmaline.

I knew Em would want to be there, but I decided I needed Billy by my side for this particular adventure. Thirty minutes after I'd eaten the last of the lemon-thyme bread,

I pulled up in front of Ruby's Old Fashioned Ice Cream Parlor, the same place I'd gone with my dad. I saw Billy from half a block away, ball cap pulled low over his eyes as if he were hiding. The slump of his shoulders and the depth of his hands in his pockets betrayed his emotions.

I pressed the heel of my palm to the center of my steering wheel, giving the horn three sharp blows. He jerked his head up at the sound. Once he saw me, he turned sideways so he could squeeze between two cars angled into tight parking spaces. He had the passenger door of my car open and had maneuvered himself into the seat before I'd rolled to a stop. Saying he was worse for wear would be an understatement. His six o'clock shadow was going on three days now, and his cheeks and raccoon eyes made him look gaunt. A little feral, truth be told.

"I thought the focus was going to be on these investors," he said, looking straight ahead as I started to drive again.

The investors in Max's condo fail were still at the top of my list, but what if it *wasn't* one of them? Losing money — even hundreds of thousands — didn't automatically make someone a murderer, so I couldn't just stop digging. "It is," I said, "but we don't even know who they are and I can't sit around just twirling my thumbs."

"Me either," he said.

He was telling the truth, but his agitation ran deeper than mine. Innocent people were often found guilty of a crime, and those convictions weren't often overturned. Billy was thinking of the life he was on the verge of losing. Even in death, Max Litman had succeeded in taking him down.

"Who else had a motive?" he asked.

I'd thought long and hard on this question — and I'd come up with a new possibility. "Mr. Zavila," I said.

Silence hung between us for a long few seconds. Finally, Billy shook his head. "Why would he kill Max? He was his informant."

"I know, but what if something had turned sour between them? It seems like Max did a lot of people wrong. What if Mr. Zavila was one of them?"

Billy stroked his chin, considering the question. "I guess it's possible," he finally said.

"Anything's possible when it comes to murder." It sounded like a hollow platitude, but since returning to Santa Sofia, it was one thing I'd learned with utter certainty.

"So, what, we're just going to barge in and grill him about Max?"

"Absolutely. We can play it casual, like he

did all those times he came sniffing around to check out your art car. Tit for tat," I said.

Billy side-eyed me. "I'm glad you're on my side."

My hands tightened on the steering wheel. "Always."

We drove in silence until we reached Santa Sofia High School. School was over for the day so there was only a spattering of cars in the student parking lot. From the looks of it, quite a bit of the faculty had left for the day, but I remembered Mr. Zavila usually staying late when I'd been in school; I figured there was a good chance he was still on campus.

I parked off in one of the side student parking lots, as far as possible from the staff lot. Neither Billy nor I wanted to come up close to the spot where our mother had died in a hit and run. Being on campus was close enough, and we didn't relish even that. Our dad still hadn't been able to set foot on the school grounds. Aunt Josie, who was not really our aunt, but had been our mom's best friend for as long as we could remember, taught history here. She, Billy, and I had packed up our mom's classroom. I'd seen her a few times since then, but always on neutral ground, someplace away from the school. Josie couldn't avoid it, so she'd

figured out how to come to terms with being here day in and day out. I was getting
there, and so was Billy. I'd been thinking
about how to help our dad; a tribute of
some sort was the obvious choice. Maybe a
plaque or a bench placed under a tree on
campus. But lately I'd been thinking that a
college scholarship in her name was the
thing to do. It would honor her and her love
of books, writing, and education in general.
I hadn't figured out how to fund it on an
ongoing basis, but it was always in the back
of my mind.

Security at the school was much tighter
than it had been when Billy and I were
students, but our mother had taught here
for years and years. We were known by most
of the teachers. If we were lucky, someone
we knew would be able to let us in. Billy
and I strode across the parking lot and
circled to the front entrance, but it was
locked up tight. We peered through the glass
of the front doors. Not a soul in sight. So
much for luck.

"Call Josie," Billy said.

"Right." She lived and breathed her job
and her students, investing every spare
minute in them. Chances were good that
she'd be here. I took out my phone, went to
my list of favorites, and activated the call.

It rang twice before she answered, not with a polite hello, but with an enthusiastic, "Ivy!"

"Hey, Aunt Josie," I said, automatically calling her the name I'd grown up with.

"What a surprise. It's always so good to hear your voice," she said, the sincerity in her voice encircling me.

"Yours too," I said. I held out the phone between my brother and me. "Billy's here, too."

"Hey, Aunt Jo," he said, using the same familiar endearment I did. We were cut from the same cloth, he and I. When we'd been students in her classroom, we'd called her Mrs. Jeffries, but otherwise it had been Aunt Josie, or in Billy's case, Aunt Jo. It was hard to teach a dog a new trick.

Her sigh was audible across the airwaves. "Darling boy, how are you holding up?"

"So I guess you've heard, then," he said, his voice turning monotone.

"It's a small town. Of course I've heard. I planned to come around to see you this week, in fact. Billy, anyone who knows you knows it's utterly ridiculous."

"But the sheriff doesn't know me. It's not ridiculous to him."

"Is Emmaline not —"

"She's deputy," he interrupted, "and she

was taken off the investigation."

I needed to redirect the conversation. "Josie, are you at school?"

She laughed. "Where else would I be?"

"Can you let us in?"

We heard a scraping sound, as if she'd shoved a chair back. "You're here?"

"Yes, we want to talk to —"

She cut me off. "I'm coming down. Don't go anywhere."

"Where does she think we'd go?" Billy asked, cracking a grin.

My heart swelled. It was the first genuine and spontaneous smile I'd seen from him since all this had begun. I shrugged, smiling with him. "It's Josie."

"Right. Enough said."

A minute later she appeared at the door. Her look was typical Josephine Jeffries: a sliver of skin between her maroon skinny jeans and black booties; an off-white peasant shirt; a karma ring necklace strung on a black piece of leather; short waves of auburn hair, blond streaks in front framing her face; red-and-black-framed glasses. She was not what most people thought of as a typical sixtysomething-year-old teacher, but she'd been Teacher of the Year for Santa Sofia High School three times, had been Teacher of the Year for the state once, and was a

239

perennial student favorite.

She leaned against the bar on the door, releasing the lock and pushing the door open. "My darlings," she said, wrapping us up in a Josie-sized bear hug, "you are a sight for sore eyes." She was a familiar comfort. Outside of our immediate family, she was the closest thing we had to a blood relative anywhere near Santa Sofia.

Her hug was as warm as a wooly blanket on a stormy night. I stretched my arms around each of them, the flat of my hands against their backs. I could have stayed in the hug forever, but I felt Billy melt into her. Then his chest heaved. I slipped myself free from them, letting Josie slide her arm from me to around Billy. He sank deeper into the embrace and she held him. He muttered something into her shoulder. "Sshh sshh," she soothed, rubbing his back. "It's going to work out, Billy. You'll see. It'll be okay."

I choked back my own emotions. Seeing how real this was for him, how scared he was strengthened my resolve. "I'll be back in a minute," I said, leaving Josie to comfort Billy. I hurried out of the main building, through the quad, and to the art building in the far southeast corner of campus.

CHAPTER 21

It had been nearly twenty years, but walking through the door to Mr. Zavila's art room was like walking through a time portal. I stood just inside the threshold, taking a moment to look around the classroom. It had the same paint-spattered tables; the same shelves loaded with art supplies and student work; the same graffiti art and murals decorating every open space. It was just as I remembered it, right down to Mr. Zavila himself hunched over a potter's wheel. His foot moved up and down on the pedal, controlling the wheel's speed. His hands worked the beige clay as he shaped what had started as a mound of nothing into what I guessed would be a vase.

"Mr. Zavila?"

He jumped, his fingers curling and mis-shaping the clay he'd been working. He cursed under his breath, smashing the clay with his fist before turning to me. "What the hell —" he started, his words cutting off as he registered who I was.

I raised one hand. "Hey, Mr. Zavila."

His aggravation disappeared. Instead he was now flustered and looked shell-shocked that I was standing here in his classroom. He took his foot from the pedal, his potter's wheel coming to a stop.

"Sorry to barge in," I continued when he didn't speak. I gestured to the mound of clay on his potter's wheel. "I hope you can salvage it."

He looked at it, his eyebrows knitting together as if he were trying to figure out just what had happened to the vase, but he still didn't utter a word. I remembered this about him, too. He was chatty when he wanted to be, like every year when he consulted with Billy about his art car. Talking to him when he was in an antisocial mood, however, had made me want to pound my forehead against a wall. It was like trying to teach a dog to speak English — nothing but blank stares and the occasional bark.

It had been less than a minute, but I could already tell that this conversation was going to be one-sided. I waited to see if he'd ask how I was, or inquire about Billy, but he offered only a vacant stare.

"Billy's here," I said, watching carefully to see his reaction. It had been several years since I had discovered that Mr. Zavila had been working against Billy, so just as many since my brother had stopped using him as a consultant.

His jaw tensed again as he looked over my shoulder.

I looked behind me, too, wondering if Billy had extricated himself from Josie's hug and followed me to the art hall. No one was there. I turned back to Mr. Zavila after registering the empty doorway. "He's with Mrs. Jeffries," I said.

Mr. Zavila's eyes relaxed slightly, but his posture was rigid. "Nice woman," he said.

He'd engaged. It was a start, so I pressed on. "She's family."

This time he didn't respond. An awkward silence fell, but I cleared my throat and shifted the conversation to the subject I was most interested in talking with him about. "I wanted to say that I'm sorry for your loss, Mr. Zavila."

"My loss?" he asked, his face blank.

"I know you were friends with Max Litman," I said. "It must have been a shock to hear that he died. That he was *murdered.*"

His head jerked ever so slightly. And then his nostrils flared. An involuntary reaction to hearing Max's name? It might be a reach, but I was here to look for any sign — any inkling — that Mr. Zavila knew something. Mentioning Max's name had caused an infinitesimal reaction. The question was *why?*

"It's not *my* loss," he said. "I didn't know him."

It was an out-and-out lie. I'd followed Mr. Zavila from our garage straight to Litman's house to give his report on Billy's car. Why would he lie about something that was probably easily provable? Surely other people had seen them together over the years. I met his gaze head-on, measuring my words. "I'm sure I've seen you with him once or twice over the years."

He blinked, his eyes darting away briefly before coming back to me. "You're mistaken. I didn't know him."

I wondered how far to push. If he had killed Max, what would stop him from killing me? I hadn't felt this tension and unease when I'd met with Vanessa Rose, or either of the Wellborns. Mr. Zavila, on the other hand, made me think of a caged animal. I needed to be on my guard. I stayed hyper-alert, ready to bolt, but made a show of checking my watch, then looking over my shoulder as if I were waiting for someone.

He wouldn't do anything to me if he thought Billy was going to show up any second. Hopefully. "Sure you did," I said as I turned back to him. "A couple of times, actually, always before the Art Car Shows."

This time he visibly balked. "You saw — ?"

He stopped, catching himself before giving himself away, but I nodded. How far should I go with my information? There was no plausible reason for me to be cruising around Malibu Hills Estates, but I had to go with a factual encounter, one he couldn't deny. "Oh yes. I saw you at his house. On the driveway, in fact."

His spine stiffened, his entire body growing tense. He looked in control, but just barely. "You are mistaken."

I leveled my gaze at him. "I don't think I am."

Behind his eyes, the wheels were turning. How far would he take his denial? "What is it you want, Ms. Culpepper?"

People were asking me that question over and over lately. Instead of the response I'd given before — that I was trying to help exonerate my brother for Max Litman's murder — I went for a sucker punch. "I know that you were never helping Billy with his cars. It was always about helping Max beat him."

"That is not true . . ." he snapped.

"It *is* true. You helped him beat Billy every year. How much did he pay you to be a spy for him?"

"He didn't —"

"I followed you!"

He started, suddenly looking not only caged, but rabid. "What do you mean, you followed me?"

I hesitated. I had put myself in danger by being here, which had been foolish. I glanced over my shoulder again, hoping Billy would materialize. He hadn't. I analyzed the situation. I'd have a head start if things here went south and I had to make a run for it. I was closer to the door by a good fifteen feet, and there was a long table he'd have to either go around or leap over. He was portly, his belly hanging over the waistband of his jeans. If he was, in fact, a killer, his belly wouldn't stop him from killing an unsuspecting victim, i.e. Max, but it gave me the advantage right now.

After calculating the risk, I forged ahead. "The last time you *helped* Billy," I said, making air quotes as I said "helped," "I was waiting in my car. I followed you to Max's house." I paused, letting him sweat before adding, "I *saw* you."

The color drained from his face. "You set

me up. Max barely won."

"We had to know for sure."

He balled his fists by his side. "Billy lied to me." His voice was laced with disdain, as if he had been the one wronged.

I heard the intake of a sharp breath behind me, turning. Billy had materialized. He stood in the doorway, Josie by his side. "You've got to be kidding. *You* lied to *me,*" he said. Scorn colored his face. "Year after year after year."

Mr. Zavila looked away, staring for a moment at the mound of clay on the wheel. "You don't understand. I'd bought a house from him, but my financing fell through. I was going to lose my deposit. He wouldn't refund the whole thing unless I helped him."

"Blackmail," I muttered. I'd always wondered why Mr. Zavila would work against Billy. Now it made sense. "Of course."

Mr. Zavila nodded in confirmation, and just like that, he gave himself a motive.

"So every time you spied for him, he gave you back some of your deposit?" Billy asked.

Josie's jaw dropped with disbelief. "Is this true, Cristopher? You cheated Billy so Max Litman could win a car competition?"

Mr. Zavila couldn't meet Josie's disbelieving face. Instead, he turned to face Billy. "You have to understand, I had no choice. I did this so I could keep my house. Take care of my family."

That was a cop-out. "You always have a choice," I said, not accepting his rationalization. "You could have said no."

"No, I couldn't. I have a *family.*"

Billy fisted his hands, the veins in his neck popping. "You screwed me over."

"I had no choice," he said again, this time not sounding so convincing.

Billy started to move around the table separating us from the art teacher. "You set me up for his murder."

I hurried to his side, putting my hand on his shoulder to stop him. "Billy, wait."

"If he killed Max —"

Mr. Zavila stepped back, his face contorting. "What are you talking about? I didn't kill him!"

Billy surged forward again. "Tell me the truth. Did Max stop paying you back when we figured out what you were doing? Did the money stop?"

Mr. Zavila shook his head. "No, no, no. That happened years ago. We worked out another deal. I helped him build his cars every year. We developed the concept for the car each year and I organized a team to execute it."

I studied his face. His posture. The way

he retreated in fear. And I believed him.

Billy stopped halfway around the long art table. "You didn't kill him," Billy said. A statement, not a question. His anger deflated and I could see that he believed him, too.

"God, no. I never wanted any of this to happen," he said. His voice dropped to a pained whisper. "I'm sorry. I really am. I'm so sorry."

There was nothing left to say. We left him to his guilt, no closer to the truth than when we'd entered the school. Mr. Zavila had been a Hail Mary, and it hadn't paid off.

CHAPTER 22

That afternoon, I convened a meeting of
The Blackbird Ladies at Yeast of Eden. I'd
dubbed them that the moment I'd first laid
eyes on them. They met regularly at the
bread shop, and when they were together,
they wore hats, each adorned with a little
blackbird.

The hats themselves, as well as the blackbirds with which each woman had festooned
her hat, I realized after I'd gotten to know
them, symbolized who she was in some
form or fashion. Mrs. Branford's wide-
brimmed hat was lavender, simple, and the
blackbird on it was small, but sat promi-
nently on the brim. She'd taught English
for half a century, a guide in the classroom,
but was prominent and impactful in her
students' lives. Her bird was symbolism at
its finest.

Alice Ryder was a little uptight, in my
opinion, and not overtly friendly, but she

was loyal to her friends and had a caring heart. The style and design of her hat reflected that. It was cool and reserved compared to the others: white, with a band of black along the outside of the down-turned brim, and black tulle forming a tasteful bundled bow off to one side. The blackbird sat, small and prim, tucked into the left side of the tulle.

And then there was Mabel Peabody. If you were to line the three women up and ask which one didn't belong, the obvious choice would be Mabel. On a bell curve, Alice Ryder was on the far end of one side, Mrs. Branford sat squarely atop the curve, and Mabel Peabody was clear on the other side, the direct opposite of Alice. I wondered sometimes how they were even friends. After a time, I realized that although they bickered, they also had each other's backs. They had a long history, and that was the glue in their friendship.

Mabel's hat, like her, was bright and unique. It was a felted concoction, she'd told me, of merino wool, decorative silk fabric, and lace; it was bohemian in style, and had a floppy brim. It ran the color spectrum from chestnut-brown to rust orange, and she'd had her blackbird sitting between sprigs of peacock feathers and vintage buttons. It was truly one of a kind, just like her.

The women — just like the birds — were utterly unique, and I adored them all.

Not long ago, Mrs. Branford had dubbed both Olaya and me honorary members of their unofficial club. We'd spent an afternoon choosing our own hats and adding little blackbirds to them, symbols of intelligence and quick wit, characteristics each of the women, including Olaya and me to some degree, possessed. Olaya looked a bit like an Aztec queen. She was slightly shorter than my own five feet eight inches, but looked statuesque with the soft curls in her steel-colored hair and warm skin tone. She'd chosen a black classic men's hat. A single feather and a blackbird sat on the left side, close to the black flat band circling the fedora. She wasn't really a "hat" person, but this one completely suited her.

True to form, I'd found my perfect hat at the antique mini mall down the street from Yeast of Eden. I'd loved how it looked a bit like a top hat, reminiscent of the Mad Hatter's. It was a rich maroon and was adorned with soft waves of organza ribbon and a few artfully placed feathers, both of the same color. The blackbird I'd chosen rested between the folds of organza as if it were hiding away, observing. Just like I tended to do.

"What's this about?" Alice asked once we were gathered around one of the bistro tables of the bread shop.

I cut right to the chase. "Max Litman."

They knew I'd been digging around, so none of them were surprised. "Have you made any progress?" Mabel asked.

I rested my chin on my fist. "Yes. But at the same time, no."

"Don't give up," Alice said. Her lips were pressed tightly together and her terse expression didn't change, so the encouraging statement was uncharacteristic coming from her.

"Don't worry, I'm not." I talked, almost without taking a breath, rattling off the things I'd learned over the last week.

1. Max was most likely killed somewhere other than the hangar that housed the art cars because he was not in it when it was delivered by Allen Trucking Company.
2. There was an unexplained broken window in the hangar.
3. Billy was there, summoned by Max, when Max's art car was loaded up to be hauled to the hangar.

4. The truck drivers didn't seem to know anything helpful.
5. Billy's *Through the Looking Glass* book was found in Max's car.
6. Billy had never won the Art Car contest, but Max always did, thanks to Mr. Zavila.
7. Max had committee members in his pocket, but some had recently left. Of course this was motive for Max to go after Billy, not the other way around. And Billy had no knowledge of the bribery.
8. According to Dixie, Max had lots of women. But my feeling was that Max had given up his revolving door for Vanessa Rose.
9. Vanessa, the spiritual advisor, believed Max had changed his ways and was making amends for all the wrongs he'd committed.
10. Mrs. Wellborn did not.
11. Max had swindled ten people out of one hundred twenty thousand dollars — each — in a condo deal that never happened.
12. Of those ten people, I only knew of Johnny Wellborn and Vicente Villanueva.
13. Emmaline was off the investigation

because of her engagement to Billy.

14. The sheriff was convinced Billy was guilty and didn't want to hear anything else.

I thought for a second before adding one more thing to the list.

15. Mr. Zavila. Max owed him, and revenge was a powerful motivator. Had Max tried to make amends with him?

I finished talking, immediately realizing that what I had was a lot of suppositions, which was another way of saying that it all amounted to nothing more than a bunch of loose pieces to a jigsaw puzzle of a Jackson Pollock painting.

Mabel Peabody leaned forward, scratching her cheek. "He was really trying to make things right?"

Alice scoffed. "How could he possibly make things right? That man was a terror."

"Do you have a story with Max Litman?" Mrs. Branford asked her.

She exhaled, giving herself a moment of reprieve, and then nodded her head. "It seems as if everyone does."

We waited for her to explain what she

meant, but Alice was done sharing. Instead of telling just how Max had financially screwed her, she offered another condemnation. "He may have wanted to cleanse his soul, but you can't hide from your sins. And you can't take back what you've already done."

"So you don't believe Vanessa's story?" I asked, glad for someone to play devil's advocate.

She adjusted her hat, closing her eyes in a long blink. "Vanessa Rose, the spiritual advisor?" Alice said, mocking. "Not even a little bit."

Mabel eyed her friend, brushing back her newly dyed strands of red hair. "You're judging her on her job title rather than her merits. She may be a perfectly wonderful spiritual advisor."

"What does that even mean? She helped Max find God?" she asked, her voice dripping with sarcasm. "I highly doubt it. Remember who we're talking about. That man never thought about anybody but himself."

I jumped in, wanting to diffuse her skepticism. I'd asked the same question, after all. "People can change, though, can't they?"

They all had a different reaction to that rhetorical question. While Mabel's optimism shone brightly — and in stark contrast to Alice's cynicism, Mrs. Branford and Olaya's expressions mirrored each other's. They met one another's gazes, nodding. They knew firsthand how radically people could change. It sounded overly dramatic, but they'd gone from sworn enemies to reluctant friends. If *they* could change, anybody could.

"They can," Olaya said. "And they do."

The thoughts circling in my head were so polar opposite to what I'd felt not so long ago. I couldn't know for certain if Max had truly been trying to make past wrongs right, but at this moment, I was choosing to believe that he was. "Max might not have been able to change the things he did in his past, but Vanessa was trying to help him be better. He was walking a spiritual path," I said, repeating the words she'd used.

"Hallelujah," Mabel said. She pointed her index finger upward, speaking with utter conviction. "He walked that spiritual path right out of this world, but he was a better person for it."

"Oh, for pity's sake, Mabel," Alice scoffed, clearly unwilling to forgive Max. "I thought you were over that ooey gooey hooey stuff."

"Why would you ever think that? How can I be over something that is in my blood and my bones?" Mabel spoke with completely seriousness, but she turned her head slightly, winking at us.

I laughed fondly. I adored Mabel, from the strands of her dyed red hair to the Birkenstocks on her narrow feet. Alice fluttered her hand as if Mabel were off her rocker, but I could also see the affection in her eyes. Theirs was an unlikely friendship, but it was as strong as two pieces of welded metal.

"I trust Ivy's judgment," Mrs. Branford said. With me, she wanted to be in the thick of every adventure. She was quick to jump into the fray, but with her friends, she was the rock. "I never was a fan of Max's, but I'm a firm believer that everyone deserves a second chance."

We all absorbed that simple sentiment. And we all nodded. Max Litman had been a thorn in Billy's side for so long, but if he had recognized the error of his ways, who was I to doubt him? I chose to believe that Vanessa had been his guide on whatever spiritual path he'd been traveling. In the end, I chose to believe that he had tried to change.

CHAPTER 23

I spent what was left of the afternoon at Santa Sofia Community Park. I tested my camera shots whenever possible, getting in as many angles as I could before the light became too harsh. By dusk, I was as prepared as I could be for the big event.

Emmaline and I had spoken just a few hours ago. Now her voice echoed in my head. "Keep your eyes and ears open at the events, Ivy. I'll be there, but Lane has me on a leash."

I wanted her off the leash, just as much as she wanted to be free of it, but if I was being honest, I could understand Sheriff Lane's perspective. He wanted to charge Billy with murder and Em had the exact opposite goal. Lane's restrictions limited what Emmaline could do and how far she could push without jeopardizing her job and the relationships she had in the department. She was trying to figure out how to help

Billy while still keeping her job and her boss off her back. It was not an easy tight rope to walk.

"What about the investors?" I asked her.

"Dead end, unfortunately. The team found the books when they searched the Litman Homes office. Jenkins said Lane checked them himself. Nothing surfaced."

Somehow I managed not to smirk. I didn't trust Lane and his investigation one iota.

"I don't suppose they'll give you the names to double-check?"

"Um, yeah, no. I can't get so much as a paper clip in the same vicinity as the case file."

Emmaline's leash was on good and tight.

The cars, with the exception of Max's, had been moved from the hangar to Santa Sofia Community Park. They were lined up, like soldiers in formation, along the perimeter of the square. The parade would be the following morning, followed by the ball and awards event. Santa Sofia had been through a lot. In order to end the event on a positive note, rather than have the pallor of Max's murder hang like low-lying dark clouds, the city had gone so far as to hire a security detail to patrol the park through the night. No one was going to tamper with another car, and no one else was going to be hurt.

Or worse.

By the end of the day, I was exhausted. With nothing else to do, I headed home. Just being on Maple Street did something to my brain. All day — all week, actually — I'd felt as if my heart was compressed, a rope wound so tightly around it that I could hardly breathe. But as I drove under the canopy of leafy trees, past the remodeled historic homes, and past the old-fashioned light posts, the bindings loosened. The weight on my shoulders didn't abate entirely, but I was definitely breathing easier. The release of anxiety would, with any luck, help me think.

My house was just as calming as my street. It had a steep gable, a high-pitched roofline, and the Tudor's traditional half-timber exterior. The wavy-edge siding at the gable peaks was a deep red, which filled me with a sense of warmth and calm. Driving up to the house was akin to wrapping myself up in a warm blanket. It could have been a gingerbread house straight out of a fairytale, the leafy trees and the cobbled walkway up to the arched front door softening the harder edges of the house. The flower beds, bursting with color, were the final touch. They'd been here when I bought the house, but Penelope Branford and I had spent many a lovely afternoon playing with the color palette, the arrangement, and the flower variety. There were still things to tweak, but I planned to live in this house for a long, long time, so there was no rush.

I was the newest resident on the historic block — and I was also about thirty years younger than most of the street's other inhabitants. I'd been taken under Maple Street's proverbial wing, with the exception of one or two fringe residents who wished I'd move far, far away and never come back. But they had their reasons. I'd suspected them of foul play recently, and while they hadn't been guilty of murder, they had plenty of other misdeeds under their belts.

At the moment, I had no time for anyone or anything but Max Litman, so I shoved my neighbors, both difficult and delightful, out of my thoughts. After the parade tomorrow in the morning, a good part of my day would be spent at Yeast of Eden helping Olaya get ready for the Art Car Ball. The rest of the evening I'd be at the ball itself, both photographing the festivities and keeping my eyes and ears open. I didn't have any specific expectations; I'd be keeping a wide-open mind.

I'd parked in the garage, but walked around to the front yard rather than going through the interior garage door to the house. Agatha would be itching to get outside, but I strayed off the cobbled walkway to pull a few stray weeds that had popped up. I straightened up, clutching the limp weeds in one hand, my camera bag and purse over my shoulder, and my keys in my other hand. I got back on track, stepping onto the walkway again, but instantly stopped in my tracks. This time it wasn't a wayward dandelion or bunch of ragweed, but the shadowy form of a body on my front porch. Man? Woman? Sitting? Standing? I couldn't be sure. Given the fact that there was a murderer on the loose, I slowed. "Hello?" I said, my voice tentative.

The scraping of a chair's legs made the hairs on the back of my neck raise, followed by the one-two thump of something hitting the ground. The form moved into the light and my heart dropped from my throat back to my chest cavity. Mrs. Branford . . . and her cane. "My dear, it's about time. You do not have time to gallivant around. We still have a murder to solve."

I heaved a sigh of relief, my knees nearly buckling. "You scared me half to death. And I am not gallivanting around. I've been getting ready for tomorrow *and* trying my best to solve a murder."

"As long as the other half of you is alive and kicking, we're looking good." She emerged from the shadows to stand squarely in front of the dark wood of my arched door. It framed her, setting off the snowy white of her hair and the bright pink of today's velour leisure suit. She'd hung up her Blackbird Ladies' hat, but otherwise looked the same as she had when I'd seen her earlier in the day.

She stepped aside as I held my key out to unlock the door. "How long have you been waiting?"

Instead of looking at a watch or cell phone, Mrs. Branford took three steps off the porch and peered up into the sky. "About twenty-five minutes, I should say. Give or take. I might have dozed for a few of them."

The groggy state of her eyes told the tale. "I think you mean definitely."

She knocked the rubber-footed cane she held against the ground as if she were miffed at my snarky remark, but I knew better. Mrs. Branford loved her power naps, and she wasn't afraid to admit it. "I needed to talk to you."

My senses went on alert. Had something happened in the hours since I'd seen her? Or, I reasoned, she could need me to get something from a cupboard in her kitchen that she couldn't reach, she could need a ride somewhere, or she could be hungry for something she didn't happen to have at the ready. I stepped aside so she could cross the threshold. With the door closed behind me, I placed my keys in a small ceramic bowl on the table I'd picked up at a shop in town. It featured ceramics and other handcrafted goods made by disabled adults in the community. I'd purchased several small bowls, each unique, and had them scattered around the house. This one was the biggest, about six inches in diameter, and sat next to another piece made by a local artist. The Galileo thermometer had been hand blown at a glass shop on the pier by Baptista's and had been a housewarming gift from Miguel. My fingers skimmed the tall glass cylinder.

"Hello." Fingers snapped in front of my face. "Earth to Ivy."

I focused on Mrs. Branford and blinked, drawing back slightly. "What?"

A twinkle sparkled her eyes and the corners of her mouth lifted mischievously. "I've been thinking about everything you said earlier," she said. "I've got an idea."

An image of The Grinch as he was figuring out what to do about the Whos and their Christmas cheer came to me. Mrs. Branford was quite clever — as clever as Dr. Seuss with his crafty rhymes and devilishly wily Mr. Grinch — and from the look of her smile, she'd come up with her own wonderful, hopefully not awful, idea. If she had come here, sitting patiently and waiting for me to return home, her idea must be a very good one indeed. I peered at her as if I could see straight through her eyes, imagining her thoughts running like a ticker tape on Wall Street.

She leaned heavily on her cane, her arthritic knuckles turning white with her grip on the handle. What was I thinking making her stand in my entryway? I took her arm and guided her out of the entryway and to the right, straight through one of the wood-framed archways that led to the parlor. "Come on and sit down, Mrs. Branford."

She let me lead her, but that didn't mean she was giving up one speck of her feistiness. "I'm going to wear you down, you know, so you might as well go ahead and bend to my will."

I couldn't hide my grin. "Are you going to cast a spell on me?" I asked as I settled her into a comfortable straight-backed chair. Agatha's crate sat in the corner of the room. I quickly set her free, opening the French doors leading from the parlor to the backyard. Agatha spun around and around in three solid circles before her little paws took purchase and she raced outside.

"As a matter of fact . . ." She tapped her index finger on the handle of her cane. "I might have to have a tête-à-tête with Olaya. Have her bake some special herb or flower into one of her breads so that you will, indeed, do as I ask."

"I don't think Olaya has any special ingredient that will make me start to call you Penelope."

She thrust her finger toward me. "Aha!"

"Oh my God!" I shook my head, cupping one hand over my forehead in a head slap She'd done it to me again, the trickster. Mrs. Branford got some sort of satisfaction from coercing me into saying her name. The thing was, I was my mother's daughter, raised with an inherent respect for my elders. I was finding it impossible to overcome that bit of my upbringing, even if I enjoyed spending time with Mrs. Branford more than anyone else. My mother, my father, and my brother — they were the family I was born with, but just as warm water and yeast and flour combined together to form the basis for myriad types of bread, the three of us combined to form an essential female bond. The two women weren't my blood, but they were the family I had chosen.

"You can trick me into saying Penelope —" She waved her hand, her mouth forming the *Aha!* she'd thrown at me a moment ago, but I beat her to it. "Aha!" I said, pointing one finger to the sky. "I can say your name in that context, but that doesn't mean I will address you by it. Mrs. Branford," I added for good measure.

"One of these days, Ivy," she said, her lips pressed together in determination like Ralph from the old *Honeymooners* show. "One of these days."

From where I sat, perched on the couch across from Mrs. Branford, I had a clear view of the yard. Agatha's nose was buried in a bush, her thin tail wound up like a curlicue. She was happy. "What's your idea" — I winked — "*Mrs. Branford?*"

Her eyebrows lifted slightly in acknowledgment of my snark, but she didn't rise to the bait. "Do you know the Picaloos?" she asked.

Did I? I mulled the name over, but it wasn't ringing a bell. "I don't think so."

Her silver curls bobbed as she nodded. "Of course you do."

Maybe she was right, maybe she wasn't, but it really didn't matter. "Okay, but remind me, then. Who are they?"

"White Queen Anne on the corner of Walnut and Liverpool."

Recognition dawned. "Cottage garden flowers along the street and the porch swing?"

She tapped the tip of her nose with the pad of her index finger. "As I said, you know them."

"Knowing their house isn't the same as knowing them," I corrected, inwardly chuckling inside at the fact that people in the historic district of town identified people not by their names, but by their homes. I was the redbrick Tudor. My neighbor had a lovely English Cottage. Across the street from me was an Arts & Craft, and next to that was a Dutch Revival. The variety made the street, and the entire historic area, unique and charming. One house might have been built in the same style as another, but beyond that similarity, no two were alike.

Mrs. Branford's house was a pretty Craftsman. It was just like her: old, but well cared for. The warm taupe exterior blended beautifully with the creamy white of the window frames. Maintaining the integrity of one's home was of paramount importance to most people who bought a historic home. The historic committee also wanted all things original kept intact. The Mastersons, across the street from Mrs. Branford, had probably had conniption fits when Mrs. Branford replaced her ancient window with modern double-paned numbers that kept the temperature inside constant. Good for Mrs. Branford's gas and electric bills, and for her arthritis. Bad for the historic purists.

I'd learned a lot about houses in the short time I'd lived in the area. I'd learned just as much about the people in them. Studying houses was a lot like studying psychology. The biggest takeaway was that a house tells an awful lot about its occupants. A certain type of person prefers a Victorian over a Colonial Revival. The person who falls in love with a clean-lined, symmetrical, rectangular Cape Cod is probably not going to buy a Queen Anne, replete with towers, turrets, and spindle work. If you like bungalows, chances are you'd like a Craftsman style house. Simple or ornate, however, we could all bond over the milestones each of us had shared.

"We need to pay the Picaloos a visit," Mrs. Branford said. Her voice was usually edged with lightheartedness. With sass. With subtle cleverness. But at the moment, her tone was ominous.

It felt like we were playing a game of chess. I moved a pawn and she moved a rook. I moved a knight and she moved a bishop. I scooted to the edge of the chair. Mrs. Branford had realized something, and I was willing to take a risk to find out just what that was. I moved my queen. "*Why* do we need to pay a visit to the Picaloos?"

And then she played her final move. "Because it turns out Max Litman was doing a job for them and was in their house the very day he died. The. Very. Day," she repeated, driving the point home.

Check. And. Mate.

CHAPTER 24

Twenty minutes later, Mrs. Branford, Agatha, and I strolled down Maple, turning onto Liverpool. Half a block later, we stood at the corner of Walnut, a majestic Queen Anne Victorian looming above us. The Picaloos' cottage garden was just starting to bloom. Daisies, roses, salvia, and alyssum filled the space between the curb and the sidewalk. It wasn't as lush as it would be in just a few short weeks, but it was still a beautiful corner.

A black wrought-iron fence circled the property. The yard was like an outdoor room. The same early spring blooms filled the flower beds in front of the raised porch. The focal areas in the yard drew the eye. Enormous boulders were strategically arranged under the two oak trees, clusters of flowers filling in the open spaces beneath the bare branches. Narrow brick paths shot off from the main walkway, wrapping around the perimeter of the house. The barren twisted trunks of wisteria climbed up trellises bordering two sections of the porch. During the summer, they acted as natural screens, shading the house; at the moment they were dormant, leaving space for light and warmth to filter through.

As I took it all in, ideas about flowers and gardens for my own house flitted around in my head. Agatha whimpered and pulled at her leash, itching to keep walking. "Shh shh shh," I said. "Just a minute." I opened up the camera app on my cell phone and took a few pictures of the curbside English cottage garden and the fully landscaped front yard. "It's beautiful," I said to Mrs. Branford.

No response. I turned, thinking she hadn't heard me, but the space she'd occupied a moment ago was vacant. I looked back the way we'd come. No sign of her. I turned, looking the other way, and drew in an exasperated breath. She'd gone through the gate and now she swung her cane, walking purposefully up the uneven brick path toward the porch. "Mrs. Branford!"

If she heard me, she didn't acknowledge it. Oh my God, what was she doing? We hadn't formulated a plan on how to approach the Picaloos. All she'd told me was that they had worked with Max Litman on the remodel of their house and it had ended badly. I'd started to ask her for details, but she'd been tight-lipped. "You should hear it from them," she said, and when I prodded her for more, she just shook her head with an emphatic no.

She reached the porch and stopped. She started to lift her foot to the first step, but stopped, rooting herself to the bricks where she stood. She seemed flummoxed. After a second, I realized why. There were no railings along the steps leading up to the front door. Potted plants, yes. A few ornamental garden statues, yup. But a railing for an elderly woman to grab on to as she climbed? No.

"Mrs. Branford," I called again, more loudly this time. "Wait." There were only five steps from the walkway to the top of the porch, but I didn't want her trying to make that climb without help. A tumble for Mrs. Branford could be debilitating. She was smart enough to know that. She turned, one hand on her hip, her foot tapping as if she was utterly impatient with me. I hurried through the gate, stopping short in front of her. "What are you doing?"

"Going to ring the doorbell, Ivy." Her tone said, *obviously.* She switched her cane to her left hand, grabbed my elbow, and put her foot on the first step. I had no choice but to go with her.

"We don't have a plan," I said, my voice low, but stern.

She gripped my arm tighter as she made the final step and then turned to face me. "You have a laundry list of possible suspects in Max Litman's murder," she said. "I'd like to narrow your list down. The Picaloos might be able to help with —"

She didn't have to finish her sentence. I was already sold. If the Picaloos knew anything, of course I wanted to hear it. Before we could turn and knock, the door opened. The woman who stepped out stood a few inches above five feet. Her plump cheeks were flushed. Her black pants tapered at the ankle and the dark red of her lips matched the crimson of her sweater. Now that she stood in front of me, I conceded to Mrs. Branford. I didn't know this woman, but I'd definitely seen her around. I'd come across her once in a while when I walked Agatha. She had a cute-as-a-button terrier, if I wasn't mistaken. From the shift in her expression, I'd venture to say that she'd recognized me, too, but when she scrunched her nose at Agatha, I realized that it wasn't me she necessarily found familiar.

"Have you come to play with Hemingway?" she asked. Agatha tilted her round little head up and gave a sharp yelp. In response, a flurry of yapping came from somewhere inside the house. I heard a familiar *clickety-clack* — the sound of a small dog's nails on a hard-surfaced floor. A second later, the little black and beige Yorkshire terrier skidded to a stop at the threshold.

Agatha yelped again, but followed it up by inching forward until she was up close and personal with the Picaloos' dog. They sniffed each other, each of them backing away before coming nose-to-nose again. I crouched down, running my hand over Agatha's back. "Hemingway, I presume?" I asked, looking up at the woman in red.

Mrs. Branford leaned heavily on her cane. I had enough experience with her to know that she didn't really need it. I suspected her motive was an invitation into the Picaloos' home. "Hemingway and Agatha," she said, the corner of her mouth quirking up. "Seems to me that these two pups are meant to be together."

Mrs. Picaloo's brows lifted in surprise. "As in Agatha Christie? It's fate!"

Fate? Possibly. Coincidence? Most likely. Either way, I took the opening and ran with it. "Agatha Christie was my favorite author growing up. I think I read every single one of her books when I was in high school." I'd spent a good number of lunches holed up in a favorite teacher's classroom devouring books, and most of them had been by the grand dame of mystery herself.

Mrs. Picaloo knitted her brows together as she considered us, zooming her focus on Mrs. Branford. "Penelope Branford, right?" she said, finally pulling my crime partner's name from her memory banks.

"And you're Mrs. Picaloo, if I'm not mistaken." If you didn't know Mrs. Branford, the comment would have come off as completely innocent and convincing, as if she'd also just remembered this woman's name. But I knew Mrs. Branford and her sneaky ways. I felt the tiniest rivulet of guilt snake through me. Mrs. Branford suspected that the Picaloos might have knowledge of Max Litman. If Mrs. Branford was right and Max Litman had been here on the day he died, it was possible they could have had a hand in it. But if they didn't, and she was wrong, then I felt badly that we were manipulating this woman and her dog.

Mrs. Picaloo's eyes dropped to Mrs. Branford's cane. "My gosh, how rude of me! You ladies should come in." She stood back, holding the door wide for us.

Agatha spun around, stopping short and sitting back on her haunches expectantly. I was about to suggest I keep her outside, but Mrs. Picaloo beat me to it. "Actually, we can stay out here on the porch. Unless you mind the chill? You can let Agatha off the leash and the dogs can run around."

"We don't want to intrude," Mrs. Branford said, but her body language begged to differ.

"Nonsense," Mrs. Picaloo said. She ushered Mrs. Branford to one of the rattan chairs facing the yard. Please, come sit down."

"Call me Penny, dear," Mrs. Branford said, but she didn't have to be asked twice. Her cane led the way with a *clunk, clunk, clunk* as she made her way to the first chair. She sank down, but I could see the satisfaction on her face. I met her gaze and notched my brows up to give her a silent *cool it* look. She'd been an English teacher forever, but she'd never set foot on a theater stage — at least not to my knowledge. If she overplayed her hand, Mrs. Picaloo would get wise.

"Penny," she said. She turned to me. "I got Agatha's name, but not yours."

I extended my arm toward her. "Ivy Culpepper."

She took my proffered hand, but in a light,

278

loose, slightly uncomfortable grip. If she noticed my quick release, she didn't let on. She just smiled. I crouched down and unharnessed Agatha. She waited, looking up at me. "Go play!"

That was all she needed to hear. She did her signature spin before bounding down the porch steps. Hemingway yelped and took off running after Agatha. They both stopped and faced each other, looking as if they were ready to duel. Instead, they each inched forward, sniffing. Testing the water. They gave each other the green light. Hemingway took off, with Agatha hot on his tail.

With the dogs squared away, I turned back to Mrs. Picaloo and Mrs. Branford. They sat side by side in a tête-à-tête, as if they had been friends forever. Was my sidekick playing at a fast friendship? I couldn't say for certain. If not, Mrs. Branford missed her calling, I thought for the second time that evening.

"This is a great porch," I said, leaning against the railing in front of their chairs. "I think I'd be out here all the time."

"It's my favorite part of the house," Mrs. Picaloo said, sitting back in her chair.

Mrs. Branford tapped the rubber end of her cane against the wood planks beneath her. "I can certainly see why. They don't make houses like this anymore, do they? Solid as a rock."

Mrs. Picaloo laughed. "It wouldn't blow over in a storm. We've been going through a remodel. Not an easy task."

Mrs. Branford gave me a surreptitious wink. She'd led Mrs. Picaloo right to the subject we'd come here to dig into. "Now that you mention it, I do recall seeing workmen here a while back," she said. So innocent. So good.

Her smile vanished. "That was a nightmare. Now, listen," she said, "I'm not one to speak ill of the dead, but —"

There was always a "but."

"— that Max Litman and Litman Homes are absolutely the worst. Worse than the worst. Don't ever use them." She seemed to realize what she'd said, placing her fingers over her mouth. "Oh my, that was in poor taste, wasn't it?"

"It's just us chickens," Mrs. Branford said. "You are certainly not the first person to be disappointed by that man."

Mrs. Picaloo breathed a sigh of relief that we hadn't been offended. "Now," Mrs. Branford said, that twinkle back in her eyes, "tell us all about it. What happened?"

Mrs. Picaloo half laughed, half scoffed.

"How long do you have?"

Her question had been rhetorical, but Mrs. Branford answered anyway. "We have *all* evening."

Mrs. Picaloo laughed outright at that. "Well, then, settle in."

She proceeded to tell us about the plans she and her husband had drawn up for a granny quarters in the backyard, as well as renovations of the main house, the hiring of Litman Homes to do the build, and Max's recommendation to rebuild the porch at the same time.

I tapped my foot on the outdoor flooring. "He did a nice job."

"On this, yes. On the rest? No. He walked off the job."

"Like, literally walked off?" I asked.

She nodded. "He got a phone call — that happened a lot — and headed right out the front door. That man was horrible."

Mrs. Branford nodded her agreement. "I can't say I liked him, but I can't fathom who might have killed him." She tilted her chin up suddenly, her eyes curious. She leaned forward, conspiratorially. "Do *you* have any ideas?"

Cut to the chase. Mrs. Branford was slick. I waited with bated breath for Mrs. Picaloo to answer.

"As a matter of fact . . ." She grinned as she splayed her fingers through her hair at the base of her neck. "Mr. Litman didn't work here for very long, but long enough for me to overhear an awful lot of his phone calls. He was on that thing all the time."

The door behind us closed with a pronounced *click,* followed by footsteps. "Who was on what all the time?"

Mrs. Picaloo stretched her arm out behind her. The man, who I assumed to be Mr. Picaloo, took her hand, giving it a squeeze. "Max Litman," she said, answering his question. "With his phone."

"In the library with Professor Plum," Mrs. Branford said under her breath. I think she intended the comment to be just for herself, but Mrs. Picaloo chuckled.

"Indeed. Ladies, this is Ralph."

"Mr. *Renatta* to her friends," he said with a wink at his wife.

Mrs. Branford extended her hand. "A pleasure, Mr. *Renatta.* You make a lovely trophy husband."

He took her hand, rather gallantly, and bowed slightly. "The pleasure is all mine."

"Of course it is," Mrs. Branford said coyly.

"As I was saying," Mrs. Picaloo continued. "He was on the phone all the time, and that man did not have a quiet voice. I heard far too much about his life than I wanted to, I'll tell you that."

I didn't believe that for a second. I'd known Renatta Picaloo for all of five minutes, but I was pretty sure she thrived on town gossip. If Mrs. Branford wasn't careful, she was going to be unseated as the neighborhood busybody. "Who was he talking to all the time?" I asked

"Who *wasn't* he talking to is a better question," Ralph Picaloo said. "He was supposed to be working on our build, but he spent half his time setting up appointments to bid other people's jobs. He struck me as somewhat of an obsessive personality. Once he got something in his head, he was stuck to it like glue."

"Until the next thing came along," Mrs. Picaloo said.

Ralph nodded. "Right. Then he dropped the first thing like a hot potato and moved on."

"Is that what he did to you all?" I asked. Being left high and dry in the middle of a remodel was not uncommon, but was it a motive for murder? "Started the renovation but —"

Ralph grimaced. "If by started you mean totally gutting several rooms, then yeah, he started. Demolished one entire wall, then left. Didn't cut the drywall or look for support beams. He took a sledgehammer and plowed right into it. But Christ, this is an old house. Drywall and a typical framing of wood wasn't used back in the twenties."

"It's shiplap!" Mrs. Picaloo exclaimed, as if she'd just won some grand prize. "You just don't destroy shiplap."

"He should have known that, right?" Ralph answered his own question by restating it. "He should have known that. His head was *not* in the game."

Mrs. Picaloo took his hand in hers and gave it a squeeze. "Because of that damnable art car of his. He was obsessed with it. Truly, I do not understand. It's a car. Half of them look ridiculous, but the other half? They're either outlandish or basic and not worth whatever it costs to enter." She looked at Mrs. Branford and me. "But the competition seemed to rule Max's life. If half of his phone calls were about new jobs, the other half were about getting materials for that car or making plans on when and where to meet to do this or that or the other. James at the staging area. Liliana at the office. Marcus at the garage."

"And the police," Mr. Picaloo said.

Mrs. Picaloo's eyebrows shot up. "That's right. They had him on speed dial."

That didn't surprise me. He screwed over enough people that the complaints had probably rolled in. "And he just walked out?"

"Without a word." She swept her arm toward the house. "We have to find someone else to finish the job."

Her husband put his hand on her shoulder. "Which will not be an easy thing to do, I might add. No contractor wants to finish a job that someone else had started."

Walking off the job was generally not a murderable offense, and the Picaloos didn't strike me as people who would snap over losing their contractor. They were upset, but they weren't unhinged.

"He walked out of here the day before his body was found," Mrs. Picaloo said. "Nobody's come to talk to us about that." She frowned. "They should have, right? Come here to see if we know anything."

Before she could think too much about the answer to that question, which was definitely yes, something made me interrupt her. "Who was he talking to?"

Mr. Picaloo jumped in. "On the phone? Can't say as I know, but whoever it was, they had some *bad* mojo."

Mrs. Picaloo's contemplative face lit up like a gas lamp on a stormy night. "That's right. It was the most volatile conversation he'd had in the time he was with us."

"Off the rails," Ralph Picaloo confirmed.

Here it was. From the way the Picaloos described Max, he could have pissed off any number of people, but an explosive conversation on his end of the line most likely meant an equally fiery response on the other end. Which very well could mean a motive.

One of the investors, perhaps?

Vanessa Rose?

Dixie Mayfield?

A new suspect?

A killer?

"Well?" Mrs. Branford leaned forward in her chair, chomping at the bit. "Don't keep us in suspense. What got him so riled up?"

Once again, Mrs. Picaloo glanced to the right side of the porch and then to the left. She looked over her shoulder before turning back to us. "Not what," she said, building the suspense. "Who."

"Who, then?" Mrs. Branford prompted.

"I remember it so clearly. Max took the phone call, talked for a minute, and then stormed out here to the porch. I could hear his footsteps clomping as he paced up and down." She paused, considering something. "Now that I think about it, I'm a bit surprised that *he* was the victim in all this

286

because *he* was the one spitting fire. Truly, he sounded like he could have killed the guy on the other end of that conversation. I thought his heart might explode then and there and I'd have a dead contractor on my hands." Her lips twisted wryly. "I guess he ended up that way, didn't he?"

"You were saying?" I prompted, wanting to get her back on track.

"Of course. I heard him, clear as a bell. He said, 'I'll be there. Back off.' Of course I had no idea what he was talking about, but now it seems so ominous. . . ."

It was as if she were dropping breadcrumbs as she told the story, stopping and starting, turning back, but then finding one of the crumbs she'd dropped and forging ahead again. "Renatta," Mrs. Branford said, graduating herself to a first-name basis. "Don't keep us in suspense. Who was he talking to?"

She looked up, her face pensive. "Someone named Billy."

CHAPTER 25

Mrs. Branford and I had extricated ourselves from the Picaloos' porch and now we
sat across from each other in my kitchen.
Normally the brick arch over the cream-
colored Aga range, the farm sink, the pale
yellow KitchenAid mixer all fill me with a
sense of well-being. But right now, my heart
was in the pit of my stomach. The kitchen,
the house, Mrs. Branford, Agatha — none
of it was comforting. Mrs. Picaloo's words
still repeated in a loop in my head. *Someone
named Billy. Someone named Billy. Someone
named Billy.*

Renatta Picaloo's other words quickly followed — the ones she'd said to her husband
— circled in my head. *We need to call the
police, don't we?*

"Why are you so worried?" Mrs. Branford
asked. "The police already know they
talked."

"But according to the Picaloos, Max

answered the phone, so that would mean *Billy* called *him,* but Billy said *Max* called him."

"Is it that —" She broke off before she could finish the question. "Everything is important."

"Billy also said Max told him he couldn't make it to meet Allen Trucking —"

"But the Picaloos said Max planned to be there — wherever *there* is."

"Two inconsistencies."

"There's no proof it was Billy on the other end of the phone call."

"But there's no proof it *wasn't,* which is the problem. The sheriff is already after Billy. If the Picaloos tell them about the phone call, he's going to think Billy lied."

I sat motionless, the hands of the clock on the wall mirroring the rapid beat of my heart; then I picked up my cell phone, went to favorites, and pressed Billy's name. I launched into it the second he answered. "Did you call Max, or did Max call you?"

"What?" The puzzlement in his voice threw me. Whatever I was feeling, he was feeling it a hundred times worse.

In my head, I'd spoken the entire question but hadn't transferred that to Billy. "You and Max talked on the phone the day he died."

"No, we didn't."

That's right. They hadn't talked, Billy had said Max texted him. "There was no phone call?"

No hesitation. I knew he'd been over this a thousand times: in his head, with our dad, with me, with Emmaline, with the sheriff. He could probably rattle off the details of Max's death day in his sleep. "No phone call. You already know that."

I heard Emmaline's voice in the background. "Know what?"

His words became muffled. I could picture him turning toward her, covering the mouthpiece of the phone. "What's this about?" he asked me a second later.

"Somebody heard you talking to Max. Or they heard Max talking to you." For a fleeting second, I wondered if it mattered which way I phrased it, but of course it did. The Picaloos hadn't heard the other side of Max's conversation. Presumably, they'd only heard Max mention Billy's name. Then they'd made the assumption that Billy was the one who'd called Max. "They're going to tell the police."

"Who's going to tell the police?"

"The Picaloos."

I heard Em whispering followed by Billy's exasperated sigh. "I give. Who are the Picaloos and what, exactly, are they going to tell the police about?"

I told him the story, which I knew Emmaline was hearing, too. "If they tell the sheriff, you're going to be under a microscope."

He gave that scornful laugh I was getting used to hearing. "I'm already under a microscope, Ivy. And Em *is* the police." But then he stopped to listen to something Emmaline was saying. "Ah. Got it," he said to her. He cleared his throat as he came back to me over the phone. "It's inconsistent."

"Exactly. Which is why you don't need more scrutiny," I said. "The Picaloos said they *heard* him talking to you."

"They're wrong," he said.

"Some people have said that he was trying to make amends for his bad behavior," I said.

Again, he scoffed. "Not with me."

"He never called you? Never tried to make up or just say sorry for spying? For Mr. Zavila? For any of it?"

Vanessa Rose had told me that Max had been saving his outreach to Billy, his lifeline, for last, but I wanted to confirm. If Vanessa was wrong, if Max had actually apologized to Billy, it would go a long way to deflating any motive the sheriff thought my brother might have.

But Billy dashed those hopes. "Nope, not a word. He texted me. Said he couldn't meet the truckers. That was it. Short and sweet."

All those years, Max had robbed him of winning the Art Car Show intentionally and diabolically. Which made Billy's potential motive good and strong.

"Jesus," Billy muttered. I could picture him dragging his hand through his hair. "I didn't kill him, Ivy."

"I know."

So who did?

CHAPTER 26

After a long night of tossing and turning, I finally gave up my attempt to get any real sleep. Just before five a.m., I got up, pulled on sweats and a T-shirt, and headed out, camera in hand. Agatha lay on the passenger's side floor of the car, happily snoring. My car drove, almost of its own accord, straight to the beach. It was deserted — because any sane person was still in bed, fast asleep.

Agatha and I walked along, her trotting along happily, her tail wrapped into a tight curl, and me lost in thought. After I'd left Santa Sofia to go to college, I never thought I'd be back here to live. But things happened. Life happened. I earned my degree, started my career, got married, ended up divorced. Now, with the waves crashing at the shoreline, the smooth silk of the morning sand under my feet, and the sunrise on the horizon, I wondered why I'd ever left.

This place was home. It always was and it always would be.

I walked along the beach and shot the sunset, capturing a barge far in the distance, a ship that was massive, but that looked as if it could fit in the palm of my hand. Distance was a funny thing, warping your perspective. It was as true with vessels moored off the coast, as it was with family half a country away. The reality was that being up close let you see things with clearer eyes. Relationships strengthened, rather than fading into afterthoughts. Faces snapped into sharp focus. The holes carved by being away from people filled again.

Finally, after forty minutes, I settled at one of my favorite spots — a cluster of rocks a few yards from the breakers. A massive flat boulder formed the tip of the formation. I let Agatha out of her harness and sat down to watch as she scampered around, stopped to frenetically dig into the freshly packed sand, sniff, and then move on to another fascinating area of the beach. It was her happy place as much as it was mine.

A cool breeze blew in off the shore. I wrapped my sweater tighter around me, letting my thoughts flit from one idea to the next in the exact way Agatha flitted from one place to another. The holes I'd had inside after being away for so many years, I realized, had closed, just like the people I loved had become entwined in my life again.

The light was still soft and lovely, full of promise and hope, by the time Agatha and I left the beach. I went home, cleaned up, and by six-thirty I was at Yeast of Eden before the sun had fully risen.

Olaya directed me to take the loaf pans filled with babka dough from the walk-in refrigerator. We'd spent time the day before making the traditional dough, letting it rise, filling it with the coffee-infused chocolate schmear, shaping it, placing each log into a prepared bread pan, and then sprinkling on the crumbly cinnamon-sugar topping We tented each loaf pan before placing them into the refrigerator.

"Why babka?" I'd asked Olaya after she showed me the baking plan for the Art Car Show. The sheet of paper listing the various baking tasks we'd have leading up to the event lay on the table between us.

"Babka. Panettone. Challah. Traditional bread. It is my specialty. No matter where it is from, what I want to share with my customers is the old way. I want them to experience bread the way it should be. The slow rise. The rustic experience, or the refined taste. Whatever it is, what I do is make bread the way it was made before bread machines and Wonder Bread." She tapped her index finger on the paper. "Babka is not a common bread here. Most say it original, is that how you say it?"

"Originated?" I said.

She nodded. "Yes, yes. It *originated* in Eastern Europe. Russian or Slavic. Originated here with Jewish immigrants. You can find it in big cities. New York. San Francisco. *Posiblemente en* Houston, even. Not in a small-town bakery or bread shop. But the babka, it is good. The people, they love it. So I make the chocolate krantz cakes for this event."

And make them she did. *We* did. Dozens and dozens and dozens of them. Yeast of Eden, along with a few other local eateries, would have a booth set up. Babkas were just one of the baked delicacies we'd offer, but Olaya clearly thought it would be high on everyone's list. Our production of the chocolate swirled bread far outnumbered the other things we were making. Once we had let them rise and they were baking, the scent of coffee, chocolate, and yeasty bread filling the kitchen, I thought she might be right. But then she handed me a slice from the first finished loaf. It had a sweetly crumbed outer edge, and the yeast bread, with its swirls of coffee-infused chocolate, melted in my mouth. I was a believer.

By the time the vans were loaded, the krantz cakes, as they were also called, were done. We took them from the ovens, placing them on the bakery racks to cool. Someone would come back for them. By eight o'clock, I followed the van to the beachfront park, where the festival booths were already set up. The bread shop did enough special off-site events that the setup and tear down were no-brainers for the small crew. I'd become part of the streamlined process, directing people as they unloaded the breads and setting up the displays for the day's events. I arranged babka, muffins, mini loaves of sweet breads, baguettes, and some of Olaya's other specialties on the white linen-covered tables.

As I worked, Olaya took the time to hide several of her sugar skull cookies amidst the bread. It was part of who she was — infusing her culture and tradition into everything she did.

I slung my camera strap over my shoulder, ready to head to the parade. Before I left, she gave me a quick hug. "Nothing is accidental, Ivy. You can see everything if you look." And then she handed me one of the skull cookies. *"Buena suerte,"* she said.

The torta Miguel had made me; the bit of sourdough I'd managed to choke down; the babka. Since Max's death, my appetite had all but disappeared, but I'd managed to get in the bare minimum. The cookie did tempt me, though. I took a bite. It was perfect, melting in my mouth, but not too sweet. The thin layer of icing, with its hint of almond, was the perfect complement. Olaya and her bread were known far and wide for their magic and healing abilities. People came from far and wide for bread from Yeast of Eden because of the healing that came with it. Lavender for anxiety, dill to help nursing mothers, passionflower to aid sleep. Whether it was mind over matter or Olaya's manipulation of herbs didn't matter. People came to her for help, and the breads she offered always seemed to do the trick.

Her words sank into me and I took them to heart. Nothing was accidental. I would keep my eyes and ears wide open. Maybe, I thought optimistically, the skull cookie, which represented love and family, really would give me the luck I needed.

I left the booths behind, wending my way through the park, past the staging area for the Art Car Parade, along the street, and to the end point. From the look of things, the entire town had come out for the event.

There were more people lined up along both sides of the street than I ever recalled seeing at past art car parades. Was it the murder of a local that had brought the masses out? It seemed to be the logical reason for the increase in attendance, but at the same time, I couldn't fathom why. Max was gone, and not well-loved, and his murderer wasn't wearing a sign to announce his — or her — presence, so that was not a sound reason for the increased attendance. Aside from the cars, there was nothing to be seen.

Olaya's voice sounded in my head. *You can see everything if you look.*

And so I looked. I turned and scanned the area behind me. Rotated to look up and down the line of cars. Peered past the art cars toward the beach. Nothing struck me. Nobody guiltily darted in between people or held up a sign proclaiming himself or herself as a killer. Despite all the people, however, the mood along the street was subdued. Not tense, exactly, but not full of energy like you might expect from a crowd. And then, like an aftershock, it hit me: People were afraid there would be another body. Another murder in Santa Sofia. If it happened, they wanted a front-row seat. People were twisted that way.

To the west, the Pacific Ocean loomed, waves crashing. The sound washed over me now, calming me, as I found a spot in the shade and waited. The subdued cheering from the staging area carried all the way down the street. The parade had begun. It wouldn't be long before the cars started rolling by. I readied my camera and waited.

As the first car rolled by, the crowd, like a sleeping giant roused by a mass of mischievous Lilliputians, awakened. They clapped and cheered. The art car drivers and passengers tossed candy out of the windows to elated children. I snapped picture after picture, moving around and darting between the cars as they passed to get the best shots, to capture faces in the crowd, to represent all facets of the annual Santa Sofia event. Max Litman's death never left my mind. I searched the crowd, but I wasn't looking for anything — or anyone — specifically, so of course nothing jumped out.

The cars drove at about fifteen miles per hour, allowing everyone to get a good look at them. Two hours had passed. I'd been on the lookout, impatient to see Billy's *Through the Looking Glass* Jabberwocky car. Finally, as the last of them came down the street, I saw it. A hush came over each section of the crowd it passed by. It was full of life, tottering whimsically as it rolled along. I'd seen it throughout its construction, of course, as well as when I'd photographed it not even a week ago. But seeing it in the context of the parade gave me a different perspective. Billy had truly outdone himself. The cheering crowd confirmed it.

But then, as suddenly as the whoops and hollers started, a hush fell over the crowd. The final car rolled into sight. Max Litman's Zombie Apocalypse was closing the parade. It was meant as a tribute, but more than anything, it felt like a metaphor. Zombies were dead, yet they lived on, just like Max.

CHAPTER 27

The only formal dress I owned was from an evening wedding I'd been in five years ago. The fabric was textured crepe with watercolor flowers, cap sleeves, a back slit, and a satin sash. The background was neutral and the flowers were muted, yet vibrant enough to stand out. The bride had told us this was the bridesmaid dress we'd wear again, but I'd had my doubts. I'd never had an occasion — until now. It was looser than it had been when I'd first worn it. The evils of divorce and death, I guess.

I messed with my hair for a solid fifteen minutes, but my spiral locks were looking particularly carroty and were untamable at the moment. In the end, I pulled the mass back, twisting it into a messy bun. I pulled a few loose strands out to frame my face and called it done. A few minutes later, I pulled up in front of Mrs. Branford's house. She was waiting for me on the sidewalk in a powder-blue gown with a chiffon skirt and tiny silver beads that sparkled in the moonlight. This was a far cry from her daily velour sweat suits. I liked making connections between things and I'd often thought that the *Sex and the City* women were the *Golden Girls* in their early years. Looking now at Mrs. Branford, she was clearly Elsa, from *Frozen,* all grown up and ready for the ball.

"Ooh la la, Mrs. Branford!" I said as I came around to the passenger side of the car to help her in. "Stunning!"

She waved me away, but blushed, clearly pleased. "The last time I wore this dress was at Jimmy and my fiftieth wedding anniversary. We treated ourselves to a cruise — with a balcony, no less — and you know the ships, they have their black tie night. All I can say is that James Bond has nothing on Jimmy in a tux."

Her husband had been gone for ten years. She didn't talk about him much, but I knew she missed him every single day. Wearing her blue chiffon dress had given her a short stroll down memory lane. "I imagine it looks just as great on you now as it did then," I said as I tucked the folds of the skirt's fabric into the car.

She looked up at me from where she sat. I

had one hand on the open door and the other on the frame. "Well, of course it does, dear."

"He was a lucky man, Mrs. Branford. A very lucky man."

She looked like she might say something sentimental, but after giving her head a little shake, the moment was gone. "Enough of this," she said as she grabbed the handle and yanked the door shut. She spun her finger in an air circle and spoke to me through the glass. "Let's get this show on the road."

Which is just what we did. Door to door, it was a fifteen-minute drive to the Santa Sofia's convention center. We'd arrived early so I could take pictures and Mrs. Branford could meet with the committee and trouble-shoot any last-minute issues. Other than the art car entries circling the outside edge, just a few cars peppered the parking lot. I found a space close to the entrance, then helped Mrs. Branford out of the car. Manipulating the flowing fabric folds of her dress would be very different than her normal track suits, and I was afraid her cane might get tangled up in the yards of chiffon. "Please be careful," I cautioned. "I don't want you to trip."

"You and me both, my dear." But she

moved slowly, acknowledging the reality of the concern. Satisfied that she would be as careful as she could, I slung my camera bag over my shoulder, hiked up my dress with one hand, and together, we headed inside.

I pulled open the door to the convention center, ushering Mrs. Branford in ahead of me. I'd scoped out the ballroom the week before so I knew exactly where I was going. Impatience crawled through me, but I kept my pace slow so Mrs. Branford could keep up. Once we were in the ballroom, she had committee details to take care of. She'd go her way and I'd go mine.

Each room in the facility was named after a California locale. From the Redwood Forest to Palm Desert to Half Moon Bay, the rooms represented the vast beauty of the state. We stopped in front of the San Francisco Bay room, but as I reached for the handle, the door wrenched open. I stumbled back and my camera bag slipped from my shoulder. I tried to catch the strap in the crook of my arm, but my ankle buckled and I lost my balance.

"Ivy!" The moment slowed and Mrs. Branford's voice sounded far away. I thrust my arm out to try to catch myself, but too late. Just when I thought I was going down, a hand gripped my upper arm. One second

I was nearly sprawled out on the corporate carpeted floor, the next I was yanked upright like a rag doll. My feet sought purchase, but they couldn't find the ground. The hand around my arm tightened, and another hand found my hip and held tight. "You're good," Miguel said. He deftly slipped the camera bag from the crook of my arm, all the while holding on to me until I could regain my balance.

I brushed the front of my dress down, tried to pat my spiraled curls back into place, and looked sheepishly at both Miguel and Mrs. Branford.

"Your knight in shining armor," she said under her breath.

I glared at her. I was not a damsel in distress, and the last thing I wanted — or needed — was a man — even Miguel — to rescue me. Still, I was certainly glad he'd caught me before I'd crashed to the ground.

Miguel placed his hands on my shoulders. "You okay?"

I waved away the concern etched on his face. "Completely fine," I said, although my ankle was sore and I wondered if I was going to make it through the evening. I loved the opportunity to dress up, but three-inch heels, which were on the conservative side for many, were extreme for me and not my normal footwear.

He leaned into me, brushing his lips lightly against my cheek. "You look beautiful."

I felt a touch of heat in my cheeks. He looked pretty dashing himself in a cream-colored guayabera, a black sport coat, and slacks. "You're quite the pair," Mrs. Branford said, "but if you're done . . . People to see, things to do, a murder to solve."

"Mrs. Branford," I scolded, but she'd said enough for Miguel to pull back and give me a side-eye.

"A *what* to *what*?" he asked, his question directed to Mrs. Branford, not to me.

Mrs. Branford gave him the look I'm sure she'd given to a thousand teenagers over the years. "Come now, Miguel. You know our Ivy well enough to understand that she's not sleeping, she's hardly eating, and she's worried sick about Billy."

I stared at her, marveling at her sixth sense, but signaling to her with my eyes to stop.

Instead she shook her head, this time at us both. "My goodness. I have spent eight and a half decades on this planet, at least five of them in direct contact with teenagers. One of my greatest strengths as a teacher was not to actually instruct, but to observe.

To watch, listen, and learn. By doing those three things, I armed myself with everything I needed to reach them. It's the same with you two. I watch. I listen. And I learn."

I started to speak, but she held up one gnarled finger and shushed me. "The older I get, the less sleep I need. Which means I spend far too many hours in my parlor reading or knitting or trying to teach myself to crochet. You wouldn't think that would be so difficult, but I find it horribly so." She fluttered her hand in front of her. "But I digress. From the vantage point of my sofa, I can see the front of your house. Which means I know when you turn your lights off at night, and when you alight in the morning."

If it were anybody other than Mrs. Branford recounting her spying activities, with me as the focus of her scrutiny, I would have been incredibly freaked out. But instead, I was mildly amused. I suspected that she knew everything about everyone on Maple Street — and that they wouldn't be nearly as interested in her deductions as I was.

She seemed to have forgotten her urgency to enter the ballroom. I wanted to get in there, too, but I suspected that learning about Mrs. Branford's skills of deduction would come in handy. "What else have you observed?"

"I know you are not sleeping the number of hours you should," she said, basking in the glow of our attention. "I know that you've already lost five pounds — maybe more — since Max's death. And these things tell me that Billy coming under scrutiny is not only taking its toll on him, but it's wearing you down, as well."

Miguel placed his hands on my shoulders, looking into my eyes. "She's right, Ivy. You're no good to Billy if you don't take care of yourself."

"I'm fine," I said.

"You're not fine." We'd gone from high school sweethearts to a brand-new relationship in progress. Not long ago, he'd told me he was all in. Looking at the concern etched on his face now, I believed him.

"Let's go," I said, reaching past them both and pulling open the door to the ballroom. I crossed the threshold, knowing they'd be right behind me. Just inside, we all came to a stop. The room had been transformed from a plain, unadorned space to a retrospective of Santa Sofia's Art Car Shows over the years. The committee had to have spent an inordinate amount of money recreating — or disassembling and reassembling — winning entries from the past. All along the perimeter of the vast room, the front halves of cars emerged from the walls as if they'd driven right through but had gotten stuck halfway.

Mrs. Branford nodded her approval. "Perfect."

"How did they do that?" I asked in awe, but she just shrugged.

"I don't know. It was Max's idea, actually. He hired a crew to make it happen."

From what I knew of Max, prior to talking to Vanessa Rose, self-interest had been the driving force behind many of his actions, which meant these were all of *his* cars on display. Excluding the wall behind us with the two double-door entrances to the room, the main walls held three cars each. Correction, three *half* cars each.

"At his own expense?" Miguel asked, taking the words straight from my mouth.

"Entirely. The committee told him in no uncertain terms that we could not even begin to take that on. He said no problem, that he'd take care of it himself as long as we approved the idea. To which, of course, we said yes. It meant less outlay for us in the decorating department."

"Penelope!" Someone from across the room waved at us, beckoning Mrs. Branford. "Oh my goodness, I'm so glad you're here! We need your thoughts."

"Be right there," she called, waving her hand at the woman. She looked at Miguel and me, dropped her voice a level, and winked. "I don't know what they'd do without me." She was clearly pleased, though, her smile curving her lips up contentedly as she sauntered off, swinging her cane.

"I don't know what *I'd* do without her," I said to Miguel. I talked to her on the phone several times a day, saw her at least once a day, and just knowing she was across the street from me kept me grounded.

Miguel wrapped his arm around my shoulders. "She's like a cat with nine lives. That woman isn't going anywhere."

That was the truth. Penelope Branford might just outlive us all.

I limped slightly, grimacing at the arch in my ankle. Ironic that I was the one hurt after working so hard to make sure Mrs. Branford wasn't. Miguel kept his hand on the small of my back. His touch sent an electric charge up my spine, but I was here to work. There was no telling where any bit of information might lead to in my effort to help free Billy from suspicion.

We circled the room, looking at each of the cars on display. I wished they held some message — some clue as to who else had a beef with him. But, of course, they didn't. They were just cars. Plaques hung on the wall next to each installment with Max's name emblazoned across the top of the engraved brass sheet and the year that particular art car had won. Alongside the wood and brass plates was a series of framed pictures from the corresponding year. In each, Max was in the driver's seat, a smug look on his face as if his winning was inevitable. In every single picture, a woman — the girlfriend du jour — sat in the copilot seat. Some smiled, some were serious, but the one thing that stood out to me was their age. I'd learned from Emmaline that Max had been fifty-six, but every single one of the girls in question looked to be a good ten years — or more — younger than him. Plenty of women hadn't seemed to care about the age difference.

"I need to document these cars before the event starts and the people come," I said after we'd made one entire loop.

I reached for my camera bag, but Miguel shook his head. "I got it," he said, holding on to the case as I retrieved my Canon. Once the bag was zipped up again, he slung the strap over his shoulder and walked with me.

"You're the perfect assistant," I said.

He gave a slightly salacious smile. "I have many untold talents."

"I just bet you do," I said, lifting one eyebrow.

He wrapped his arm around me, pulling me close. "I'll show you, one by one by one."

My feet came to a standstill. In my heels, I could look at him eye to eye. And meet him lips to lips. I could imagine his many talents. I *wanted* to imagine them. Hell, I wanted to *experience* them. But not yet.

He seemed to read my mind. Or my face. He dropped his hand from my waist, interlacing his fingers with mine. "I'm all in, Ivy, remember?"

I nodded, squeezing my hand around his. "I know."

His gaze intensified. "Are you?"

And then some. "I am."

He flashed that crooked grin of his and nodded. "Good."

He stayed by my side as I retraced our steps to photograph the plaques, the pictures, and the corresponding cars. I shot from different angles, looking for artistic composition to complement the artistic nature of the cars themselves. At one point, I managed to crouch down, shooting one of

Max's past creations from the bottom looking up to capture the feeling of being under the sea.

"This is why I don't wear high heels very often," I said, needing to take Miguel's proffered hand to stand up again.

Before he could respond to that with some witty remark, the distinct sound of something breakable hitting the ground came from behind us followed by a sharp "Shit!"

We turned to see a young man dressed in black slacks and a white dress shirt swiftly picking up shards of a white plate. Another server hurried to him with a broom and dustpan. In less than two minutes, it was cleaned up. As they stood to leave, a small group of people entered through the same double doors we had. Emmaline, with the tight spiraled curls of her black hair, her porcelain-like cocoa skin, and the sharp angle of her jawline giving her face a heart shape. Her cream dress was elegant, and with her shoulders thrown back and her confident stride, she looked like a movie star on the red carpet. She laced her arm through Billy's, who looked dapper in a dark suit. From their expressions, neither one looked particularly glad to be here, but they came into the ballroom, stopping as they saw all of Max's cars on display.

"Look," Miguel said, lightly touching the back of my arm. I turned, then sighed with dismay. Sheriff Lane and one of his deputies had slipped in without my noticing and stood tucked in the shadows of a back corner. Their attention was firmly rooted on Emmaline and Billy, who had started the slow promenade around the room to look at each car. "He's determined," I said, hoping the sheriff didn't have some grandiose plan of arresting Billy and making a spectacle in the middle of the event.

Miguel and I stopped at one of the three hors d'oeuvres tables set up along the west side of the room. Mrs. Branford was nowhere to be seen, but while Miguel and I had been circling the room, Olaya and her crew had started setting up their portion of the buffet tables. For this particular event, The Fish Market had prepared carrot and tuna bites, smoked salmon on chunky slices of cucumber and garnished with sprigs of dill, thinly baked potato pancakes topped with gravlax and Dijon mustard and dill, seared scallops wrapped in prosciutto, and lobster salad to accompany Olaya's mini sourdough boules. Yeast of Eden had also supplied bruschetta for The Fish Market's tuna salad, and thin slices of toasted French bread for a hot crab dip and herbed shrimp dip. If I had any sort of an appetite, I'd have one of everything.

Olaya and the head chef of The Fish Market, Walter Jessup, stood to one side, evaluating their creations. Miguel gave a low whistle. "Looks pretty damn good."

Walter had one arm folded across his chest, stroking his chin with his other hand. "I agree."

But Olaya narrowed her eyes, stood back, and cocked her head. And then, as if she'd had some great epiphany, she launched into action, building more height by adding boxes on top of boxes, draping cloth, tulle, and burlap over them, and then rearranging platters. I snapped a few pictures of her as she worked. She was an artist in the kitchen and with her bread, but she was also an artist in her presentation. I wanted to document all of it.

Finally, she stepped back, looking satisfied. Miguel, Walter, and I looked at each other, then at her. She gave a final nod. *"Listo,"* she said.

I crouched down again, taking pictures from interesting angles to capture the pink of the salmon and the contrasting green of the dill, the golden crust of the sourdough boules, and every other little detail Olaya and Walter had put into their food.

Through it all, I kept an eye on Billy and Em as they worked their way slowly around the room, as well as the sheriff and deputy. They hadn't moved from their spot in the corner. At least the sheriff had turned toward the door rather than burning a hole in Billy's back with the intensity of his earlier stare. I watched him as he watched the townspeople begin to spill into the ballroom. Just like he'd been at the hangar, he seemed to be studying each and every person, gauging the likelihood that any given one of them could have murdered Max Litman.

I turned my attention to them, listening to the cacophony of their chatter. The pall that had been like a dark cloud over the crowd at the parade had given way to excitement. It filled the air like the aroma of baking bread steaming from an open oven door, wafting through the room until every corner was infused with it. The women's dresses glittered. The men's sleek coats dazzled. The Art Car Show and Ball was an opportunity for the people of our quaint beach town to sparkle, and they were doing it magnificently.

"No one holds a candle to you," Miguel said, his voice low, his breath warm on my ear.

I leaned into him coquettishly, but only for a moment, because from across the room, I spotted someone I hadn't expected to be here.

Vanessa Rose.

Each time I'd seen the spiritual advisor, she put on an entirely different persona, as if she were donning a different hat. First, she'd been frazzled and acting as if she had secrets to hide. Then she'd been an earthy fortune-teller. Now she was doe-eyed and innocent, yet a knockout in her low-cut and form-fitting dress.

"That's Vanessa Rose," I said to Miguel.

"The life coach slash spiritual advisor?" he asked, following my gaze.

"The same."

"Did you know she'd be here?"

I quickly schooled my expression. "I didn't, although I guess I'm not surprised."

"Maybe she'd been planning on coming with Max?"

That was quite possible, actually. Not for the first time, I wondered how their relationship had evolved over the time they'd known each other. I didn't have any inkling of what her motive might be, but I revisited the idea that Vanessa could have killed Max.

I caught a glimpse of the sheriff. He'd

moved to a different location. Even in civilian clothes, he looked like the law. He rocked back on his heels, his arms folded over his chest. Body language spoke volumes. He wasn't interested in talking to anyone. His stance and his scowl ensured that no one would approach him.

But then a man did approach him. I couldn't see him well, but I placed him in his early sixties, dark but thinning hair, and a thin frame. The man said something to Lane, who shook his head sharply, and as if he'd been shamed, the man slunk away.

I made a split-second decision, handing my camera to Miguel. "I'll be right back."

"Where are you —"

But with the music and constant chatter, I was already out of earshot. I ignored the dull ache in my ankle, kept my head up, shoulders back, and my stride confident.

Up close I noticed that Sheriff Lane's scowl carved the vertical lines between his eyebrows into deep crevices, and his lips were pulled into a thin line. Definitely unapproachable. But his "don't even think about coming near me" stance wasn't going to deter me.

"Sheriff," I said, coming up to him.

He acknowledged me with a single nod and a frown. "Ms. Culpepper."

I didn't waste any time with pleasantries. "Look, I know you think Billy killed Max, but he didn't. There are plenty of people with motives."

I had his full attention now. "Is that right?"

"It is."

"I've heard about your detectiving prowess," he said.

I heard the faint mocking tone, but chose to ignore it. I also chose not to downplay the two murders — three if you counted my mother — I'd had a hand in solving. "That's right. Which is why I think you should listen to me."

One side of his taut mouth curved up, not in a real smile, but in an indulgent gesture, as if he were telling a child to go ahead and explain the tax code. "By all means."

I was surprisingly calm, given how much I wanted him to take what I had to say and run with it. "I know Em — er — Detective Davis shared the investment fraud with the condo deal with you. There are a lot of people who each lost a lot of money thanks to Max."

He nodded, again, just once, but it wasn't an affirmation. With the raised eyebrows, it was more of a "Is that all you've got?" expression. "Max being dead wouldn't help them retrieve their money, though, would it?"

I had to concede that point. "But at this point, is there any hope of recouping it?" I asked. The sheriff chose not to reply, as if it had been rhetorical, so I forged ahead. "He had a spiritual advisor. Or a life coach." I pointed to Vanessa Rose across the room. She stood at one of the mounted cars, completely motionless.

The sheriff dropped his arms to his side. "Is that right?" He turned to his deputy. "How did we not know about this?"

The deputy's brown eyes grew wide. "You said to, er, we've been focusing on —"

His words broke off when the sheriff raised his hand, palm out, but I'd heard enough to know that the deputy had simply been following orders. He'd investigated what he'd been told to investigate, nothing more, nothing less.

"Is there anything else, Ms. Culpepper?" he asked.

I nodded. I hated to think that it could be true, but Mr. Zavila, high school art teacher and Billy's former art car consultant, had a motive. "Cristopher Zavila. He helped Max cheat with his art cars. His wins were not legitimate, you know. Mr. Zavila was a spy. He was paid well, but then Max fired him."

The sheriff narrowed his eyes before shaking his head. "There again, you can't get blood from a stone. With Max alive, there would have been a chance for other work. With him dead, that pipeline is closed up. Not a sound motive."

"I see your point," I said. He was a tiny bit smarter than I'd given him credit for. Max's death meant that the mysterious investors — mysterious with the exception of Johnny Wellborn and Vicente Villanueva — Vanessa Rose, and Cristopher Zavila had no more chance of regaining or, in the case of Vanessa, earning any more money from Max. And if Vanessa and Max had been in a real relationship, then her motive weakened. "People have killed for a lot of stupid reasons," I said, playing devil's advocate. I'd watched *Law & Order,* after all. I'd seen stories ripped from the headlines. I'd read about murders committed for no reason at all. Anger and revenge for perceived wrongs was not that much of a stretch. It was the same motive the sheriff was attaching to Billy.

But the sheriff wasn't willing to concede that point. "This isn't a TV show, or a make-believe crime novel, Ms. Culpepper. It's real life. I'm looking for real things that lead to real motives."

No, I thought, you're looking for anything that will corroborate your opinion that Billy is guilty. For a fleeting moment, I'd hoped that maybe I'd mischaracterized the sheriff. I'd hoped that maybe he *was* open to seeing what happened at the event tonight that might connect back to Max. I'd believed for the briefest second that maybe, just maybe, Sheriff Lane hadn't bet his entire hand on Billy.

But then I remembered what Emmaline had said so often about Lane's skill and, to use his made-up word, *detectiving*. He'd never see it my way.

Chapter 28

I hadn't come to the ball with any sort of an orchestrated plan. The music pulsing and the people circulating didn't give me any other bright ideas. The art cars Max Litman had painstakingly arranged to install for the event hadn't told me anything. Maybe the photos he'd displayed with each installment would.

I told Miguel my thoughts. "Let's take one more look at them. You game?"

Of course, he was. My ankle ached a little less, but we took it slowly, skirting past the people gathered around each creation. I looked for Vanessa, but she'd vanished into the crowd. I'd caught a glimpse of Dixie, flipping her hair and sashaying around like Marilyn Monroe. That woman was one of a kind. The one person I hadn't seen was Mr. Zavila. I wasn't sure how much I considered him a true suspect, but he stayed in the back of my mind.

Miguel and I peered more closely at the photos. As we stood in front of the first one, Miguel leaned in next to me, hands in his pockets. "What are you looking for?"

I didn't have anything explicit on my mind, but sometimes things came to light when you weren't even looking. "What if one of the women pictured with Max could give us some sort of clue?"

"We already have a pretty healthy list of potential suspects," he said. "Do we need more?"

"We have ten investors, all dismissed as suspects by the sheriff. We have a spiritual advisor with no ascertainable motive. We have the art teacher who gets out from under Max's thumb with his death, but also has no more chance to earn extra money. We have my brother, who we know is innocent. A picture speaks a thousand words, they say. What if one of these can tell us something?"

We made our way around the perimeter of the room, stopping at each car to study the pictures. It didn't take long to ascertain that what we needed to focus on was the women. I had to give it to Max. He kept it interesting. Some had black wavy hair; blond locks; auburn curls; even strawberry ginger. Pale skin, coffee-colored, freckled,

325

and olive. It seemed that Max Litman had liked his women in every flavor.

"Maybe Vanessa does have a motive," I said slowly, thinking as I talked. I swept my hand wide to encompass the room as a whole.

Miguel, however, knew what I meant. "You think she was jealous?"

She hadn't struck me as the green-eyed type, but I'd been surprised before. People played against type all the time. "It's possible, isn't it?"

"Anything is."

One by one, we looked more closely at the pictures. After we'd studied a few, something struck me about one of the women. Her head angled toward the camera, the crystal blue of her eyes boring into me. Her hair was distinctly red, her lips painted crimson, but it was the eyes that I came back to. I backtracked to the previous photo. "That's the same woman," I said.

"No, it can't be." He was skeptical, but peered closer. "Can it?"

"The hair is different" — I pointed to the first photo — "but they have the same jawline. The same skin tone."

Miguel leaned one shoulder against the wall. "Okay, but what if it is the same woman? That doesn't make her a murderer."

I ignored his logic, instead hurrying to the next picture. It didn't matter why, but I wanted it to be the same woman.

"Look at the eyes."

As he considered, I went on to the next car and photograph. The same vibrant blue eyes stared at me. She was in three of the pictures. I held my breath as I turned to face the room, scanning each face. Searching each corner of the room, I considered each woman.

"Three of them seem to be the same," Miguel said as he came up beside me.

I nodded, but exhaled slowly, disappointed. "She's not here." Which, truthfully, shouldn't have surprised me. Nothing about absolving Billy of Max's murder was easy.

Miguel, however, wasn't so willing to throw in the towel. I knew he was keeping his eyes peeled as we walked. I was, too, but the women's faces had blurred together, their murky features filling my head until it swam. The nausea that had taken root in my gut churned to life. I wanted to end the evening by identifying a murderer.

Miguel and I had come full circle, ending at the buffet table. Olaya and Walter had their crews, dressed in crisp black and white, working the room, platters in hand. They navigated through the clusters of people with the ease of runway models, passing each other, pivoting, and returning, all with effortless ease. Two others kept the buffet table stocked, blending into the background as they disappeared into the kitchen, returning to refill platter after platter.

Miguel held a small plate out to me full of a sampling of hors d'oeuvres. The aroma. The colors. Everything on it looked delectable and I could have eaten every bit of it if it weren't for the hole in the pit of my stomach.

I shook my head, pushing it away with the pads of my fingertips. "I can't."

"You need to eat, Ivy."

He was right, of course, but I was afraid that after it went down, it would come right back up. "Maybe just a piece of bread," I said, reaching for one of Olaya's boules. The outer crust crumbled as I broke off a piece, the sourdough scent wafting up from the warm, soft center. If there was anything I could stomach, it was freshly baked bread from Yeast of Eden. I pulled a tuft from the center, but hesitated before eating it. It was just a simple rustic sourdough; would it work its magic, easing my unrest and anxiety over the dark cloud hanging above Billy? I took a bite, hoping against hope that it would.

Miguel was clearly relieved that I was eating. "Wine?"

With a mouthful of bread, I nodded my assent.

"Red or white?"

I considered as I finished my next bite. "White," I said, but then I hesitated. "Er, no red." I took another bite and shook my head. "No, yes. Red."

He notched one side of his mouth up in amusement, but waited a beat to be sure I wasn't going to change my mind again. "Red it is," he said when he was sure I wouldn't, and in a matter of seconds, he was sucked into the crowd, disappearing from my line of sight. I turned back to the buffet table and weighed pros and cons of eating something else. Miraculously, the knots in my stomach had loosened. Olaya's bread had been known to work in a split second, relieving mind-numbing depression or alleviating a heartache that ran deeper than the earth's core. It wouldn't surprise me if my newfound calm was due to her.

Still, not wanting to rile anything up, I decided to wait until the wine came. I turned back to face the dance floor, searching the crowd for Miguel. I didn't see him, so I shifted my attention to the revelers and let my mind drift to Billy. With Max gone, he was a shoe-in for first place. But actually winning would only serve to underscore the motive I knew people had in the forefront of their minds — that, as ridiculous as it sounded, my brother was actually capable of killing in order to win a car contest. It would solidify the motive that the sheriff already had him pegged for.

I scanned the crowd, but there was no sign of Billy. No sign of Emmaline, either. Where had they disappeared to?

There were plenty of familiar faces, though. People I'd seen at the bread shop, or wandering through the antique mini mall, or at Baptista's. People who'd been at the Winter Wonderland Festival. There were people, people everywhere. And then, like the Red Sea parting, one face came into startling focus. I started. I was staring straight into the piercing eyes of the woman featured in several of Max Litman's photos.

Miguel materialized by my side, but I stayed focused on the woman. Slowly, I lifted my hand, pointing. "Look," I whispered, hardly able to believe it. "That's her."

He put the two wineglasses he held down and followed me across the dance floor, heading straight to her. In the photographs, she'd had shoulder-length auburn hair, a short shaggy blond do, and long strawberry-blond locks. The woman I saw in front of me had the jawline and the blue eyes, but her hair was jet black.

She saw us coming. Watched, twisting her small gold clutch in her hands, looking puzzled.

I smiled, hoping to diffuse any tension as I approached. "Hey," I said, keeping my voice light.

She took a step backward. "Yes?"

"You're in some of the pictures," I said, letting my smile widen.

She frowned. "I — how do you — ?"

I tapped my temple. "The eyes. They're stunning. Truly."

She blinked, five or six times in quick succession, but didn't respond.

"You and Max must have been close," I said.

"I'm sorry, do I know you?" she said, evading responding to my statement.

"I grew up in Santa Sofia. Ivy," I said, extending my hand.

She took it, albeit with some trepidation. Her grip was loose. Nervous. "Isabel."

"This is Miguel," I said. He'd been hanging back, but I twisted slightly to put my

331

hand on his arm and nudge him forward.

"Nice to meet you," he said.

"Did you know Max?" she asked, her sparkling blue eyes hooded.

How did I answer that? Sure! He screwed my brother so he'd never win the Art Car Show award. He spied on him. Every. Single. Year. I went with the safe answer, though. "Not exactly."

She looked at Miguel, who shrugged. "He came into my restaurant sometimes. Baptista's."

She swallowed, looking a little too guilty, if you asked me. "Do you know it? Best restaurant in town," I said.

Miguel cocked his head. "You look familiar."

She swallowed again, shaking her head. "I don't, um, no. Baptista's? No, never."

He snapped his fingers. "Yes, I'm sure of it. Last week, right?"

I looked at him, my mind racing. I didn't know if he was serious or if he was playing at something. And then it dawned on me. I remembered what his mother had told him. Four people at the restaurant. Max's name mentioned. A man who spoke Spanish. Someone who said they were better off with Max dead. One of them had to have been Johnny Wellborn. And a woman with dark hair and bright eyes.

This woman. This Isabel. "*You're* one of the investors," I said. My heart raced. I'd gone back and forth between the idea of jealousy and revenge. I didn't know if IDing the investors meant anything, if it would lead to solving Max's murder, but it felt like a victory.

She did her rapid eye blinking again, rubbed the back of her neck, and swallowed. "I don't know what you're talking about."

Just then, an involuntary squeaking sound came from the base of her throat. Her bright blue eyes bugged and she turned her body slightly just as we were joined by two people. Martina Solis, looking sleek and sophisticated in a pale-green beaded dress, her dark hair slicked back into a tight bun, came up next to me. "I have been looking for you, Ivy. I want to introduce you to *mi novio*. This is Vicente."

I nearly dropped my camera. "Vicente Villanueva?"

He extended his hand to me. *"Mucho gusto,"* he said.

The next few seconds were a blur. I know I took his hand. My handshake had to be as limp as Isabel's had been.

Vicente Villanueva drew his head back, clearly perplexed by my reaction to him, but he was a gentleman. Miguel looked just as baffled, but he returned the handshake and responded with his own, *"Mucho gusto."*

Four things hit me all at once. The first was that Miguel's mother had told him that one of the men she'd seen at Baptista's spoke Spanish. The second was our belief that Isabel had also been at Baptista's, and therefore was one of the investors. And then there was Johnny Wellborn.

It was the fourth realization that hit me like a ten-pound bag of King Arthur Flour to the head. This man, Martina's boyfriend, was the man I'd just seen talking with Sheriff Lane.

CHAPTER 29

My head spun. It had to mean something, but what? How did Martina's boyfriend know the sheriff? I kept an eye on Vicente Villanueva and his brief — and awkward — greeting to Isabel, at the same time angling my head toward Miguel. "Take a picture of Isabel and Vicente," I whispered. "And the sheriff."

One eyebrow arched up. But then his eyes narrowed as he processed what I had said. He gave the briefest of nods, taking his cell phone from his pocket. *"Con permiso,"* he said, and held up his phone. "My mother."

Isabel gave a forced laugh. Vicente and Martina both nodded as if they understood. The three of them had a shared culture, so Vicente and Martina understood the importance of family and the matriarch of a Mexican family.

Miguel brushed my cheek with his lip, quickly whispering, "I'll find out."

We were in tune, thank God. We might not finish each other's sentences like Laura and her husband, but we were on our way. I felt my face heat with anxiety. Was I right? Did Max's death have nothing to do with jealousy and Vanessa Rose, and everything to do with the condo deal Johnny Wellborn had told us about, and the investors losing their nest eggs?

Something Emmaline had told me came jetting to the forefront of my thoughts. The sheriff had stopped being involved in the field when he'd inherited some sum of money. That meant he'd have had enough to invest — and lose — in Max's condo deal.

We made idle small talk, my heart racing the whole time. What was taking Miguel so long? Surely he'd managed to unobtrusively snap pictures of the *suspects* and text them to his mom. But, it occurred to me, his mother wasn't terribly tech savvy. Miguel had gotten her the latest smartphone, but she used it to call people and play games. She hadn't mastered the finger dexterity needed to text.

I scanned the room for him, spotting him back by the food, his phone pressed to his ear. So he'd called her instead. Brilliant.

I turned back to find our little conversation circle had grown. Emmaline and Billy had joined us, along with Mrs. Branford and another octogenarian, Mason Caldwell. She had her hand on his arm, a smile on her face, and a blush on her cheeks. They'd taught together at Santa Sofia High School and from the looks of it, they had reconnected. "Time to announce the Art Car winners!" Mrs. Branford said.

A man's voice came through the speakers. From the orientation of the crowd, whoever it was stood in front of one of Max's cars directly opposite from the food tables. He started by regaling the room with the background of the Art Car Show, launching into descriptions of some of the most memorable cars over the years. Naturally, this led to a retrospective of Max Litman and the exhibition of his cars around the room.

The conversation of our little group stopped as we all listened. Only Em started to say something, but her words cut off the second she looked at my face. "Ivy, are you okay?" she asked, taking my hand. Do you need to sit down?"

"I'm okay," I said, instantly changing my mind. "Actually, I think some water . . ."

Em communicated silently with Billy. He nodded, coming around to my other side. "I'll be back," I said to the others. "Just getting a drink."

They each gave a quick acknowledgment that I'd spoken, returning their focus to the voice over the speakers. "Fifth place . . ." the man was saying, but I couldn't think about the contest. The three of us started across the dance floor, maneuvering around people. We intercepted Miguel. "Well?" I asked.

"She said yes."

Em and Billy looked from me to Miguel. "Who said yes?"

I dragged them out of the crowd and to a shadowy corner of the room. "Here's what I think," I said. "Max screwed people over. He may have been trying to put things right, thanks to Vanessa —"

"The spiritual advisor," Em said.

"Exactly. But someone saying they're sorry for losing your one hundred twenty thousand dollars isn't going to cut it, is it?"

Cheering and clapping erupted in the crowd as the MC went on to announce fourth place.

"The people who invested with Max trusted him. Take Isabel over there. They had some sort of long-term relationship. She's in three of the Art Car photos with Max. Johnny Wellborn was a professional rival, but he considered Max savvy. You don't have to be someone's friend to do business with them."

Miguel took over the narrative. "Vicente Villanueva is a VP for a hotel chain. He and Max had a professional relationship. If he was willing to hand over one hundred twenty K, there must have been some level of trust, right?"

Em's posture had changed. Gone was the woman in the ball gown out on the town with her fiancé. Instead, dress and heels notwithstanding, she had morphed into Deputy Emmaline Davis. "So who's the fourth?" she asked, looking like she was ready to pounce.

I drew in a deep breath, looking to Miguel for confirmation. He gave a succinct nod; then we both spoke at once. "Sheriff Robert Lane."

Emmaline nearly dropped the wineglass she held. "Are you sure?"

"My mother saw the four of them at Baptista's talking about Max and the money they'd lost. She didn't know who they were, but I took pictures and texted them to my sister to show my mom. It's the four of them."

Billy shook his head. "The sheriff's high-profile." He turned to Miguel. "Your mom didn't recognize him?"

339

He laughed. "Have you met my mom? She watches telenovelas and works at the restaurant. That's it. I love her, but she'd barely recognize me if I wasn't her son."

Emmaline waved away the recognition skills of Miguel's mother. "Let me get this straight. Are you suggesting that the sheriff killed Max?"

I'd worked it out in my head. Now I spoke my thoughts aloud, hoping they didn't sound ridiculous. "He inherited so he had money to invest. I don't know how he knew Max, but he's the sheriff. He knows everyone, doesn't he? Think about it. He said he looked into all the other investors and discredited them. Everything for him has been about finding Billy guilty. He went in with his mind made up, but why?"

Another idea hit me. "Wait. What if Max went to make amends with Lane. What if he told Lane where the money was? Lane might have killed Max before he could tell anyone else so —"

"He could keep the money for himself," Billy said.

The color drained from Emmaline's face, taking it from a rich cocoa color to something a little green and pale by comparison. "Oh my God."

We all stared at her. "What is it, babe?"

Billy asked, his hand finding her lower back.

"He said the money was gone. He was really pissed one day. Not pissed. Livid. He was pacing around. He kicked a chair. He even threw a glass. He said, 'So much for retirement,' but fuming."

"That was the money he lost. The money Max invested," I said.

"So it was revenge," Billy said.

"Plain and simple."

"And the zombie car?"

"Remember the broken window in the hangar?" I said to Em. "You said something was off about it."

She nodded. "It was. It *is*. The glass was inside, but it didn't look like anyone had stepped on it. It didn't look like anyone had actually climbed through that window at all, in fact."

"The place was locked up tight, though, wasn't it?" Miguel asked.

We paused to think about that one; then it came to me. "My dad told me that all kinds of events have been held at the hangar over the years. What did he say?" I thought for a second before continuing. "A vintage market. A school gala. And police auctions."

Billy's face changed, the life coming back into it. "That's right. I bought some of my art cars there in the early days. They were like blank canvases. Beat-up and ready for the junkyard. But anything can become art."

"If police events were held there," I continued, "it would have been fairly easy for Lane to get himself a copy of the keys, wouldn't it?"

Em nodded. "Presumably."

"So Lane murdered Max to get revenge for the condo fraud."

"And who better to frame for it than you," I said to Billy. "Max's longtime nemesis."

We stood there, stupefied. Could it be? Was it really Sheriff Lane? As I processed through it again, the second place winner was announced.

It wasn't Billy.

We all stared toward the front of the room, but we couldn't see the speaker. Couldn't gauge what was happening. Either Billy had won, at long last, or the judges had overlooked him because he was a person of interest in Max's murder.

The cheering died down and the voice came over the microphone speakers. "And, folks, the moment we've all been waiting for. This year, the grand prize winner for the Santa Sofia Art Car competition goes to . . ."

A collective silence came over the room.

". . . Billy Culpepper."

There was a delayed reaction, but then a loud clap came from the double doors. I looked over to see my dad standing in the threshold, a proud expression on his face, his eyes glistening. Billy's art car was a tribute to our mother. To our father's wife. To the love of his life. And it had won. Billy had won.

We joined in the applause, and before long the crowd separated to allow Billy to walk to the front. We all joined him, but I scanned the room for the sheriff in the process.

I needn't have bothered. He was at the front of the room, just off to the side from where the Eiffel Tower-sized trophies were being handed to the winners. Billy stepped up to shake the hand of the MC as my father, Olaya, Mrs. Branford, and Mason Caldwell joined me.

Sheriff Lane stepped up to the front at the same time. With one hand on a pair of handcuffs clipped to his belt, he spoke more to the crowd than to Billy. "William Culpepper, you're —"

"Sheriff," Emmaline said, coming up behind him.

He stopped. "Deputy, what are you doing?"

She said something to him quietly. I couldn't hear, but I knew what she was doing. Emmaline had integrity. She didn't need to make a show of things. What she needed was to exact justice. And that didn't need to be done publically. She was giving him a chance to save face and not go down in front of the whole town.

Lane's nostrils flared. His face instantly turned a blotchy red. He dropped his hand from the handcuffs, reaching instead for his holster. Someone from the crowd yelled, "Gun!" and just like that, the room erupted into chaos. People screamed. Rushed around. Pushed and shoved to get out of the way.

I stayed focused on the three people in front. "Robert, stop," Emmaline barked. It didn't matter that she was in eveningwear and not looking anything remotely like a cop. She was still intimidating.

The sheriff, however, didn't listen. He yanked his gun from his holster. I didn't know who he planned to shoot. Everything happened all at once. Miguel wrapped his arm around my waist to pull me out of the line of fire. Billy moved with lightning speed, grabbing him in a chokehold, which allowed Em to lunge for the sheriff's outstretched arm and knock the gun from it. She grabbed hold of the handcuffs at Lane's waist and snapped one on the wrist that had held the gun. "Robert Lane," she said. A hush had fallen over the crowd. You could hear a pin drop. "You're under arrest for the murder of Maxwell Litman."

CHAPTER 30

It was one o'clock in the morning before the chaos of the night was over. Emmaline had taken over, directing the deputy present to call for backup. Lane was subdued, but she wanted crowd control, damage control, and she wanted to read the sheriff his Miranda Rights so he could hear every last word.

Billy was officially cleared, Lane was officially under arrest, and we were all officially exhausted. A lot of people might have found an open bar. Taken a good stiff drink to decompress. But not us. We headed back to Yeast of Eden. Olaya made pot after pot after pot of coffee, we'd pushed the bistro tables together, and now we all sat, experiencing the letdown.

Mrs. Branford had changed from her chiffon dress to a dark gray and subdued velour lounge suit. She was a slave to her generation's view of propriety . . . but with her

346

own twist. The rest of us were still in our finest. Mrs. Branford clasped the wooden handle of her cane. The walking stick was usually for show, but at this moment, I thought she actually needed it to help keep her steady. She had long ago retired, but she hadn't lost her poise or confidence. "Every person deserves to rest in peace," she said. "Now Max will get that blessing."

We raised our coffee cups. "To Max," Emmaline said.

"To Max," Miguel and I said at the same time.

My father, Olaya, Mason Caldwell, Martina, and Vicente Villanueva, who'd helped Olaya tear down her tables at the ball, all chimed in. But it was Billy who kept his cup raised for an extra second. "To Max," he said. "Rest in peace."

The next morning, I stood in my dad's house gazing at the trophy on the kitchen table. Billy came up behind me, draping his arm over my shoulders. "It was a long time coming, eh?"

"Too long," my dad said, his baritone light and satisfied. "Your mom would be proud of you, son."

He took hold of it, holding it above his head, pumping his arm. "Yo, Mom, this is for you!" he said in his best Sylvester Stallone imitation.

"Where are you going to put it?" my dad asked.

Billy put it back down on the table and then leaned against the counter. "On a shelf in the lobby of my new showroom," he said, a grin spreading on his face.

My dad and I stared at him. "Your new what?" I asked.

"Litman Homes is up for sale," he said. "I'm always cautious —"

"Too cautious," I interjected.

"You work hard, Billy," my dad said, "but Litman's?"

He shook his head, the grin still in place. "That spiritual advisor of Max's —"

"Vanessa Rose," I said.

"The stuff about Max making amends? I kind of think it might be true," he said. "Vanessa told me about me being his lifeline. Taking over his business feels . . . right. Like coming full circle. I'm going to put the trophy next to mom's book," he said. "I think she'd like that."

We stood side by side, arms around each other, smiling and relishing the peace that we all felt. It was as if we'd all been in Wonderland, but now we were full size again and back in the real world, together.

Wonderland, it turns out, was overrated.

■ ■ ■ ■

RECIPES

■ ■ ■ ■

CHOCOLATE BABKA
(recipe credit to King Arthur Flour)

Dough
1 to 1 1/4 cups lukewarm water
2 large eggs
6 1/4 cups all-purpose flour
1/3 cup nonfat dry milk
2 tablespoons instant yeast
1/2 teaspoon ground cinnamon
1/2 cup sugar
2 1/2 teaspoons salt
10 tablespoons unsalted butter, at room
   temperature*
1 tablespoon vanilla extract

Filling
1/2 cup sugar
1/2 teaspoon ground cinnamon

* Reduce the salt to 2 1/4 teaspoons if you use
salted butter.

1/3 cup cocoa powder of your choice, Dutch-process or natural

1/2 teaspoon espresso powder

1/4 cup melted butter

1 cup finely chopped semisweet chocolate or semisweet chocolate chips, mini chips preferred

1 cup diced pecans or walnuts, optional

Glaze

1 large egg beaten with a pinch of salt until well-combined

Topping

4 tablespoons melted butter

1/2 teaspoon cinnamon

2/3 cup confectioners' sugar

1/2 cup all-purpose flour

1. Combine all of the dough ingredients (add water gradually), mixing until everything is moistened. Add additional water if necessary to enable the dough to come together. Cover the bowl and let the dough rest for 20 minutes. Then mix/knead it until it is soft and smooth.

2. Place the dough in a lightly greased bowl and then cover the bowl. The dough is going to rise for about 1 1/2 to 2 hours, until it is quite puffy.

3. Gently deflate the dough and divide it in half. Set the pieces aside, covered, while you make the filling.

4. To make the filling, combine the sugar, cinnamon, cocoa, and espresso. Stir in the melted butter. The mixture will look grainy and slick; that's okay.

5. Shape each half of the dough into a 9" × 18" 1/4" rectangle. If the dough "fights back," let it rest for 10 minutes to relax the gluten, then stretch it some more. Don't be fussy about this; 19" or 20" is as good as 18".

6. Smear each piece of the dough with half of the filling, coming to within an inch of the edges.

7. Scatter half the nuts and half the chopped chocolate/chips over each piece. If using standard-size chips, process them in a food processor first, to create smaller bits of chocolate and a less chunky filling.

8. Starting with a short end, roll each piece gently into a log, sealing the seam and ends. Working with one log at a time, use a pair of scissors or a sharp knife to cut the log in half lengthwise (not crosswise) to make two pieces of dough about 10" long each; cut carefully, to prevent too much filling from spilling out. With the exposed filling side up, twist the two

pieces into a braid, tucking the ends underneath. Repeat with the other log. Place each log into a lightly greased 9″ × 5″ loaf pan.

9. Brush each loaf with the egg glaze. Mix together the topping ingredients until crumbly, then sprinkle half of the topping over each loaf.

10. Tent each pan with plastic wrap and let the loaves rise until they're very puffy and have crowned a good inch over the rim of the pan, about 1 1/2 to 2 1/2 hours. Toward the end of the rising time, preheat your oven to 300°F.

11. Bake the bread for 35 minutes. Tent lightly with foil and bake for an additional 15 to 25 minutes (for a total of 50 to 60 minutes); the loaves should be a deep golden brown.

12. To ensure the loaves are baked through, insert a digital thermometer into the center of one loaf. It should register at least 190°F.

13. Remove the loaves from the oven and immediately loosen the edges with a heat-proof spatula or table knife. Let the loaves cool for 10 minutes, then turn them out of the pans onto a rack to cool completely.

14. Slice the babka and serve it at room temperature; or rewarm individual slices

briefly in a toaster, if desired. Store any leftovers, well-wrapped, at room temperature for several days; freeze for longer storage.

Or make it gluten free! It's really delicious.

GLUTEN-FREE CHOCOLATE BABKA
(adapted from recipe by
King Arthur Flour)

Dough
2 3/4 cups gluten-free flour (I use either
King Arthurs's or Pamela's all-purpose
gluten-free flour)
3 tablespoons sugar
1 teaspoon salt
1 teaspoon xanthan gum
2 teaspoons instant yeast
4 tablespoons (1/4 cup) soft butter
2 tablespoons vegetable oil
1 cup warm milk
1 large egg
1 teaspoon vanilla

Filling
1/4 cup sugar
1/4 teaspoon ground cinnamon
1/2 teaspoon espresso powder, optional; for
enhanced chocolate flavor
2 1/4 tablespoons Dutch-process cocoa
powder
2 tablespoons melted butter
1/3 to 1/2 cup semisweet chocolate chips
1/2 cup diced pecans or walnuts, toasted if
desired

Glaze

1 large egg beaten with a pinch of salt until well-combined

Topping

1/3 cup gluten-free all-purpose flour
4 tablespoons brown sugar
1 teaspoon ground cinnamon
2 1/2 tablespoons melted butter

1. To make the dough, combine all the dry ingredients in your mixer bowl. Add the soft butter, blending on low speed until you have coarse crumbs.
2. Add the oil, milk, egg, and vanilla, beating until incorporated. Scrape down the sides of the bowl. Beat on medium-high speed for 2 to 3 minutes; scrape the bowl down again. Cover the dough and let it rise for about 1 to 1 1/2 hours, or until visibly puffy.
3. When the dough has risen, turn it out onto a lightly greased piece of parchment paper (or waxed paper) and press it gently into an 8″ × 16″ rectangle.
4. To make the chocolate filling, combine the sugar, cinnamon, espresso powder, and cocoa. Stir in the melted butter. The mixture will look grainy and slick; that's okay.

5. Spread the filling over the dough, leaving a 1/2" to 1" border of filling-free dough around the edges. Scatter the chips and nuts atop the filling. If desired, process the chips in a food processor first, to create smaller bits of chocolate and a less chunky filling.

6. You may choose two ways to shape the babka. Either way, use the greased parchment (or waxed paper) to help you; don't try to shape the dough by removing it from the paper. The easiest way to shape is to start with a short end and simply roll the filled dough into a log, as though you were making cinnamon swirl bread. The dough should release from the paper as you roll. Alternatively (and if you're feeling a bit more adventuresome!), start with a long edge of dough, roll the dough forward into a log, then cut the log in half crosswise.

7. Lightly grease an 8 1/2" × 4 1/2" loaf pan. If desired, line the pan with a parchment paper sling, which will help you remove the loaf once it's baked. Gently place the dough log into the lined pan. If you've rolled the long way and cut the log in half, snuggle both halves, side by side, into the pan. This will give you a somewhat more intricate swirl.

8. Cover the pan and let the dough rise in a warm spot until it's puffy and risen about 1″ over the rim of the pan, about 60 to 90 minutes. Toward the end of the rising time, preheat the oven to 325°F.
9. To make the topping, combine all of the ingredients to form coarse crumbs. Brush the top of the loaf with the egg glaze, then sprinkle with the topping.
10. Bake the bread for 40 minutes. Tent lightly with foil, and bake for an additional 20 to 35 minutes (for a total of 60 to 75 minutes); it should be nicely browned, and a digital thermometer inserted into the center should read 205°F to 210°F.
11. Remove the bread from the oven, and if you haven't used a parchment sling, immediately loosen the edges with a heat-proof spatula or table knife. Let it cool for 10 minutes, then turn the loaf out of the pan onto a rack to cool completely.
12. Store the babka for 2 to 3 days at room temperature, well wrapped; freeze for longer storage. For best texture, reheat individual slices briefly before serving; the toaster works fine for this.

CHILE ANCHO SOPA DE CHOCOLATE
(adapted from SAVEUR)

This is an unusual soup inspired by mole, a Mexican condiment traditionally served with chicken. The hint of chocolate turns it into something special. This soup is rich and delicious! Serves six to eight.

3 dried ancho chiles (the dried version of the poblano pepper; pasilla is the dried version of the chilaca pepper. Ancho is a bit sweeter, but pasilla is used in traditional mole. Either will work for this soup.)

4 medium plum tomatoes, diced

1 small white or yellow onion, cut into chunks for sautéing

2 cloves garlic, peeled

1 tbsp. olive oil

1-2 tsp. ground cinnamon

2 tsp. sugar (I prefer Sugar in the Raw, if available)

1 tsp. ground cumin

6 cups chicken or vegetable stock

3 oz. semisweet chocolate, finely chopped (I like to use *Abuelita's* Mexican Chocolate)

Salt and pepper

1. Heat a saucepan over medium heat. Add chiles and cook, toasting lightly. Transfer to a bowl, add 1 cup boiling water, and let sit until soft, about 30 minutes. This step is important in order to avoid the flakes of the chili skin.
2. Meanwhile, sauté tomatoes and onion until slightly blackened.
3. Drain chiles (set aside the soaking liquid), remove stems and seeds, and put chiles in blender with onion and tomatoes.
4. Add garlic, cinnamon, sugar, and cumin; puree until very smooth.
5. Add oil to a soup pot. When hot, add the chile puree. Sauté, stirring constantly, until mixture is slightly reduced. Add chicken or vegetable stock and bring to boiling. Finally, remove from heat, stir in chopped chocolate. Season to taste with salt and pepper, and serve.
6. Garnish with sour cream, avocado, cilantro, green onions, and either fried strips of corn tortillas or crumbled tortilla chips.

ABOUT THE AUTHOR

The indefatigable **Winnie Archer** is a middle school teacher by day and a writer by night. Born in a beach town in California, she now lives in an inspiring century-old house in North Texas and loves being surrounded by real-life history. She fantasizes about spending summers writing in quaint, cozy locales, has a love/hate relationship with both yoga and chocolate, adores pumpkin spice lattes, is devoted to her five kids and husband, and can't believe she's lucky enough to be living the life of her dreams. Visit her online at WinnieArcher .com.